Prasie for Lucy and Stephen Hawking's

GEORGE

'Like a Doctor W

'Delig

'Gripping, informative and funny' *The Bookseller*

'Dramatic' *Guardian*

'A true beginner's guide to *A Brief History of Time*'
Publishers Weekly

Also available by Lucy and Stephen Hawking:

George's Secret Key to the Universe
George's Cosmic Treasure Hunt
George and the Big Bang
George and the Unbreakable Code

You can find Lucy at:

lucyhawking.com
@journeytospace

For details of Stephen Hawking's
books for adult readers, see:

www.hawking.org.uk

LUCY &
STEPHEN HAWKING

Illustrated by Garry Parsons

CORGI BOOKS

CORGI BOOKS

UK | USA | Canada | Ireland | Australia
India | New Zealand | South Africa

Corgi Books is part of the Penguin Random House group of companies
whose addresses can be found at global.penguinrandomhouse.com.

www.penguin.co.uk
www.puffin.co.uk
www.ladybird.co.uk

Penguin
Random House
UK

First published in hardback by Doubleday 2016
This edition published in paperback by Corgi Books 2017

001

Typeset in Stempel Garamond by Falcon Oast Graphic and Dickidot
Printed in Great Britain by Clays Ltd, St Ives plc

A CIP catalogue record for this book is available from the British Library

ISBN: 978–0–552–57597–3

All correspondence to:
Corgi Books
Penguin Random House Children's
80 Strand, London WC2R ORL

I don't know what I may seem to the world, but as to myself, I seem to have been only like a boy playing on the sea-shore and diverting myself in now and then finding a smoother pebble or a prettier shell than ordinary, whilst the great ocean of truth lay all undiscovered before me.

Isaac Newton

THE LATEST SCIENTIFIC IDEAS!

As you read the story, you will come across some fabulous science essays and information. These will really help bring the topics you read about to life, and are written by the following well-respected experts:

*With very special thanks to Sue Cook,
the George series non-fiction editor*

And to Stuart Rankin.

Chapter One

The pink-fringed coral waved gently in the soft blue ocean as a shoal of millions of tiny silver fish dived past it. Swimming as one, the swarm of fish jackknifed and suddenly shot upwards and away, towards the turquoise water above George's head. A larger fish lay up there, hovering between George and the sunshine on the surface of the ocean. The huge fish moved slowly across his field of vision, as stately and as well armoured as any battleship.

On the floor of the ocean bed, where the coral reef dropped away to the sandy ground, little creatures scuttled along, waving their pincers furiously as though a catch would swim straight into them. Wriggly sand worms snaked around them, creating curly patterns in the loose material on the sea bed.

The Oceans of Earth

Earth – our blue planet – is exceptional in our solar system as it is nearly three quarters covered by the oceans. But why are our oceans here? Intriguingly, Earth's oceans arrived from outer space. When the Earth was forming, it was too hot for water to condense on the planet. Just as tall mountains have snowy white tops above the 'snow-line', where the cooling of the atmosphere with height allows snow to persist, so too was there a gradient of cooling to a snow-line away from the ferociously hot early Sun.

Temperatures cold enough for ice grains to form were only reached further out in the solar system, in the asteroid belt somewhere between Mars and Jupiter. Earth's oceans, therefore, had to be *imported*: many think this happened with a shower of water-rich meteorites or comets from the asteroid belt bombarding the early Earth.

Since then these extraterrestrial water molecules have been neither created nor destroyed! For the subsequent 3.8 billion years (the first evidence for liquid water comes from sediments of this age on southwest Greenland), our oceans have been trapped on the Earth's surface, where they go round in two cycles.

First, the warmth of the Sun in the tropics turns some of the ocean to vapour (just as you see coming from a boiling kettle or steam engine) and clouds. Rising clouds cool and create rain, which trickles across the land and into streams and rivers before gushing back into the oceans.

Second, small amounts of water pop down into Earth's interior, through deep-sea trenches in the ocean crust. This water rapidly returns to the surface through volcanoes or hydrothermal vents.

So the very same water molecules coming out of your taps at home have witnessed *every second* of Earth's history, from before the start of self-reproducing life itself to the emergence of multi-celled organisms. Most probably, these water molecules passed through a dinosaur at some point. You could be making a cup of tea out of water that was once slurped down by a thirsty T. Rex!

What makes water so extraordinary and the oceans so key to life is its ability to dissolve things. Put some salt in a glass of water, or sugar in your tea, and those crystals will disappear or dissolve. This is because of the slight charge or 'polarity' of water molecules, which attracts elements into solution.

Water is even better at dissolving things if it is made a little acidic, by reacting with something like carbon dioxide to make carbonic acid. Take a sip of fizzy water (those bubbles are carbon dioxide) and see if you can taste the acidity; both my sons wrinkle their noses on doing so. Now, when water cycles from the oceans to clouds, then to rain and down rivers, it becomes a bit acidic by reacting with carbon dioxide in our atmosphere. As a result, this carbonated rainwater dissolves elements out of the land (this is called *weathering*), takes them into the rivers, and the elements end up going into the oceans. Have you ever seen reddish-brown rivers? These are full of *iron* which has been leached out of the rocks.

The oceans accumulate all the elements dissolved from the land (and from reaction with the deep ocean floor at hydrothermal vents, such as spectacular black smokers). But only the water molecules themselves keep on cycling back to clouds – the elements are left behind. Some elements get so concentrated in the ocean that they turn back into minerals and fall out as sediments, notably limestone (*calcium carbonate*) and cherts (*silica*), a process which limits their concentration in the sea.

Unlike most elements, however, the elements sodium or chlorine – the two ingredients of salt – only fall out from the ocean episodically and in exceptional circumstances. For example, the entire Mediterranean dried up to a puddle about 6 million years ago, leaving huge salt deposits. The lack of a natural continuous 'sink' for *sodium* and *chlorine* means that the sea is always salty.

The weathering of land by water is the very reason why life could appear and remain on Earth: it acts as a thermostat for Earth's temperature. The speed of weathering depends on Earth's temperature. So if, for any reason, the temperature rises – due to the increase in solar luminosity over Earth's history, for example – or if there is an increase of carbon dioxide (a greenhouse gas which warms the Earth) in the planet's atmosphere, then the rocks on land dissolve more quickly. This leads to a rush of elements (and carbon) into the oceans – which in turn speeds up the formation of sediment. This locks additional carbon dioxide into limestones, thus resetting the planet to its previous conditions and stopping everything from overheating. How do you think weathering works to stop the Earth completely freezing over?

While weathering maintained temperatures favourable for life to appear, we do not know, and perhaps might never know, where life did begin on our Earth (now there's a challenge for you!). Was it in some 'warm little pond', as the great naturalist Darwin suggested, or at the depths of the ocean? Whichever it was, one thing we do know is that life's origins and evolution depended on water. Elements are bound rigidly in rocks in the Earth's crust, but the ocean is a watery cocktail of all those rocky elements (and organic molecules) highly available, all free to diffuse and react. This is the key to initiating life.

It is believed that the deeper oceans likely provided a safe haven for life's very first stirrings – the surface of the early Earth would have been a much harsher environment. Down in the oceans, harmful radiation was filtered out, and the seas provided buffering against extreme temperatures, and protected the development of life against bombardments of meteorites and intense volcanic outpourings.

From uncertain origins perhaps 2.7 billion years ago, scientists believe that the first 2 billion years of life's history almost certainly then played out in the ocean. But an inescapable feedback spurred life to become more and more complex. The increasing success of microbes created more chemical byproducts (notably oxygen in the atmosphere), most of which were initially toxic. So to afford more and better control of internal chemistry, simple cells became compartmentalized (these kinds of cells are called *eukaryotes*) and ultimately differentiated.

This appearance of multicellularity coincided with the most spectacular of life's inventions - that of the *skeleton*. During this 'Cambrian explosion', 0.54 billion years ago, the rock record of life shows a change from faint ambiguous imprints to a diversity of robust yet intricate shell fossils, undoubtedly sculpted by organisms of complexity (indeed Darwin misread this explosion as the dawn of life).

The solution of Earth's minerals concentrated in the ocean – as explained before - made making hard parts like shells relatively easy. Just as the horned dinosaurs developed ever more elaborate ornamentation against the increasing ferocity of the Tyrannosaurs, these first 'biominerals' afforded armoured protection against forces, poisons and, importantly, predators.

Skeletons – shells and bones – gave rigidity to support animal life in the first steps onto land!

Over Earth's history, the weathering thermostat has maintained a *balance* between the amount of acidity (the carbon dioxide) and the amount of alkalinity (the dissolved ions in the ocean). You might think of the continents as an indigestion remedy or 'antacid' for the ocean. As long as the oceans have been present, they have always been slightly alkaline – perfect for making skeletons.

But we – and future generations on Earth – face a growing problem.

The booming of mankind and our thirst for fossil fuels is adding carbon dioxide – hence *acidity* – to the ocean at an unprecedented rate. In a million years or so, the dissolution of the land masses of our continents will accelerate sufficiently to start to neutralize this great burp of carbon dioxide into our waters. But this weathering is inherently slow, so in the meantime, the oceans are becoming a bit less alkaline and a bit less saturated. This process is often termed ocean *acidification*. 'Ocean slightly less alkalization' would be a more accurate description, though less headline-grabbing!

Vulnerable organisms such as coral reefs will find skeleton generation increasingly challenging. This could have enormous ramifications across the marine ecosystem. Unless organisms can adapt – and fast!

Some scientists believe we should intervene to redress global warming and acidification by 'geoengineering' carbon dioxide removal. This could include manipulating the weathering of the land, to release more alkaline elements into the seas.

But should we really embark on yet another global-scale experiment with our Earth?

What do you think?

Ros

Another group of fish swam past, so close to George's nose that he thought he could reach out and touch them! These fish were brightly coloured, like a little carnival passing through, with stripes of red, blue, yellow and orange. In the far distance, George thought he saw an immense flippered turtle turn and stare at him with its ancient unblinking dark eyes. The turtle opened its mouth, and to George's astonishment, it seemed to be calling him! It seemed to know his name!

George, the turtle said. *George!* Strangely, the turtle seemed to have reached out a hand and was shaking his shoulder.

A hand? How would a turtle have a hand? George was just pondering this from his underwater idyll when . . .

'George!' It was his best friend Annie standing in front of him, holding the cardboard 3D virtual reality headset he had been wearing until just a few moments before.

George blinked, adjusting to the bright sunlight of a summer afternoon in Foxbridge rather than the murky blue gloaming in the depths of the Coral Sea, off the coast of Australia. He felt completely disorientated. A moment ago, he'd been floating by the Great Barrier

Reef. Now he was back in the treehouse at the bottom of his garden, rather than at the bottom of the ocean. There was no turtle talking to him – just his best friend Annie from next door, and she certainly seemed to have a lot to say.

'I'm taking back my VR headset!' she complained. 'I should never have let you have it! You spend all your time underwater now! And I want you to look at this.' She waved her tablet at him and then pressed a button so the screen came to life. George looked down at it, but he was still seeing fish-shaped blue clouds in front of his eyes so it took him a few moments to focus his

vision. Compared to the marvels of the reef, it looked *very* dull.

'You made me come out of VR to read a form!' he protested. 'Like you fill in to get a railcard.'

'No, silly,' persisted Annie. 'You didn't look properly.'

George looked again. 'Oh!' he said, realization dawning like the sunrise on a planet with two suns in the sky.

'See?' said Annie. 'What does it say?'

'*Astronauts wanted!*'  he read. '*Astronauts wanted!*' he repeated. 'That's *so* cool!' He carried on reading out loud. '*Do you have what it takes to leave Earth behind and travel further than any human being has gone before? Could you start a human habitation on the red planet? Could you save the future of the human race by helping it spread out into space and colonize a whole new planet? Do you have the skills to take us into a new era of manned space travel?*' George rattled off quickly. '*If so, apply here . . .* Hang on,' he said suspiciously. 'If they want astronauts, don't you think they mean grown-up ones?'

'No!' said Annie triumphantly. 'This is for junior astronauts! It says so – between the ages of eleven and fifteen!'

'Bit weird, isn't it?' asked George. 'Why would you send a bunch of kids to Mars?'

'Duh!' replied Annie. 'Any mission to Mars won't be ready for years – by the time it lifts off, we won't be kids any more. But they must want to start the training now so they've got lots of time to pick the best candidates . . . Can you fill them out?' She handed him the tablet.

'Them?' said George.

'One for you, one for me,' said Annie.

'Why am I – ?' he started to ask.

'You can't change what you've typed,' said Annie, who was getting more confident now about admitting she was dyslexic. 'And there's no autocorrect – the form goes automatically, as soon as you've typed it. So it would be way better if you did it.'

'Will spelling really matter on Mars?' questioned George. 'There are far more important things for travelling in space, you know that.'

'No,' said Annie firmly. 'It won't. But I might not get there if I call it the planet "Rams" by mistake.'

'This form is quite long,' said George, scrolling down.

'Of course it is!' scoffed Annie. 'You don't think they are going to let just anyone fly to Mars?'

'Or Rams,' added George with a cheeky grin.

'Yes, Rams, the new home of the human race!' cried Annie. 'Right, come on. What's the first thing?'

'Erm . . . *Explain in your own words why you would be a great candidate to join a trial programme for junior astronaut training in preparation for a Mars mission in 2025.*'

'Easy!' cried Annie. 'I've got a very high IQ, I'm excellent at problem solving, I have lots of experience of travelling in space—'

'Can we put that?' interrupted George. While it was definitely true that he and Annie had travelled in space before, no one was supposed to know about their out-of-this-universe adventures. 'When does training start?' he asked. 'Hang on! It starts really soon. How are we going to get places on this? Haven't they chosen people already?'

'Hey, chill out! It says that a few places have come vacant,' said Annie. 'I can't believe we missed the advert the first time. And it's timed to start at the beginning of the school holidays.'

'That's in a few days' time!' said George.

At that moment, the screen pinged with an incoming message.

'Don't read that!' Annie cried out.

Glancing up in surprise, finger frozen above the tablet, George saw that Annie had turned white. 'C'mon, I . . . I . . . wouldn't read your text messages!' he said.

'Well, don't!' said Annie. 'Just . . . don't. Go back to *Astronauts Wanted . . .*'

But the screen pinged again. And again. And again, until there was a whole list of incoming unread messages, all from the same number.

'Right. Mars,' said Annie defiantly, brushing her long fringe out of her eyes, clearly determined to ignore the messages, which were piling up by the minute. 'Let's leave this planet behind. I don't want to stay here with the horrible people.'

'What horrible people?' said George slowly. 'Annie, what's going on?'

'NOTHING!' said Annie. 'Why has something always got to be going on? No Thing is Going On. Except me, leaving Earth for ever to become a space superhero so I can look down on those earthy worm idiots.'

Silently George swiped one of the messages at random.

U R STUPID AND EVIL AND NO 1 LIKES U.

'Yuk!' he exclaimed, recoiling from the screen. 'That's nasty! I'm going to write back . . .'

Before Annie could snatch back her tablet, George tapped out, WHO ARE YOU?

U NO, came a message only seconds later. U NO AND U R SCARED OF US COS U R WEAK AND SILLY AND WE HATE U.

WHY DON'T YOU SHUT UP, UGLY FACE? George tapped back furiously.

UGLY LOL! AS IF. U R THE UGLIEST PERSON ON EARTH came back at him.

'Stop it!' said Annie furiously. 'Messaging back only makes it worse!'

'Have you told your mum and dad about this?' asked George.

'No way!' cried Annie. 'They'll think it's my fault!'

'Why would they think that?' asked George. He was so disgusted by the messages that he flinched away from the screen as though it was burning hot. 'I don't understand.'

'I don't either,' said Annie miserably. 'I thought I was friends with everyone.' She seemed to find it hard to explain at first, but then the words came tumbling out. 'This group of girls suddenly started whispering about me. As soon as I came into the room, they all started muttering behind their hands, and when I asked them why, they just laughed in my face and said they weren't whispering about me and I had a really big head to think they were talking about me. But as soon as I went out of the room, they stopped.'

'Did you tell your teacher?'

'She just said that she would look into it – and it would help if I could identify the ringleaders, which I *can't*. But the best thing is to be mature enough not to react, because if I ignored the bullies they would stop. And if I didn't they would keep on bullying me. I figured that meant it was my fault for paying them any attention.'

'That's stupid!' said George. 'Bullies don't just stop because you ignore them!'

'And then I started getting left out of everything,' said Annie. 'Like, everyone else would be going somewhere at lunch time or after school. And I'd be the only person who wasn't invited. If I tried to sit next to anyone in my class, they would get up and walk away and everyone else would laugh.'

'But why?' said George, bewildered. 'I don't get it.' Annie was the coolest person he'd ever met and he couldn't begin to imagine how anyone would think differently.

'I don't either,' said Annie.

'It's so random and weird!' exclaimed George.

'And, like, there are all these stories about me at school now.' Annie looked distraught. 'I heard some girls saying that everyone knew I was actually really thick, but my dad did all my homework for me, which is why I'm top of the class.'

'Well, that's not true!' said George. 'They're probably just jealous. Do you know who is sending these messages?'

'It's one of *them*,' said Annie. 'It's got to be. But I don't know which one.' She wrapped her arms around her knees and buried her head so that George could just see a blonde crown above shaking shoulders. 'I've only got like one or two friends left now, and even they don't dare hang around with me too much.'

'So that's why you haven't wanted to do anything lately!' George realized. Every time he'd asked Annie to come to the skate park or go to the cinema with him, she'd made up some kind of really obviously flimsy excuse. 'In case you see any of those girls?'

'Yup,' said Annie's muffled voice. 'It would just make it worse.' She sounded like she was crying now. 'I don't want to go any place or do anything.' She swallowed, then added fervently, 'Except space. I still want to go into space.'

'Right, that's enough,' said George fiercely, snatching up the laptop. 'C'mon.'

He scaled quickly down the ladder, the tablet under his arm pinging all the time, while Annie followed him at top speed shouting, 'Where are you going?'

George jumped through the hole in the fence which divided the next-door gardens belonging to his and Annie's families, and ran up the overgrown path to Annie's back door. 'Eric!' he hollered.

Annie's dad was on the phone. 'Yes, I know, Rika,' he was saying rather testily. 'I haven't been a scientist for all this time without understanding how experiments work. I'm just saying that I don't think your suggestion is going to produce the kind of results we need.'

The two friends heard a furious high-pitched squeaking from the other end of the phone.

'If you'll just let me make some simple changes to your plan for the space mission . . .' he said. 'Rika . . . ?

Rika? Are you there?' He put the phone down. 'Can you believe it?' he said, spotting Annie and George. 'Rika seems to have hung up on me. We used to get on so well. I don't understand why she's changed so much.'

He took off his glasses and started cleaning them on his shirt, a process which only seemed to make them filmier. 'I do wish I had a second-in-command who liked me a little more,' he complained. 'It is making everything incredibly complicated, not to mention embarrassing now, that my deputy treats me like I am some kind of dangerous fool.' He put his glasses back on and looked at Annie and George and noticed they were both very upset. 'But that isn't what you've come to see me about it, is it? What's wrong?'

'Eric!' said George. 'Annie's getting nasty messages! And she won't tell you because she thinks you will blame her.'

Annie stood beside George, unable to wrestle the tablet back from him as he was now holding it with both hands over his head.

'It's all right, Dad,' she said bravely. 'George is making too big a deal out of it. They're jokes. It's just silly. A lot of it is my fault really. And I've got it all under control.'

'I'll be the judge of that,' said Eric. 'Give me the tablet.' He took the computer and looked at the messages on the screen. His face changed instantly from sunny and friendly to thunderous.

'Don't!' wailed Annie, who was mortified. 'I don't want you to read them.' She collapsed into sobs while Eric read the contents of her inbox, his eyes widening in disbelief.

'These aren't jokes,' he said angrily. 'This is not funny. And it's certainly *not* your fault. Have you told your mum about this?'

Annie shook her head and said nothing.

'What can we do?' asked George.

'I've got an idea,' said Eric. 'Follow me.' The two friends trooped behind him into his study, where Cosmos – the world's greatest supercomputer – was humming to himself on the desk.

'WAKEY WAKEY!' Eric summoned his hi-tech helper.

'Professor!' replied Cosmos cordially, his screen springing into artificial life.

'Cosmos, me old mate,' said Eric, leaning on the desk. 'The youngest member of the Order of Science, Annie Bellis here, has an issue with which we require your assistance.'

'My pleasure.' Cosmos glowed. The supercomputer

had a special fondness for Eric's daughter. 'What can I assist you with today?'

'Annie is receiving malicious communications,' said Eric seriously. 'On this tablet, through an internet messaging service.'

'Has this matter been referred to you by another member of the Order?' asked Cosmos.

'Thank you, yes, by George Greenby, also a member of the Order, the second youngest scientist in our number.'

'In that case, under the International Agreement for the Use of Supercomputers in matters pertaining to the Order of Science, part two, paragraph three, sub-clause b, amended in 2015 by annexe k,' reeled off Cosmos. 'I find . . .' He paused while his circuits chuntered.

Eric waited, as did the two friends. They knew from Eric's constant grumbling that he and Cosmos – since new regulations over supercomputer use had come into force – now had to work with far more rules and regulations about everything he did than they had done in the past. Before, Eric had been pretty much free to be as creative with how he used Cosmos as he had wished.

'I find I can act on your behalf!' said Cosmos delightedly. 'Please attach the tablet so I can download the information.'

George ran forward and plugged the tablet into the supercomputer.

'What's Cosmos going to do?' Annie whispered to her dad.

'I don't know!' said Eric gleefully. 'But I bet it will be fabulous! Within,' he added hastily, 'the provisions of the International Agreement for Response to Defamatory Statements about scientists within the Order, as mandated in—'

'Yes, we know,' said Annie. 'Paragraph Y, annexe X and sub-clause Z.'

'Something like that,' agreed Eric. 'Annie, perhaps you should be a lawyer when you grow up.'

'No thank you, Dad!' exclaimed Annie. 'I'm going to be a scientist! I told you already.'

'OK, OK,' said Eric, shaking his head. 'Just saying – maybe there will be more jobs in the future for lawyers than there will be for scientists . . .'

'Well, don't,' said Annie firmly. 'I bet Nana and Grandad didn't say to you: "Don't be a cosmologist, little Eric, 'cos you'll never get a job that way" . . .'

'Actually they did,' said Eric mildly. 'But I took no notice.'

'Well, now you know how that feels,' said Annie firmly. George was very pleased to see how much more cheerful she looked.

'I don't think I ever spoke to my parents the way you speak to me,' complained Eric.

'Perhaps they inspired respect?' asked Annie innocently.

Eric gave her a mock cross look, but George knew he wasn't angry with Annie. It was just how they were, bickering endlessly about everything but in a funny and friendly way. Mostly.

Standing right next to Cosmos and Annie's tablet, George was the first to see an outgoing message on the tablet screen, sent by Cosmos via the tablet to the same number that had been harassing Annie. But there wasn't just one message; there was a first one, which was followed instantly by another and another and another.

'Cosmos, what are you doing?' asked George in wonder.

'I,' the supercomputer replied happily, 'am sending over, in one hundred and sixty character chunks, the full text of *Principia Mathematica*, the great work of Isaac Newton. Once that has been sent, I will continue with Charles Darwin's *On the Origin of Species*, which will be superseded by the collected works of Einstein. It should take around one hundred and fifteen hours for all the text to go through. I do not think you will hear from this correspondent again, not given the amount of interesting reading matter we have supplied.'

'Genius!' cried Eric. 'You have invoked the "Respond by Education, Not Threat" clause of the agreement!'

'To the very letter,' said Cosmos. 'Would you like me to show you from whence your messages originated?'

'Yes!' said Annie. 'You know who sent them then?

Oh, Cosmos, lovely Cosmos, I wish I'd asked you to find out stuff about this for me before.'

Cosmos didn't answer, but simply posted a map on his screen with a big red arrow pointing to a nearby address. 'Is this location known to you?' he asked.

Annie had turned a sickly whitish-green again. 'That's Belinda's house! I thought *she* was my friend,' she whispered, sounding broken-hearted. 'I thought she wasn't joining in with the others. She said they were awful and should know better.'

Her dad put his arm round her. 'I'm sorry, darling,' he said. 'We think we know people, but . . .' His face brightened up. 'Cosmos! Can you continue performing this action and open the portal at the same time?'

Cosmos snorted. 'Of course, Professor,' he said. 'This task uses around 0.000000000001 per cent of my full capacity.'

'Good!' said Eric. 'Under the "Entertainment and Welfare" section of the agreement in relation to scientists suffering from distress, I have a request!'

He winked at the two friends. They knew he was treating them like real grown-ups, like proper members of the Order of Science in order to cheer them up – and it was working! They both loved pretending that they were adult scientists with important experiments and ideas that might change the future of the world. Annie and George looked at each other, not daring to hope.

'Dr Bellis, I presume,' murmured George.

'Professor Greenby,' replied Annie politely. 'Such an honour to know your work.'

'Put your spacesuits on,' said Eric firmly. 'Cosmos, open the portal. I will give you the coordinates. Because, fellow scientists of the Order of Science, we are going on a field trip.'

Chapter Two

'A field trip!' Annie was overjoyed. 'You haven't let us use the space portal in, like, for ever!'

The portal, Cosmos's computer-generated doorway to space, had been closed to George and Annie for some time now. When Annie was a little girl, her father used to take her for spacewalks quite often, in the way other dads would take their kids to the park. But since the new regulations about supercomputers, Eric had been very firm that Cosmos was a tool for professional research only and not for exciting activities on rainy Earth days.

Annie and George hadn't really been listening to the whole long and rather boring rigmarole that Eric had poured out one day, in one of his endless complaints about the now-hated Rika Dur, his second-in-command, and how she insisted on writing a special new rule for everything that used to just happen by itself in the past. But they had certainly listened when Eric told them that the upshot of all of this was no more journeys into space for Annie and George using supercomputer Cosmos and his amazing portal.

And yet now, to their delight, it looked as though Eric himself was fed up with the rules and regulations and wanted to go out to space too in order to make Annie feel better after her horrible experience on Earth.

But Cosmos didn't seem so sure this was a good idea. A computer, even a supercomputer, can't actually look down its nose, but that was exactly what Cosmos seemed to be doing.

'Professor,' he said. 'I have a compliance issue with your request.'

George's heart sank. It felt as though they were so close to getting out into space and now Cosmos was putting the brakes on! It was unbearable! George could almost taste space in his mouth he was so excited about the prospect of exploring with Annie and Eric beside him. He just couldn't wait for that extraordinary feeling when he stepped over the threshold of Cosmos's doorway and once again was free floating above some incredible cosmic planet-scape. And now, after all, it might not happen. His shoulders drooped.

But Eric, who was halfway into his spacesuit, which he put on over his normal clothes, simply asked, 'Why?'

'It does not meet the criteria under the provisions of the agreement. I find no specific mention of field trips into space merely in order to cheer people up.'

'It's not "people",' protested Annie. 'It's me and George.'

'Regretfully,' said Cosmos, 'that makes it even worse.'

Eric paused. He was clearly trying to think of a way to get round the problem. The two friends watched him, willing him to find a really clever solution that would let them get out into space, even if just for a minute or two. But as Eric sighed and started to slip off his spacesuit again, they realized it wasn't going to happen.

'Cosmos is right,' he said sadly. 'We'll all be in huge trouble if anyone finds out I used a supercomputer to take kids—'

Annie interrupted. 'Not kids; two members of the Order of Science! We became members of the Order of Science years ago – you got us to join so we could help you understand what kids want to know about science to make the future world a better place.'

'– into space,' Eric finished.

'Trouble with who?' asked George longingly. 'We won't get into trouble with anyone, will we? I don't see how that could happen.' But he didn't sound very convincing. Memories of space trips he had taken which hadn't worked out very well – and got them into lots of trouble with all sorts of people – surfaced in his mind.

Eric frowned. 'Some of the Order wouldn't mind,' he said. 'But if *Rika*' – he almost spat the name out – 'found out, she'd rocket me into space from Kosmodrome 2 on a one-way ticket.'

Kosmodrome 2 was the name of Eric's new-ish place of work. Recently, he'd taken over as head of

Kosmodrome 2 – an international space facility and joint enterprise involving lots of countries and private companies, trying to bring the plans for robotic and manned space travel together into one gigantic whole. Annie and George had pestered Eric to take them to his 'office' but Eric had regretfully refused. Kosmodrome 2 was a closed facility, he explained. Only in exceptional circumstances could they have visitors. However many exceptional circumstances Annie and George dreamed up, none of them seemed to make the grade.

'To think I was so pleased when I got that job,' said Eric, folding his spacesuit up surprisingly neatly and putting it back in the cupboard. 'I really thought I could help coordinate the world's efforts to get further into space. Turns out, I can't even manage the person who is supposed to be helping me.'

Annie looked at her dad sympathetically. 'Are you being bullied too?' she asked.

'You could say that,' admitted Eric. 'I'm being bullied at work. Except it's all so clever and so sneaky that I sometimes I wonder if

I'm going mad and imagining things. Everything I do at work goes wrong somehow, and yet I don't understand why, except that it all started when Rika came back from her holidays. She was normal, friendly, helpful, nice before – and then after she wasn't ... it's so very, very odd.'

'Are they whispering about you as well?' asked Annie solemnly.

'Yes!' said Eric, as though this was a revelation to him. 'They are! Whenever I pass people in the corridors – and Jupiter knows, we have enough corridors at Kosmodrome 2 – they seem to be whispering, but they stop while I walk past and then start again!'

'Horrid,' said Annie. 'Do they make up stories about you as well?'

'Goodness, yes,' said Eric fervently. 'Completely bonkers ones too! Why would I deliberately trigger the space elevator to malfunction when we have a group of important international guests? I just wouldn't do that!'

George was startled. He hadn't heard anything about an incident with a space elevator – he was pretty sure he'd remember if he had; it wasn't the sort of thing he would forget in a hurry. In fact, he hadn't heard anything about a space elevator at all! This was really important and exciting stuff that they were missing out on!

'Poor you, Dad,' sympathized Annie. 'I know just

how you feel. Have a hug!'

There was a moment's silence as Eric and Annie hugged and George stood around wondering what to do next. And that's when he had his new idea.

'I know!' he exclaimed. 'I've got a plan! It's like a thing we did before: we opened the portal with Cosmos but we didn't go through it – we just *looked*! It was way more exciting than watching stuff on YouTube because it was real! Could we do that? Could Cosmos just show us something, rather than let us actually travel?'

'Aha!' Eric's eyes brightened up. 'Now that may well be within the bounds of possibility!'

'Like, in other words, yes?' said Annie.

'Cosmos?' asked Eric. 'Can you *show* us a space voyage, even if you can't let us physically transport to the location we choose?'

Cosmos tutted to himself while he checked his operating rules. 'I find that I can!' he cried, clearly unhappy to have blocked his friends earlier. 'What would you like to view?'

Annie and George

went into a huddle together.

'What do *you* want to see?' George asked Annie eagerly.

'Well, I really don't want to just look through the portal,' admitted Annie. 'I won't feel like I've left everything behind if we're stuck on this side of the doorway.'

'Maybe just knowing that space is out there – because you can see it for real, in 3D, and sort of feel it and touch it – will make you happier,' said George hopefully, trying to persuade her.

'Maybe,' said Annie. But she looked doubtful.

'I think we should look at a place in our solar system, so it's somewhere we could maybe visit one day,' said George. 'Then you can imagine stepping through the space doorway and crunching down onto the surface of another planet and it will be sort of like going there for real.'

'Oooh, yes,' said Annie, brightening. 'That's a cool idea.'

'What about one of Jupiter's moons?' George suggested. 'They're super-icy and weird and strange – and who knows what we might see!'

'It's a plan,' said Annie decisively. 'I know! I know!' She jumped up and down, squeaking suddenly. 'When we got the VR thingy, I did some research on marine life – and I found out that there might be extra-terrestrial aliens swimming around under the icy crust on Europa! Let's go and see for ourselves.'

'Oh, yeah,' said George. 'Now that would be awesome.' He thought back to the VR headset and the views he had seen of the underwater world around the Great Barrier Reef. Could it look like that in space too?

'Yay! Dolphins in space!' said Annie. 'Can we, Dad? Can we?'

'Well, it's cheaper than a trip to the aquarium,' said Eric cheerfully. 'But don't expect to actually see dolphins, mind you. We don't really know whether there are any beings anything like dolphins or minke whales in space, you know.'

'Then let's find out!' said Annie.

'Permission granted,' said Cosmos. 'Security checking . . .'

This was a new phase in Cosmos's space doorway creation activity, which Eric himself had added after Cosmos had been hacked by an evil-doer called Alioth Merak, who had turned their friendly supercomputer into a dangerous enemy.

'Security check complete!' Cosmos sang out. 'Prepare portal.'

'Cosmos,' said Eric, as the now-familiar twin beams of light shot out from the little computer and started to draw a door shape in the air. 'Make sure you add a radiation shield to protect us, given how close to Jupiter we will be.'

'Affirmative,' replied Cosmos, who had gone into operational mode, during which time he tended to

LUCY & STEPHEN HAWKING

become more automatic than personable.

George threw a glance over at Annie's tablet computer and noticed that the outgoing messages, made up of chunks of text taken from some of the greatest scientific books, were still pouring relentlessly onto the screen. 'Your "friend",' he said, using his fingers to make inverted commas, 'must be going crazy by now.'

'Hope so!' said Annie crossly. 'Just the other day, she was telling me how she was, like, my BFF. And that she wasn't taking part in all the mean stuff happening at school. But then it turns out that she's worse than all the others! I bet she was sending those messages to keep in with the bullies. But she didn't dare admit to me that she couldn't be my friend any more, so she was pretending to me as well . . .'

'Look,' said George, pointing. The hairs on his neck stood on end. 'Cosmos is opening the portal!'

The door-like shape, which Cosmos had drawn out of beams of light, had now turned solid and was swinging very slowly open. All three of them – Eric included – watched with open mouths as the door opened fully, to reveal behind it the pitted and cracked icy surface of one of Jupiter's moons. It was a sight that never disappointed.

'Wow! Could we skate on Europa?' asked Annie in a breathless voice as she gazed through the portal doorway at the rough, icy landscape beyond. The view stretched all the way to the horizon, peaceful and calm – just an uninhabited ice-bound celestial body in orbit around its planet, Jupiter. From Europa, the two friends and Eric could see the magnificent gas planet

hanging in the sky like a massive stripy ball. The light was dim on Europa, this moon world being so much further away from the brilliance of the Sun than the Earth, but they could still see strange ridged and squiggly formations in the ice. With a gentle 'pfoof' in the air, as though the moon was doing a tiny exhale, a burst of gassy liquid escaped upwards from the crusty surface into the thin atmosphere. Against the black backdrop of space – peppered with billions of tiny stars in every direction – the fountain made a lacy pattern as it froze and fell back down to the surface in gentle flakes.

'Ooh, it's just like when we were on Enceladus!' said Annie happily. Her father was looking at her quizzically, but she carried on regardless.

George started coughing very loudly to try and drown out what she was saying – he just knew this wasn't the time to let her father know they'd been on unauthorized space voyages in the recent past – like that particular trip to Enceladus, one of Saturn's moons.

But Annie just patted him on the back and carried on talking over his volley of splutters. 'Only this time, we're all snug at home, not standing on a volcano that's about to erupt under us—' She realized her mistake too late and fell silent.

George stopped coughing and gave her a puce-faced glare. He couldn't believe she had been so stupid! Annie just shrugged back at him again.

Is there really life on Europa, the 'blue' moon of Jupiter? Right now, we don't know! Thanks to the Galileo mission, launched in 1989, which sent back lots of new information about Jupiter's fourth largest moon, we think there is a subsurface ocean under the thick icy crust, which could contain a form of life. But whether we would actually find dolphins swimming about if we could land on Europa and drill down through the several-kilometre-thick carpet of ice, is anyone's guess! It would be far more probable – and actually, equally exciting to scientists – that any life found would be more like microbes.

But we may get some clearer answers in the next decade! A new mission called JUICE (Jupiter Icy Moon Explorer) is planned to set off in 2022 to take a closer look at this mysterious moon. JUICE is a robotic spacecraft designed by the European Space Agency. It will take around eight years to reach Jupiter, arriving in 2030, and will spend about three years looking at the giant gas planet and three of its largest moons, Callisto, Ganymede and Europa. Hopefully JUICE and a simultaneous NASA mission, Europa Clipper, will tell us much, much more about Europa.

What do we know now?

Well, we know that:

(Europa is an icy moon in orbit around Jupiter, the largest planet in our solar system.

(Jupiter has a total of 67 moons, but the four largest of them - including Europa - are called the *Galilean moons*, because they were discovered in 1610 by the astronomer Galileo Galilei. When Galileo spotted these moons orbiting around Jupiter, he realized that not everything in the solar system went around the Earth, as previously thought! This completely changed perceptions of our place in the solar system and the Universe itself.

(Europa is only slightly smaller than our Moon but has a much smoother surface. In fact, Europa may have the fewest lumps and bumps of any object in the solar system as it doesn't seem to have mountains or craters!

(It has an icy crust surface. Scientists believe the ocean underneath could be 100 kilometres - or 62 miles - deep. Compare this to the deepest ocean on Earth – the Marianas Trench in the Pacific Ocean, which is 6.8 miles deep!

(The crust has distinctive markings in the form of dark stripes which may be ridges formed by eruptions of warm ice at an earlier stage in Europa's life.

'When did you go to Enceladus?' demanded her father. 'There are some unaccounted space voyages in the supercomputer log and if it turns out that it was you all along . . .'

'We went to Enceladus in our minds,' Annie lied, crossing her fingers behind her back. She and George had, in fact, visited that weird little snooker ball of a moon on a secret mission to collect the building blocks of life. It had been an unhappy and dangerous visit and they had been desperate to escape, especially when a cryovolcano had nearly exploded through a fault line under their feet.

'You know, Dad,' Annie continued, 'you're always saying, "I travel across the Universe in my mind!" Well, we've been doing that too. And it's really great. You were right all along.'

Her father gave her a disbelieving look. George stared hard at Europa through the doorway. He knew if he glanced at Eric he'd look guilty and give the game away, so he searched the surface of the moon instead. He hoped to spot something to ask Eric about in order to make the tricky moment go away. And just as he was trying to form a clever question about the gravity there, or the orbit of Europa, or the possibility of alien life, he saw something for real.

'What's that!' he said, pointing.

'What's what?' said Eric, peering through the doorway. 'What have you seen!'

'Over there,' said George. 'There's a hole in the ice!'

'I expect there are lots of holes in the ice,' said Annie, confused as to why George was suddenly sounding so excitable. 'That's how the geysers escape from the underwater ocean.'

'Not like that one!' he said.

Annie gazed in the direction of his outstretched finger and saw exactly what he meant. 'OMG!' she breathed. George had indeed spotted a hole in the crinkly, greenish-white ice, but it wasn't just any hole. It was perfectly round, as though someone had taken a cookie cutter and sliced out a circle of thick ice. 'Could that happen naturally?' she asked her dad.

Eric was staring in horror at George's discovery. 'No,' he said, shaking his head. 'I don't believe it could. That's not the effect of an impact. That looks like it was done mechanically.'

'Mechanically?' said Annie. 'Like, by a robot?'

Volcanoes on Earth, in our Solar System and Beyond

Imagine what it would be like to visit an erupting volcano. Perhaps you even have? The ground shakes with tiny earthquakes as molten lava forces its way from the Earth's insides and hums as volcanic gases struggle to escape. Booming explosions vibrate through your body and ears. Acid fumes sting your eyes and nostrils, and even your skin and sweat begin to smell of sulphur (a mix of rotten eggs and struck matches). Up ahead, red-hot rocks fly high into the air, turning black as they cool and plummet to the ground. Some of them join the growing cone of rubble. Others feed a lava flow that snakes, clinking and fuming, downhill. This is what it was like for me visiting Mount Etna in Sicily in 2006. It was actually quite a small eruption (otherwise it would not have been safe to get so close!), but breath-taking, even for a volcano scientist (known as a volcanologist).

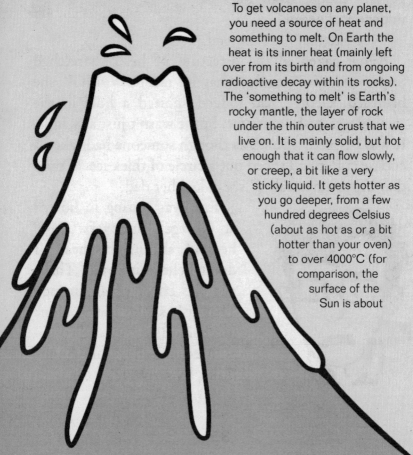

To get volcanoes on any planet, you need a source of heat and something to melt. On Earth the heat is its inner heat (mainly left over from its birth and from ongoing radioactive decay within its rocks). The 'something to melt' is Earth's rocky mantle, the layer of rock under the thin outer crust that we live on. It is mainly solid, but hot enough that it can flow slowly, or creep, a bit like a very sticky liquid. It gets hotter as you go deeper, from a few hundred degrees Celsius (about as hot as or a bit hotter than your oven) to over 4000°C (for comparison, the surface of the Sun is about

5500°C) just before you reach the molten outer core. Pressure also increases as you go deeper inside the Earth, like an exaggeration of the pressure you feel when you dive to the bottom of a swimming pool.

So the mantle is already very hot, but it is solid. On Earth there are two ways that nature melts it. In some places, like Iceland, where tectonic plates split apart from each other, or beneath Hawaii, where blobs of deep, hot mantle flow slowly upwards like a lava lamp, the pressure on the mantle *decreases*. This makes the mantle's melting point drop. You might have seen how kettles boil at a lower temperature up a mountain as pressure drops. In other places, like under Japan and Indonesia, things get *added* to the mantle and make it melt, just as we add salt to roads and pavements in winter to melt ice. This happens at 'subduction zones' where two tectonic plates push together. One sinks below the other and into the mantle, releasing water and other stuff into the mantle rocks above.

When the mantle melts, it produces a liquid rock called *magma*. This magma is less dense than the surrounding rock, and so it starts to move up towards the surface. This journey can be relatively quick, especially beneath the oceans where Earth's crust is thin. Or it can be longer, especially where the crust is thicker, like on the continents. The longer this journey takes, the more time the magma has to cool and change, becoming stickier and stickier.

But what makes magma explode out of the ground rather than just oozing like jam out of a doughnut? Magma has gases like steam and carbon dioxide dissolved in it. As magma rises and the pressure drops, the gases can't stay dissolved and they form bubbles. As they rise further, these bubbles grow bigger and bigger until they reach the surface and sometimes explode. Something similar happens when you open a bottle of cola quickly, especially if someone has been kind enough to shake the bottle first! Sticky magmas are better at trapping gas bubbles. This is one of the reasons why some volcanic eruptions are much more explosive than others.

That's how we explain most volcanism on Earth. But Earth is not the only place in our solar system that has volcanoes. Just look at a full Moon on a clear night. The large, dark patches you can see are solidified lava beds. They are called *Mare*, from the Latin word for sea, because early astronomers thought they really were seas.

37

Volcanoes on Earth, in our Solar System and Beyond

On Mars there are huge volcanoes, including Olympus Mons, the largest known volcano (over 20 km high and about the size of the state of Arizona in the USA).

Being smaller bodies than the Earth, both our Moon and the planet Mars cooled more quickly, so their volcanoes are now dead. Venus is a similar size to Earth, and the latest results from the Venus Express mission show exciting new evidence of possible active lava flows on this planet.

Further out in the Solar System we see more exotic forms of volcanism on moons orbiting the giant gas planets. The planet Jupiter has volcanoes on several of its more than 60 confirmed moons. Io, the innermost of the planet's larger moons, is the most volcanically active body we know of in the Solar System. Io heats up – like a squash ball in your hand – as it is stretched and squeezed under immense tidal forces from the giant planet it orbits. Io's volcanoes are spectacularly alive, sending plumes of gas and dust hundreds of kilometres into space. Europa, Jupiter's ice-covered moon, is also of great interest. It has a very young surface, with very few craters. This suggests that ice volcanism is continually covering the surface with watery magmas.

In 2005 the Cassini space probe spotted fountains of vapour and ice shooting into space from one of Saturn's moons, Enceladus. And even further away from the Sun, the Voyager 2 space probe saw dark plumes rising high above one of Neptune's moons, Triton, maybe made of nitrogen ice and driven by heat from the distant Sun itself.

Recent discoveries of rocky planets outside our solar system mean that whole new types of volcanism might also exist in the Universe that we and scientists of the future – like you perhaps – have yet to discover. Light that reaches Earth from these planets can hold clues about their atmospheres. As volcanoes release distinctive gases, volcanism could be the first geological process that we confirm outside our solar system.

I am often awestruck by how much remains to be understood about volcanoes on our own planet. The idea of a whole universe of volcanism still out there to explore is mind-boggling!

Tamsin

'But there are no missions to Europa,' said George, who knew his solar system pretty well by now. 'We've never sent a robot mission to Europa – just a space probe flying *past* – so how could a machine have made that hole?'

'Cosmos,' said Eric. 'Give me the coordinates of the area we can see on Europa right now.' Obligingly, Cosmos flashed up on his screen a string of numbers, which Eric read quickly. 'Yes, yes, yes,' he muttered to himself. He looked back at the hole in the ice completely baffled.

'What is it, Dad?' asked Annie.

'The coordinates are right, they fit the location, but this shouldn't happen for years yet . . .' Eric wasn't really making sense to the two friends.

'What shouldn't happen?' asked George.

'Artemis,' replied Eric. 'This is the location and the plan for Artemis . . . but Artemis hasn't happened yet. I don't understand. This is literally *impossible*.'

'What is Artemis?' asked Annie.

But Eric was already busy, closing down the portal doorway by tapping commands on Cosmos's keyboard. 'I have to go,' he said distractedly. 'I have to—' He was already halfway out of the door.

'Where?' Annie called after him. 'Where are you going?'

But it was too late – her father had already disappeared.

Chapter Three

'What's Artemis?' George repeated as the front door banged behind Eric. As they heard his footsteps fade away, they made out another noise – that of the landline ringing and Annie's mum picking up.

'Hmm,' said Annie. 'I think I know who or what Artemis is, but let's ask Cosmos to be sure.'

'Artemis – Greek goddess of hunting . . .' the super-computer supplied helpfully. 'Also the name of an expedition in a popular sci-fi novel, which told of a trip to Europa to see whether life could exist in an air bubble under the icy crust.'

'Well, can it?' asked George eagerly. He wiggled his toes inside his trainers with excitement.

'In theory,' replied Cosmos.

George groaned. All the most gripping things in science, like wormholes or time travel, seemed to exist 'in theory'. But when you said, 'So could that actually happen?' scientists usually said no.

'And in reality?' Annie persisted. 'Seriously, there really could be things swimming around in the oceans

40

on Europa, and if there's an air bubble between the ocean and the icy crust, then it's got to be possible that life could exist in that gap too.'

'What kind of things?' said George.

'Y'know, the kind of life forms that might have swum about in the oceans on Earth when life began,' said Annie knowledgeably. 'Like in my project last term on the Building Blocks of Life . . . what would have developed. Isn't that right, Cosmos?'

'Affirmative,' said Cosmos. 'In the book, Artemis was a project designed to take human life out into space, and at the same time investigate the existence of life in the Solar System.'

'So humans would go to Europa to see if there are life forms already there and then study them in their natural environment?' said Annie.

'But humans can't live on Europa!' said George. 'That's silly! We just saw it! It's all icy and there's nothing there!'

'Maybe the humans don't try and stay there for ever,' said Annie thoughtfully. 'Perhaps they just stay long enough to find out whether there are any underwater aliens swimming around under the ice.'

'Do they bring the aliens back with them?' asked George. 'In the story?'

'I don't know,' said Annie. 'But I expect they would want to – wouldn't they? So humans on Earth could examine them and find out more about how life began?'

'Wouldn't that be dangerous?' said George dubiously.'

'For the aliens,' said Cosmos. 'Definitely. But the possibilities of what we might learn are incredible. It might unlock the secrets of life itself.'

'Wow! . . . What if it isn't just sci-fi any more?' asked George. 'What if Artemis is actually happening?'

'Dad would know, right?' said Annie. 'That's his job – to run space missions. So how could "Artemis", whatever that is, be on Europa without him knowing?'

Annie's mum appeared in the doorway, holding the phone in her hand. 'It's your friend Belinda's mother,' she said. 'She wants to know why her daughter is getting a text from you more than once a second.'

George and Annie exchanged meaningful looks. Annie pulled an 'Ugh' face, but she did it with a sort of cheery look so George knew she wasn't so upset any more.

'Susan.' George decided to speak up for his friend. 'Annie's being cyber bullied by Belinda – she's sent loads of really mean messages to her.'

'We can show you the messages!' Annie piped up.

'I think you'd better!' said her mother.

'So Eric,' continued George, 'got Cosmos to stop her.'

Susan's eyebrows shot right up to her hairline. 'Stop her! How?' she said, her hand still covering the phone so Belinda's mother couldn't hear.

'Cosmos is sending her the works of Isaac Newton by text,' explained Annie, her eyes sparkling now.

Annie's mother smiled. 'Cosmos' – she addressed the supercomputer directly – 'I never thought I would say this, but well done!'

Susan and Cosmos were old enemies as neither

trusted the other nor truly wished to cohabit in the way they did. Cosmos lived in fear that Susan would unplug him in the middle of a vital operation, as she had threatened to do many times before, or send him to the computer junk yard; Susan disliked the central role that a computer played in her household and worried about having such a powerful piece of technology under her roof.

'Thank you, Mrs Bellis,' said Cosmos politely. 'I am pleased to be of service.'

Annie's mum walked away but the two friends could hear her on the phone, speaking crisply. 'I would advise you to look at the messages Belinda has been sending my daughter. And when you've done that, and Belinda has fully apologized and promised never to do this

CYBER BULLYING

The internet is an amazing tool for us to use. We can find out information, keep up with our friends, share photos, go shopping or play games.

But the internet also has a dark side. One aspect of internet life which is hurtful and scary is called *cyber bullying*. This means bullying, but online or through your mobile phone.

It is so widespread that the British charity Bullying UK (www.bullying.co.uk) reports most young people will suffer from it at some point. There are similar charities worldwide wherever young people use the internet.

Kids who are cyber bullied receive nasty messages through instant messaging services, find horrible, untrue comments posted about them on social networking sites or may even find a 'hate' site set up specifically about them. Unfortunately, bullies love the internet because it helps them to get their vicious messages and false posts seen by as many people as possible.

According to Bullying UK, it often turns out that the bullies may have once been best friends with their victims so they know lots of information about them.

But some internet users also find that 'new' friends, made on the internet aren't what they seem. They may not even be kids at all, but grown-ups, pretending to be kids to lure you in. Threats or requests for lots of personal photos or videos may start arriving. Sometimes these 'new friends' say they will contact your parents and say bad things about you if you don't do what they ask. This is called *grooming* and it means use of the internet to try and persuade you to behave in inappropriate or revealing ways.

If you believe you or someone you know is a victim of either cyber bullying or grooming, it is important to tell a trusted adult as soon as you can. *Never think it is your fault in any way, whatever the bullies might suggest.*

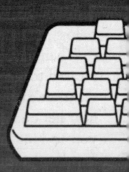

Here are some other important points about internet use
to help protect yourself from problems like this:

- **Don't share embarrassing photos of yourself with any internet users, especially not with ones who you don't really know.**

- **Don't say things online that you wouldn't say in person.**

- **Remember: there are strong laws that cover behaviour on the internet and the police can trace messages and posts, even anonymous ones.**

- **Don't reply to false posts or nasty messages – this is called flaming and bullies love it.**

- **Keep the evidence – there are strong laws which cover cyber bullying and the police may want to see the posts or messages.**

again to my daughter or anyone else, we will instruct our computer to stop messaging you!'

They heard furious squeaking from the other end of the phone.

'Yes, good, thank you,' Susan replied. 'Please ask your daughter to write that down, in pen and ink, and send it as a letter to Annie as I do not want your daughter communicating electronically with mine any further. And I will stop our computer from messaging you. But if this should start again, against Annie or anyone else at school, please know we will take this further.'

Susan hung up. She put her head round the door and gave the two friends the thumbs-up sign. 'Cosmos, you can stop now. And thank you again,' she said, then she went away to take up her violin practice again.

Cosmos cancelled the operation and the outgoing text messages ceased.

'Wow, that was cool!' said George.

'Yeah, you were right to tell Mum and Dad,' sighed Annie. 'I wanted to . . . but I couldn't. I just felt really embarrassed – like I should be able to handle all this school stuff myself, now that we're at secondary. I didn't want my parents barging into school and making a great big fuss – I thought that would make everything so much worse. But I'm so like mega phew that we told them. It is better, after all.'

'Yup,' said George. 'And if you hadn't told anyone, it would still be happening.'

'Exactly,' said Annie. 'Thank you.'

'I have the entire contents of the world's libraries at my disposal,' added Cosmos. 'So if you need me to start again, just give the command.'

'Hope not,' said Annie. 'I think the human–computer combo has solved this one for now. And as for the other mean girls, I don't go back to school for ages, and by then I'll be an astronaut, training to go to Mars. So whatevs to them anyway!'

'YOLO!' said George, pleased to hear Annie sounding chirpy again. 'Does that mean we can do Artemis now?'

'Yay!' said Annie. 'Cosmos, can you show us a screen shot of Europa so we can look at that circle in the ice again?'

'Of course,' said Cosmos. The image flashed briefly onto his screen but disintegrated very quickly into pixelated boxes in green and black. 'Reloading . . .' But the same thing happened. 'The data has been corrupted,' he said. 'I am not able to access this image.'

'Oh!' said Annie. 'Can you open the portal again and show us Europa, like you did before?'

'Negative,' said Cosmos. 'I am unable to accept a portal command from junior members of the Order.'

'Oh, bum,' said Annie crossly. 'You mean we have to get Dad back and he has to tell you?'

'Affirmative.'

'Can he do it by phone?' asked Annie. 'If I call him, can he tell you over speakerphone?'

'Theoretically . . .' said Cosmos. 'Except that all data streams to and from Europa have been blocked. Even with the correct authorization, I can no longer access any information about that moon.'

'Can you still see other planets and moons in the Solar System?' asked George.

'Mercury – check! Venus – check! Mars, asteroid belt, Jupiter itself, Saturn, frozen gas planets, dwarf planets, Oort cloud – all present and correct,' said Cosmos. 'The Solar System is all in place – except for that one moon, which seems to have gone AWOL.'

'Europa . . . is missing?' said Annie in disbelief.

'Currently,' said Cosmos. 'It would seem so. Europa is – no longer there!'

'But that's impossible,' said George. 'A moon the size of Europa can't just disappear!'

'No,' replied Cosmos. 'It can't. But it has.'

'Poor dolphins in space!' said Annie. 'Do you think

Europa's been captured by aliens? Why would aliens want it?'

'For the same reason that we would want to go there, I suppose,' said George. 'So they can find out more about how life began. Maybe they're gonna create a new life form of their own?'

'A Franken-dolph?' said Annie. 'That would be scary.'

'Better than a Franken-shark,' said George. 'That would be super-scary.'

'Ew!' said Annie.

'Maybe that was a fishing hole, like the Inuit make in the ice,' said George thoughtfully. 'Perhaps "Artemis" is like a fishing boat, but it's gone to sea on Europa instead of in the Atlantic.'

Annie whipped out her phone and pressed 'Dad' in the contacts screen. He picked up immediately. 'Annie?' he said urgently. 'Close down Cosmos – now!'

'Why?' she asked. 'We were just—'

'Annie, just do it.' Eric's voice dropped to an urgent whisper. 'Close him down immediately and do not search for any further information until I get home tonight.' He rang off, then rang back almost straight away. 'You have never observed, er, Europe,' he said in the same serious tone.

'But I have!' said Annie in confusion. 'I've been to France and Germany, and Spain and Italy, and— Oh!' She caught on. '*That* Europe. No, of course not. Never.' Her father rang off again.

George had the same tingly sensation he had felt before, when they were on the brink of an adventure.

'Sorry,' said Annie to Cosmos, feeling like an *X-Factor* judge telling a contestant to go home. 'I don't want to do this but I have to.' She pressed the exit button and Cosmos's screen turned gently to a dead black.

'What now?' asked George. 'We'd better not even look up Europa – or Artemis – on the internet until your dad tells us we can.'

'Hmmm,' said Annie. 'Clearly there's a mystery here.' She looked thoughtful. 'I know!' She brightened up. 'Let's do *Astronauts Wanted*! If we can't go into space with Cosmos any more, we'd better find another way to get out there – and this is our best chance!'

'OK,' said George. 'But it doesn't really help us with Artemis. Mars is still quite a long way from Europa. And we wouldn't even get there for eons.'

'But,' exclaimed Annie, 'we would get into Kosmodrome 2, if we got onto the training programme!'

'*Astronauts Wanted* is at Kosmodrome 2?' George wrinkled his nose in surprise. Eric's place of work was so secret that it didn't even feature on any maps. If you looked it up on Google Earth, all you saw was the old factory near Foxbridge stood where Annie had him that Kosmodrome 2 had later been built.

'It is,' confirmed Annie. 'And I bet "Artemis" HQ is at Kosmodrome 2 as well. That's why Dad's gone off in such a flurry. He's gone to find out what gives on Europa.'

'Why is it called Kosmodrome 2?' asked George. 'What happened to Kosmodrome 1?'

'They built it in the desert,' said Annie. 'And it got too hot! So they decided to move.'

'Epic fail!' said George. 'Are you sure they know how to build a colony on Mars?'

'Nope,' said Annie. 'That's why the loser grown-ups need clever kids to help them out. Clearly. They need digital natives to arrive and show them what to do.' She unplugged the tablet from Cosmos, and laughed as she looked at the thousands of messages that Cosmos had managed to send in such a short time to her former friend Belinda. In reply, there was one short message sent thirty seconds before which simply said: SORRY.

'Oh, Earthlings,' sighed Annie. 'We make everything so complicated!'

'Life on Rams will be simpler,' agreed George, taking the tablet from her and opening up the *Astronauts Wanted* application. 'Just you and me and our robotic explorers, looking out over the Martian desert.'

'Heaven,' sighed Annie. 'C'mon, scribe. Let's tell them why you and I should be the very first people to walk on the red planet . . .'

Chapter Four

When George got home from school the next day, he ran straight through his house, pausing only to scoop up one of his mother's kale, lentil and carrot muffins, leaping over the Lego structures his young sisters – Juno and Hera – had left all over the kitchen floor, and out into the garden. Muffin between his teeth, he clambered up into his treehouse, hoping that Annie would already be there. He wasn't disappointed.

'Have a muffin.' He took it out from between his teeth.

'Ew, no thanks!' Annie recoiled. 'It's got your spit on it!' She looked a bit grumpy and out of sorts.

George's heart sank a little. He was hoping she'd be all cheery, like she had been by the end of the day before. He tried to jolly her along. 'It tastes nice,' he protested. 'And you always say you like my mum's cooking!'

'She's very *now*,' mused Annie. 'Your parents are kind of cool these days.'

It was true that the world seemed to have caught up with Terence and Daisy, George's parents. Once, they had been laughed at for their eco beliefs, their home-made clothes, their vegetable patch, Terence's bushy beard and the beehive in the garden. In the short time that Annie and George had known each other, the world had changed so much that Terence and Daisy had come into fashion. Their food cooperative, Daily Bread, had featured in a glossy magazine, Terence had been asked to give lectures about their 'way of life', and Daisy had published a cookbook based on foraging food from the wild.

'Yeah, who would have thought!' said George. When he was little and wanted to be like every other kid, his parents had been a source of almost constant embarrassment. But now that he was older – and the world took a kinder view of his mum and dad – he felt proud of them instead. He still wasn't quite sure he had forgiven them for making him spend his infanthood in an encampment where they tried to live as though in the time of the Iron Age. At least they had left in the end, even if it had taken the intervention of Mabel, George's fierce grandmother, to pull them (literally) out of the mud. But he still remembered what it felt like to be the kid who got left out. He remembered that hot feeling of shame when he was the last person to be picked for any team, or when other kids turned away as he tried to talk to them. And he knew that the best thing he could do for Annie now was get her mind off what happened with her school mates and get her interested in something completely different. Something space-related, he reflected, would be perfect. Especially, he buzzed, if it had a mystery attached.

'How's Europa? Still missing? Or has your dad found it again?' he asked, stuffing the rest of the muffin into his mouth, spraying crumbs around him.

'No idea,' said Annie. 'Dad told us to do nothing, remember?'

'So, no motion in the ocean by Artemis either?' asked George, who was disappointed. He couldn't quite believe that Eric had told Annie not to investigate this peculiar incident and Annie had agreed. It was not like her to ignore the prospect of a space-themed detective opportunity. George figured she really was still feeling bad.

'Who knows?' sighed Annie. 'No sighting of the exotic "father bird" since first mention of the space mission that must not be named.'

'What? Eric hasn't come home?' said George.

'I asked Mum that and she said she'd be surprised if he remembered where "home" is.' Annie sounded very flat.

'Ouch!' exclaimed George.

'She said' – Annie looked uncomfortable – 'that she used to feel like she had married Cosmos by mistake. And now she feels like she's married to Ebot.'

Ebot was Eric's personalized android and had been customized to resemble Eric so exactly that in a dim light it was hard to tell the two apart.

'That's so weird,' said George. 'You can't marry a computer! What's your mum talking about?'

'Try living in my house for a while,' sighed Annie, twiddling with the end of her ponytail in a dispirited manner. 'The grown-ups make literally no sense most of the time.'

'And where *is* Ebot?' said George, realizing he hadn't seen Eric's double either.

'Umm, I don't know,' hummed Annie casually.

George wasn't fooled. 'You *do* know!' he said. 'Where is he?'

'Erm.' Annie looked embarrassed. 'I sent him out to buy some Haribo two days ago and he hasn't come back yet.'

'How can Ebot buy stuff?' asked George.

'Microchip,' said Annie, who was now picking up the crumbs of George's muffin off the treehouse floor with a damp finger, then eating them. 'He's got one fitted. It's like a "contactless" payment thingy.'

'And he hasn't been in touch?' asked George, even though he wasn't quite sure how Ebot could make contact with them from wherever he was stocking up on supplies of fizzy sweets.

'Radio silence!' said Annie.

George racked his brain for yet another topic which might spark his friend back to life. 'Oh!' he said, remembering. '*Astronauts Wanted!* Did you get a reply?'

'I didn't check my messages!' exclaimed Annie, as though waking up from a dream. 'That's so weird. I've literally *never* not checked my messages.'

George passed over her tablet, which was on the treehouse floor. She scrolled through and found the reply.

'OMG!' She read it, perking up immediately. 'We might do it, George! We're through the first checks! On the shortlist! They've just got to make the final decisions in the next few days, but I bet that really means we are in!'

'Awesome!' yelled George. 'So when does it all start?'

'Next week,' said Annie. 'They've only got two places left but I just *know* it's going to be us! Oh wow, oh wow! We're going to be astronauts! We're going to Mars! Yay!' She bounced off the bean bag and jumped around the treehouse.

At that moment they heard a tremendous squeal of brakes coming from the street outside Annie's house, followed by the slamming of a car door and hasty footsteps.

'Hey!' said Annie happily. 'Dad's home in his driverless car! Let's go tell him!' They clambered down the ladder, jumping off before the last few rungs, and ran over to Annie's house, arriving at the back door just as Eric stomped into the kitchen.

Faced with Eric in the kitchen, Annie and George both ground to a very sudden halt. He was holding a cardboard box containing a mouldy assortment of possessions, including a droopy pot plant and a few framed photos. He slammed the box down on the kitchen table, causing the poor plant to shed its last few remaining leaves. Eric's mouth was twisted into an angry shape that the two friends didn't know a mouth could make. He had high spots of colour on his usually pale cheeks and his eyes were glittering behind his thick glasses. He snatched a mug out of his box and handed it to Annie. 'A gift,' he announced bitterly.

Emblazoned on the mug were the words WORLD'S GREATEST SCIENTISTS! Annie turned it round and round, reading the names. '*Bohr, Darwin, Einstein, Dirac,*' she said out loud before stopping. 'Your name's not on it!' she exclaimed.

'No,' said Eric. 'It's the perfect final touch, really.'

Annie put the mug quietly down on the kitchen table.

'Shall I make you a cup of tea?' asked George.

'Why not?' said Eric rather wildly. 'After all, I have *nothing* else to do now but drink tea. So yes, George, make me some tea, thank you.'

Annie's mum appeared in the doorway behind Eric. 'What's this?' she said suspiciously. 'Why are you home?'

'Because I live here?' said Eric in a wobbly voice, wheeling round to face her.

'Awks,' muttered Annie to George. 'You'd better scram!'

George started to tiptoe towards the back door, hoping he could just sidle out and run home. But it wasn't to be.

'George!' exclaimed Eric with forced and slightly mad jollity. 'Don't leave on my account!'

'I, er, really need to get home!' squeaked George, and continued edging towards the door. 'Thanks anyway, Eric.'

'Don't go,' pleaded Eric. 'If you do, then my wife and daughter will claim I've scared you away!' His eyes looked very large and bright behind his thick glasses.

George felt terrible. He was desperate to go, but on the other hand, he didn't want to upset Eric and cause a problem for Annie and Susan. He stood on one foot and then the other, trying to decide which of the two options was the least bad.

'Eric,' sighed Susan, intervening. 'Why are you here now when I thought you were at work?'

'Because . . . I don't . . .' he said.

'You don't what?' asked Annie in the long pause.

'Work!' burst out Eric. 'I don't work! I don't have a job! Any more.'

'You've been sacked?' said Susan in horror.

'Worse than that,' said Eric grimly. 'I've been . . . *retired*.'

'Retired?' said Annie. 'I know you're old, but you're not *that* ancient!'

'That mug,' said Eric, pointing with a trembling finger at the offending item, which no one would ever dare touch again, 'is my retirement present. From Kosmodrome 2. The most expensive space facility in the world. And they gave me a mug. Which doesn't even have my name on it.'

'GO!' Annie mouthed to George.

George started shuffling towards the back door again.

'You're retired?' said Susan in astonishment, seeming to catch on at last. 'You mean, you're going to be at home?'

'I suppose so,' said Eric, who didn't seem like he had thought about it at all. 'Why are you asking?'

'It's . . .' Susan hesitated. Then she blurted out, 'Well, I got a call just now.' She seemed too shocked by Eric's news to know what she was saying. 'There's an orchestra tour.' She twirled a finger in her hair in exactly the same way Annie did when she had to admit something. 'Worldwide. And they need another player. A soloist too! They offered it to me. Well, I said, of course I can't do it! There would be no one to look after Annie in the holidays.'

'I don't need looking after,' said Annie. 'I'm not a child!'

'Yes you are!' said her mum. 'I can't leave you here with no adult in charge. I would ask Daisy and Terence but they are so busy with the little ones. It doesn't seem fair.'

'Excuse me,' said Eric. 'Do I not count as an adult now?'

'I just meant you are always at work,' said Susan quietly.

'I can certainly look after my own daughter while you are away,' said Eric haughtily. 'I'm amazed you even need to ask.'

'But I don't understand!' George, who had been quiet up to now, burst out from near the back door. 'Why have you been made to retire?'

'Why?' asked Eric wonderingly. 'I have spent my

whole life asking, "Why?" And suddenly I find I am no longer interested in "why". If you will excuse me, I am going outside to do some gardening . . .' He stalked out into the back garden – a patch of land more like a jungle than a garden – head held high, not meeting anyone's eye.

'Wow!' said Annie after he had left. 'Mega wow! That's terrible.'

'It is, it is,' sympathized Susan. 'It really is.' She seemed stunned. She sat down on a kitchen chair. 'I don't know what we do now.'

'I do,' said Annie decisively. 'You should go on your world tour, Mum. You've always wanted to tour with your orchestra. You told me it was your greatest ambition!'

'Don't be silly, Annie,' said her mum. 'I can't really go. It's just a dream.'

'No, it's not,' said Annie. 'Dad just told you to say yes. Anyway, I'll look after Dad while you're away.'

'I think it's meant to be the other way round,' said Susan, with a tiny smile.

'You should phone them back and say you're coming,' said Annie.

'But it starts tomorrow!' said Susan.

'So?' said Annie. 'Go, get packing, Mum!' Annie being bossy, thought George, was a good sign. It meant she was just a little bit more like the Annie he knew.

Susan hurried out of the room and they heard her running up the stairs to her room, followed by the sound of cupboards being flung open.

'C'mon,' said George. They both headed back towards the treehouse and climbed the ladder in silence.

They got to the top, where Annie flopped into the bean bag.

'What now?' said George. 'What's your dad going to do now he isn't a scientist any more?'

As if in answer to the question, a terrible noise started up from Annie's back garden. They both peered over from the vantage point of the treehouse. Down in the overgrown garden, they could see Eric, now clad in his laboratory safety goggles and the heavy insulated gloves that he used for handling dry ice and other very cold or hot substances, wielding a chainsaw. He had started attacking the jungle-like garden and fronds of greenery, sticks and even small branches were flying about as he delved into the thick undergrowth.

'I think he's doing some gardening,' Annie

tried to say over the noise, but George motioned to her that he couldn't hear a word.

Let's go in! he typed out on Annie's smartphone. **Before we go deaf!**

They shinned down and ran into George's house, trying to escape the horrible noise and find somewhere they could talk in peace.

They picked the wrong house. As they burst in through the back door, they found Terence and Daisy in the kitchen.

'George!' they cried excitedly. 'You'll never guess what!'

Chapter Five

Terence and Daisy were beaming from ear to ear. George didn't know what to say but Annie wasn't so shy.

'What is it?' she said excitedly. 'Is Daisy's cookery book number one on iTunes?'

'Better than that,' said Terence.

Annie looked baffled. Not much, in her view, could happen to Daisy and Terence that could be more exciting than that.

'Er, you've got the electricity generator working?' asked George hopefully. A regular supply of electricity in the house would be unlikely but amazing. Terence had been trying to supply the house with power himself, using old socks and cooking oil as fuel, but so far he hadn't been reliably successful.

'No, not quite as good as that,' admitted Terence.

Annie looked even more confused. She loved George's parents, but sometimes they were even stranger than her own.

'We've been given places as WOOFers!' burst out

Daisy. 'Isn't that great?'

Annie stole a look at her friend. George looked horrified. 'What's a WOOFer?' she whispered.

'Willing Worker on an Organic Farm,' he hissed back. 'This is really bad news.' He looked suspiciously at his parents. 'Where?' he asked them.

'On an island just north of the Faroes!' his mum said.

'There isn't an island north of the Faroes,' said George. 'Unless you mean the North Pole.' His face had fallen so far, it was now somewhere around his shoes.

'George!' tutted his father. 'We'd like you to show some enthusiasm! We can spend all summer there, taking part in a wonderful organic farming experiment. There are no mobile or internet communications allowed so we will be able to get back to nature and experience Mother Earth as she intended us to! Wonderful!'

George felt furious. Just when he thought he could trust his parents, they were letting him down completely. But he wasn't going to stand for it. And he certainly wasn't going to miss space camp for this.

'I'm not coming,' he said defiantly.

'Yes, you are!' said his father. 'We are all going. It will be a wonderful family bonding experience. Some time for you to spend with your little sisters out in the wonders of nature, with no technology! Just fresh air and farming – what more could you ask for a whole summer long? It will be incredible.'

'No, it won't,' said George. 'Not for me.' Usually so polite and helpful, this time he had had enough. He was going to space camp and that was that.

'George!' said his mother in concern. 'I don't understand! I thought you'd be thrilled.'

'Well, I'm not,' he said. 'I don't want to come, and what's more, I'm not going to.' Memories of the Iron Age encampment flashed before his eyes. Never ever again would he let his parents do that to him.

Annie decided to dive in. 'The thing is,' she said, 'George and I have applied to go to space camp this summer!'

'You have?' asked his mother. 'You didn't say!'

'It just happened,' said Annie. 'It's a bit my fault really. But we're through the first round and we might actually get picked.'

'But what would you do at space camp?' asked George's mum, looking perplexed. 'How can you camp in space? I don't understand. Won't your tent just float away?'

'No, Daisy,' said Annie nicely. 'I don't think we actually do camping or go to space just yet. I think we stay in dormitories. And every day we have special training sessions for different skills we need to learn in order to fly in space when we're grown-ups.'

'Like what?' asked Daisy.

'Well,' said Annie. 'From what I read, we would have to learn about robotics and how to work the Rovers; we would learn about flight systems for spacecraft, how to survive on another planet, lots of fitness stuff, lots of communications, loads of ICT stuff too. It's really cool and we would learn so much. It would be like being at school but with super-bright kids who love space too.'

'Huh, space again!' huffed Terence, who wasn't a fan of exploring the cosmos. 'I wish you would show the same interest in farming, George.'

'I'm interested in farming on Mars,' said George.

But this just seemed to make his father even more annoyed.

'And you see,' Annie carried on blithely, 'Dad's

going to be at home all summer! He's not working at the moment.'

'I don't believe that,' said Daisy. 'Your father's always working.'

'He's on gardening leave,' said Annie.

'Oh, is that what that terrible noise was?' asked Terence.

'So he'll be here, and he can look after me and George and take us to space camp. If we get in,' carried on Annie, pleased that she had found a solution which suited everyone. 'And my dad can look after your garden while you're away!' Terence turned pale at the thought of Eric looking after his precious vegetable patch. 'And George will help him,' said Annie hastily, realizing her mistake.

'I need to talk to your mum,' said Daisy, exchanging glances with Terence.

'You'd better hurry,' said Annie. 'She's off on a concert tour.'

'Are you sure this is what you want, George?' asked his mum, gently brushing his fringe back.

Usually he would push her away, but when he looked into her eyes, he knew she understood why he couldn't come with her. Embarrassingly, he felt very close to tears, so he just nodded in reply.

'It wouldn't be like before,' she said softly. 'It would be different this time.'

'I can't,' he whispered.

'I understand,' she said, and he knew she hadn't forgotten the Iron Age encampment either. Which made him feel so much better. She hugged him and he felt a tiny tear sneak out of the corner of his eye. She whispered into his ear, 'We love you so much.'

'I'm calling Mum now!' said Annie. She got out her smartphone and dialled her mother.

Daisy let go of George and took the phone from Annie. 'Susan?' she said. 'It's Daisy. Annie's just given us an idea . . .' Daisy went off into a different room to continue the Mum-to-Mum talk about the new plan for the summer. Meanwhile Terence stomped out into the garden to see if he could do something about Eric's near total destruction of the garden next door before it was too late and not a single leaf remained.

It was very quiet after Annie's mum and George's parents, separately, left to go their different ways.

Before they departed, George's parents locked their house up and George moved his things next door, into Annie's house, where he had the spare bedroom. Every morning George set off for his last few days at school, leaving the inhabitants of his new home to their own activities – and returned in the afternoon to while away time with Annie, waiting for the final verdict from *Astronauts Wanted*.

Annie, thought George, still wasn't quite her usual self. She didn't seem to want to do stuff in the way she had in the past. She didn't pester Eric to take her to the Science Museum or to the skate park. She seemed happy just to spend time in the treehouse, sitting and thinking while the summer days mooched along.

But the most challenging part of living next door – it had always been a dream of George's to live in the same house as Eric, with all his scientific objects and knowledge – turned out, rather unexpectedly, to be Eric himself.

George never quite knew what he would find. On the last day of school he wandered into the house to find a stepladder and a paintbrush and pot abandoned just inside the front door. Half of the hallway wall had been painted lime green, the other half raspberry pink, with an awkward bit in the middle where the paints seemed to have mixed and turned brown. George moved cautiously past and up the hall towards the kitchen, where a sickly, fruity smell greeted him.

Eric was standing at the stove, feverishly stirring a huge bubbling pot of something purple and gluey. Extra-loud opera music blared out from a radio, which had been left in the kitchen sink under the window. George could see, even from behind, that Eric had splashes of bright green paint on his clothes and his hands. Suddenly the music switched off and Eric wheeled round; Annie was coming into the kitchen  from the back door just as George was entering from the hall. Eric, who even had paint on his glasses, smiled broadly at the two friends.

'Dad,' said Annie, pointing. 'What is that?' George just knew his friend hoped it would be a scientific experiment.

'It's dinner!' said Eric brightly, waving a wooden spoon around so wildly that it caused great globules of sticky mauve goo to splatter over the walls.

Annie and George gathered by the stove and peered, with worried faces, into the cauldron.

'You made this?' said Annie, poking it with a teaspoon. 'To eat?'

George felt a little sick. He was used to eating odd food because of his mother's unusual cooking style – but at least his mother could actually cook, and however unusual her ingredients, her food tasted pretty good.

'Cherry confit,' said Eric. 'Made with fifty-eight spices, fish protein, kale, powdered seaweed and vitamins. You'll love it – it's taken me all day. I got the recipe from a book by a former chemist who is now a cook. It's given me lots of ideas. I shall try them out on you all summer and perhaps I'll write my own cook-book at the end of it!'

George and Annie exchanged looks of horror.

'Is there anything else?' asked Annie. 'To eat?'

'No,' said her dad, looking offended. 'This is a complete meal. It contains everything you need. You could survive a nuclear winter on this jam.'

'YIKES!' mouthed Annie to George. They had both found Eric quite tricky since he had been at home full-time. When he used to dash in and out, trailing clouds of glamour as one of the world's leading scientists, he had always been cheery and interested in them, if sometimes a bit absent-minded. But now he was home the whole time, Eric tended to be rather moody, a bit grumpy, and quite difficult to please.

They had tried talking to Eric about what had happened at Kosmodrome 2 – and they had asked him about the mystery of Artemis and the missing Europa. But Eric didn't want to talk about any of it. Every time they asked him a question he didn't want to answer, he blanked them, changed the subject and started talking about something else.

Annie grabbed her phone. 'Dialling for a pizza,' she said. 'Veggie for George, pepperoni for me . . . what about you, Dad? Dad?'

'No need,' said Eric, turning back to the stove. 'I shall be having super-jam for my dinner tonight.'

But just as George was wondering if he should have gone with his family to the Faroe Islands after all, and Annie was debating whether she could join her mother on her concert tour, wherever Susan might be by now, two things happened . . .

First of all, Ebot came home! The two friends were delighted to see the android again. He strolled through the door, right behind the pizza delivery man, looking a little ruffled but otherwise exactly like himself – which meant just like Eric only in robot form.

'Ebot!' cried Annie, running to give him a hug

'Gree—' Ebot started to speak, but stopped. His limbs went floppy as he collapsed in the hallway.

'He's run out of power,' said George, kneeling down by the robot, getting a little bit of green paint on both of them. 'We need to plug him in!'

Annie put the pizzas down on the floor, and between them they carried the android into her father's study, now an almost empty room. Before, it had been full of books, photos, telescopes, Eric's prizes and certificates and a huge blackboard covered in chalk squiggles. Now just a desk and a chair remained. A SWAT team from Kosmodrome 2 had arrived to reclaim any items that had been deemed 'official property' – which, alarmingly, had included Cosmos the supercomputer.

Ebot had been away at the time, sent by Annie on the 'shopping trip', so he was one of the few items that the team had failed to requisition. They hadn't found the driverless car either because that day, fortunately, it had run out of charge and Eric had to leave it in Sainsbury's car park while he was stocking up on paint or spices or whatever other exotic items he imagined his wife bought when she went shopping.

But they had taken pretty much everything else.

The two friends laid Ebot out on the desk while George rummaged around in the drawers, hoping against hope that they still had Ebot's power cable. To her relief, Annie found it and plugged Ebot into the wall. A dim light flickered in the android's previously dead eyes as he started slowly to recharge.

Suddenly, Annie gave a shout of joy. While they were

waiting for Ebot to reboot, she had flicked open her messages on her smartphone.

'Wassup?' said George.

'We're in, George! We made it! We're definitely on the Mars training programme!'

'Woo-hoo!' George leaped about with joy. It was the most exciting piece of news he had ever received. 'I'm going to be an astronaut! I'm going to fly in space! I'm going up in a rocket! YAY!'

'I must text Mum . . .' muttered Annie.

She tapped out a quick text to her mother while George realized he couldn't let his mum and dad know because they didn't have any form of communication on their island. He wondered if he should write them a letter with pen and ink. Or send a carrier pigeon. He missed them more than he thought he would.

Annie finished sending her text but kept on looking at her phone, hoping for a quick reply. None came. For a moment the two friends felt a little sad that they had no one to tell – and then it hit them! They were going to be astronauts! They might end up being the first human beings to walk on the red planet!

'What do we need to do?' asked George in great excitement. 'What do we need to take? We've got to get ready! We're just sitting around! We need to do things!'

'No we don't!' said Annie. 'It says here we need to bring nothing with us.'

'That's good,' said George, 'as all we have is some

vitamin jam and a robot that doesn't work. When does it start?'

'Tomorrow!' said Annie. 'Wow! We have to get to Kosmodrome 2 and— Oh.' Her face fell.

'What?' asked George.

'We need an adult to sign us in,' she said. 'We can't take part without a parent to give permission.'

'Your dad can do that,' said George sensibly. 'My mum and dad gave him that loco thingy so he could do stuff for me if he needed while they were away.'

'Oh yeah!' said Annie, brightening. They heard a squelch in the hallway outside as Eric walked past and trod in the pizzas. 'Dad!' she called. He poked his head round the doorway of his study. 'We got into space camp!'

'Oh, good,' said Eric. There was pizza stuck to his sandals and socks, but he didn't seem to notice.

'Can you take us there tomorrow?' asked Annie. 'To Kosmodrome 2?'

'Kosmodrome 2?' said Eric, his face darkening. 'No. I cannot. And neither will you go. I won't go there and I won't let you either. That's all.' He turned on his heel and walked away, shedding little strings of cheese as he went.

'Eek, gloomy news,' said Annie, but she looked thoughtful rather than crushed – and *crushed* was how George felt. He couldn't bear to be so near and yet so far – again! – from space travel.

CONDITIONS ON MARS

We know that Mars is now a cold desert planet with no signs of life, simple or complex, on its surface. But was it once a wet warm world where life flourished? Clues found by man-made Martian Rovers, sent out to the red planet to investigate, tell us that Mars was once a very different place.

But could Mars become a fertile, oxygen-rich planet once more, where we could grow crops, breathe the atmosphere and enjoy a balmy Martian summer? Could we 'terraform' Mars so that its atmosphere, its climate and its surface would be suitable for life as we recognize it?

'Terraforming' means making enormous changes to a whole planet in order to create an environment habitable by humans, plants and animals.

In the case of Mars, we would need to build an atmosphere and heat the temperature of the planet.

To heat up Mars, we would need to add greenhouse gases to the atmosphere to trap energy from the Sun – it's almost the opposite of the problem on Earth where we have too many greenhouses gases in the atmosphere and we want the planet to cool down a little rather than heat up!

But does Mars have enough gravity to retain an atmosphere thick enough for us? Once, it had a magnetic field, but that decayed 4 billion years ago, meaning that Mars was stripped of most of its atmosphere, leaving it with only 1% of the pressure of the Earth's atmosphere. Much lower gravity, then.

In the past, the atmospheric pressure – which means the weight of the air above you in the atmosphere – must have been higher though because we see what appear to be dried-up channels and lakes. Liquid water cannot exist on Mars now as it would just evaporate. To live there, we would need water – there is lots of water in the form of ice at two poles. If we went to live on Mars, we could use this. We could also use the minerals and metals that volcanoes have brought to the surface.

So there is lots of potential out there on the red planet, but it's going to be a very difficult job for the first astronauts. Before they can even think about the long-term task of terraforming – if that is even possible - they will have lots of work to do to survive in the pink dusty world of our rocky neighbour, Mars. It would be very much like living in some kind of dome with a controlled atmosphere – going out would only be possible with a respirator!

Those astronauts are going to need to be clever, resourceful, brave and persistent however, in order to build the foundations of a colony or a human habitation on Mars.

Does that sound like you?

BREAKING NEWS!

On 28 September 2015, NASA scientists made an announcement that stunned the world! It turns out that Mars – for long, thought of as a cold desert planet with ice only at the poles – has liquid water on its surface!

What does this mean for the existence of Martians?

In the summer months, NASA scientists revealed, water flows down canyons and crater walls before drying up in the colder autumn temperatures. We don't yet know where this water comes from – perhaps it rises up from the ground or maybe it condenses from the thin Martian atmosphere. But excitingly, this takes our journey of discovery to find life in the Solar System onwards by another step.

> **Where there is liquid water, scientists think we will find life!**

Our future colonies

This discovery also means that it might be much easier to found a colony of human life on Mars! If water could be collected from a local supply that would solve one major headache for future missions to the red planet.

> **Life on Mars just got a step closer!**

'What if,' Annie said, 'we just pop in for the first day. And then we can come home in the evening or something so Dad won't know . . .'

'Won't work,' said George, shaking his head as he felt the full force of the disappointment hit him. 'We won't get in if we go alone. We still need an adult to sign us in.'

'Rats,' said Annie. 'If only we had a parent-like being who wasn't either hopeless or away . . .'

At that moment Ebot's rapid charging must have finished as he sat up from the desk, like a mummy rising from a tomb and said, 'Hello, friends! I have returned.'

Later that evening, the duo rendezvoused in the kitchen. Ebot was still enjoying his power charge after days of battery-draining activity. Just like his robot, Eric had also nodded off, exhausted by his jam-making activities, meaning the two friends had the place all to themselves.

'Careful,' said Annie as George went to sit down at the kitchen table. 'It's really sticky. There's jam everywhere.'

Even since that afternoon, the jam seemed to have degraded into different colours – the splotches on the kitchen counter had turned a vivid blue whereas the bits on the floor were orange and the flecks on the ceiling were the colour of avocado.

'I wish your dad would go back to being a scientist,' grumbled George. 'There's only room for one crazy cook on this street and that's my mum.'

'Yeah, he must be able to do something,' said Annie. 'I mean, there must be a *real* job he could do. Physicists can't be entirely useless.'

'He always says the Universe is just a question of plumbing,' said George. 'Could he be a plumber?'

'Hmm,' said Annie. 'I think he'd be better as a DJ. Or a pop star.' They both burst out laughing.

'Ew, I am sticking to everything,' said George. 'Can we go back to the treehouse?' But in true British summer style, the rain was pouring down outside in great big fat ropes of water, and the evening was cold and bleak. 'Hey!' he said, pointing to the keys to his house, which were hanging on a hook. 'Let's go to my house! We might even find some food there.'

'I'm starving!' said Annie. 'Let's go!'

They dashed down the garden, through the bucketing rain, to the hole in the fence that divided their two gardens. They dived through and sprinted up to George's back door. Rattling the keys, he let them both in and they stood dripping in his kitchen, the same size and shape as the one next door and yet completely and utterly different. For George, it had the familiar smell of dried herbs, baking, grated carrots and lemon peel, with a faint tang of soil. It smelled like home. When George flicked the light switch, a comforting dim glow came from the eco bulbs, so unlike the super-bright LED lights that Eric used to illuminate his house.

'Phew.' Annie flopped down in one of the kitchen chairs. 'A normal house.'

It was quite something, thought George, when his friend called his house normal. It really did mean that things had gone crazy next door.

'We need a plan,' he said, rummaging through the kitchen cupboards for something edible. He came across a tin with only slightly stale biscuits in it. 'Catch!' He threw one at Annie, who fielded it deftly.

'Yum!' she said. 'Daisy's award-winning cookies!'

'Better than Eric's "Survive-the-Nuclear-Winter" jam,' said George.

'Tomorrow we'll be at space camp!' said Annie gleefully. 'Eating space rations!'

'We will?' said George. 'It says that? We have to live on space food on Earth?'

'Of course,' said Annie. 'To get us used to preparing dehydrated rations as meals.'

'I didn't know that about space camp,' said George, who really loved his food. 'I didn't know we'd be eating dust for – how long? How long *is* space camp?'

'Um, well, that's weird,' said Annie. 'Because it doesn't say. It says it will be over by the end of the summer but it doesn't give a date.'

'And we seriously take nothing with us?'

'Nope,' said Annie. 'They provide everything.'

'And it's really at Kosmodrome 2? The place we're not allowed to go, even with your dad?'

'If you don't believe me,' said Annie, 'you can read it for yourself. Why are you asking so many questions?'

George sighed. 'I really want to go to space camp and I want to go to Mars,' he said. 'I really really do, more than anything. But something just doesn't feel right.' All the tingly excitement he had felt at first when he thought a new adventure was beginning had started to turn into a queasy, icky feeling in his stomach.

'Yeah, I know,' admitted Annie. 'It's like the things you know to be true even though you can't see them.'

'Like electricity,' said George, pointing at the lights.

'And bad feelings,' said Annie. 'But we have to go to space camp because it might be the most amazing thing we've ever done. It might work out to be totally brilliant and completely OK. And—'

'We need to get into Kosmodrome 2 to find out what happened on Europa, and what Artemis is,' added George.

'As far as we know, my dad got kicked out of Kosmodrome 2 when he asked about Europa and that hole in the ice. So we have to go, even if we don't want to,' said Annie.

'But we sort of do,' said George.

'We definitely do!'

'Like no way we would miss this!' George felt much better now he knew that Annie had the same thoughts as him about space camp. It helped to know he wasn't alone in having doubts. 'But we have to find out as much as we can while we're at Kosmodrome 2.'

'And we have to try and get my dad his job back,' said Annie. 'Before he makes any more jam!'

'Or paints any more walls,' said George, who had just noticed he had bright green paint on his hand.

'It's a lot to do,' said Annie. '*And* get to Mars at the same time.'

'We can manage,' said George. 'But one thing – we've got to watch out for your dad's deputy, Rika Dur. I bet she's somehow involved in this.'

'I think she's just all about rules and regulations,' said Annie doubtfully. 'Like a nuisance school prefect. I expect Dad just got up her nose somehow. You know how he can be. But I don't think she's properly evil. Is she?'

'I don't know!' George replied. 'But I bet we're about to find out.'

Chapter Six

'George!' A brilliant light shone over his tightly closed eyes. He felt like he was swimming up from the very bottom of the ocean, struggling towards the surface. 'George,' the voice hissed again, and this time a hand shook his shoulder.

He tried to turn over.

'No!' whispered the voice furiously. 'You have to get up! It's time to go! Your clothes are downstairs. Let's go!'

Wrapping his duvet around him like a super-

hero cape, George staggered blearily out of his room and down the stairs. He stumbled into Eric's study where, sure enough, his clothes lay on the only chair in the nearly empty room. Even in his sleepy state,

George still got a shock when he saw how different this room was now that all Eric's things had gone.

He got dressed and went through to the kitchen, where Annie was already fully dressed in her combat trousers, T-shirt and sparkly trainers, her long blonde hair tied up in a ponytail. She looked more cheerful than George had seen her for ages.

'This is it!' she said. 'Time to go!'

George nodded. They had agreed the plan the night before. It was so unlikely, they figured, that they might just pull it off. 'Where's Ebot?' he mumbled.

'He went to get the car,' said Annie. 'He should be outside – about now! Go go go!' With that, she half ran, half pushed George down the hallway to the front door and they jumped out onto the pavement.

Sure enough, Eric's little pale blue driverless car, rescued and recharged by Ebot, sat outside with the friendly android in the front seat. They had already decided that Ebot should take the driver's seat. That way, anyone passing them wouldn't notice anything unusual about the car or its passengers. They would think Ebot was an adult driving two kids in the car; just a normal everyday outing . . .

Of course, there was nothing normal about an android impersonating a parent while pretending to drive a car which was actually driving itself. But Annie figured that no one needed to know that.

DRIVERLESS CARS

Driverless cars – surely only in science fiction?

Amazingly, driverless cars already exist! Also known as robotic or self-driving cars, these are vehicles that can perform the main functions of a normal car without a human being in charge. They can sense the environment around them, using radar, computer systems and GPS, so they can navigate as well as get round obstacles or deal with changing conditions on the roads.

The Google Self-Driving Car – powered by software called Google Chauffeur, for instance, has been running for a number of years already and their latest car has no steering wheel or pedals!

Driverless cars could be really useful – they do long journeys without getting tired, and they could help disabled or blind people who can't drive ordinary cars to get around. Cars driven by robots, if they function properly, might be safer than cars driven by humans: robots don't look out of the window or fiddle around changing the radio station, answer a mobile phone or have arguments with passengers!

But some people think they could be dangerous in other ways. If a driverless car malfunctions while in motion, it's possible the passengers in the car wouldn't be able to control the vehicle. And what would happen if we all forgot how to drive? Would that be a good idea? What would happen to all the bus, coach and taxi drivers? What jobs would they do if robots took over the road?

Some countries in Europe are already drawing up plans to create transport networks for driverless cars. Keep your eyes peeled – you might see a driverless car near you soon.

'How are we going to actually find Kosmodrome 2?' George asked, wondering why he hadn't thought of this last night. It was so early that the bright planet Venus was still visible in the morning sky. 'We don't even know where it is!'

'No,' said Annie gleefully. 'But the car does! Watch!'

To start the car, all Ebot, who had the same fingerprints as Eric, had to do was touch the central pad of the steering wheel with his index finger. Once the engine sprang to life, Annie guided Ebot's finger to select, from the dashboard computer, the last destination, which was saved as 'Kosmodrome 2'.

'Would it work if I used *my* finger?' asked George, more awake by now and starting to feel like they might actually get somewhere!

'Nope,' said Annie. 'It's touch-controlled, but only Dad's, or Ebot's' – she grinned over her shoulder at George, who had taken the cramped back seat – 'fingerprints can operate it.'

With that, the little car put on its indicators.

'Buckle up!' said Annie, putting on her seat belt. George reached for his own seat belt and strapped himself in. Annie arranged Ebot's hands on the steering wheel. He wouldn't actually be steering as Annie had been very careful to disable the car's manual option, but she still thought she should make sure all the details were in place. 'And we're off!' she said as the car pulled out into the road and started the journey

to Kosmodrome 2.

It wasn't the most relaxing car trip of George's life so far – he wasn't sure he really trusted either Annie or Ebot in charge of a moving vehicle. It was also very fast. Whichever setting Eric had last used for his racing, angry return from his final day at Kosmodrome 2 was obviously still active. The car sped onwards, weaving through the sparse early morning traffic until they were on the main road out of Foxbridge. At one point, the car cornered so sharply that two wheels actually lifted off the tarmac as it shot round a bend!

'AWIEEE!' Annie screamed in the front seat as the

car accelerated yet faster. But she seemed to scream out of joy and excitement rather than fear.

'Hold tight!' mumbled George from the back. He was being thrown about from left to right and hoped he wasn't going to be sick. His parents didn't even have a normal car, the kind you drove yourself, so he definitely wasn't used to this kind of travel. Even Annie had her eyes tightly squeezed shut and was clinging onto her seat belt.

'Can you slow it down?' shouted George from the back.

'No!' said Annie. 'I don't dare touch anything! The car might stop or go backwards or take us to the wrong destination if I try and change anything. Or go even faster!'

The fields outside were whizzing past so quickly that they were just a blur of green, yellow and brown. If they accelerated even just a tiny bit, George feared they might actually lift off! He wanted to fly, but in a proper craft built for that purpose, not in Eric's funny little car.

The only person who seemed to be enjoying the ride was Ebot who, being mechanical, had no stomach to churn. His hair was blowing back in the breeze from his open window and he looked relaxed, carefree and even rather stylish at the wheel of the speeding car.

At last they felt the car slow down as it made the final turn into a long unmarked driveway between two very tall hedges, which led to the hidden space facility,

Kosmodrome 2. It looked like a farm track, leading nowhere in particular. It was a good thing the car knew where it was going, because its passengers certainly did not!

Eventually the road was barred by a red and white striped pole with a small black box on a stand either side of the road. Signs dotted around read: RESTRICTED AREA! NO UNAUTHORIZED ACCESS! Stretching away on both sides was the highest chain-link fence the two friends had ever seen.

'What now?' asked George. 'How do we get through?'

Annie wound down her window and scrutinized

the box on her side of the road. There was just a small screen on it. 'I know!' she said. She got out her phone, scrolled through it, found what she was looking for and held her phone against the screen. George craned over from the back seat to get a better look. The screen behind Annie's phone glowed green, and as she took back her phone, George could see writing on the brightly lit screen.

Welcome, astronauts! it read. *Welcome, George Greenby. Welcome, Annie Bellis! Please make your way to the main building.*

The red and white pole rose, and the little car shot forward again, nipping under before the barrier could come crashing down on it.

'How did it know?' said George.

'They sent us barcodes,' said Annie, 'when we got our acceptances. They said all we needed to bring was the barcodes.'

'Well, that worked!' said George. 'Not much security, though. There's nobody here.'

But as they drove towards a distant shape, standing in the middle of the fields, he noticed what he at first thought were black birds flying around the car. But as they flew closer, diving right in front of the windscreen and around the windows, he saw they weren't birds at all. They looked like tiny airborne cameras, each with one winking red eye.

'Drones!' said Annie. 'And they're filming us!'

She fluffed her ponytail and smiled brilliantly, in case anyone was actually watching.

'And if we weren't the people they wanted,' said George, only half joking, 'they would unleash robot guards!'

In the front seat, Annie shivered. As they got closer, they saw the main building gleaming

in the sunshine. It was an extraordinary sight – it looked like it was made of lattice-work: millions of bars of steel arranged in a geometric pattern over a central dome. To either side were buildings, mostly made of bald concrete with no windows. Not a single person could be seen anywhere. None of Eric's previous workplaces had looked like this. They had all been busy, scruffy, bustling places, full of life and energy, with parks and gardens where students ate sandwiches while reading books, and professors strolled about, deep in conversation with each other. Not like this empty, sterile and futuristic venue at all.

The car guided itself into a packed car park and pulled into a spot where the name 'Professor Bellis' had been rudely scratched off a placard.

'Here we are!' said Annie, leaping out of the car. She went round to Ebot's side, opened his door and shoved him out, with George clambering out of the back seat behind the android. They followed a sign saying ASTRO-NAUTS – THIS WAY! which took them to a grand entrance in the main building.

'It's a bit creepy,' said George as they stood in its shadow, looking up at the silhouette against the perfect blue sky.

'It's very beautiful,' said Annie reflectively. 'But not in a way that makes you like it.'

'I hope Eric won't be really angry when he reads our note,' said George. He sighed, thinking of the letter he and Annie had written to Eric and left on the kitchen table, explaining that they had gone to space camp but that they would try and call him from Kosmodrome 2 and let him know how they were getting on.

'Oh well! Shall we go and find Artem—' he started to say, but Annie interrupted him.

'Shush!' she said frantically, pointing to the drone. 'Don't say that word.'

With that, they trooped slowly through the main doorway and took their first steps, they hoped, into space – and into another adventure.

Chapter Seven

Annie and George pushed open the big heavy doors into the main building and found a nearly deserted hallway. The roof arched up above them, made of thousands of metal struts, covered in gleaming glass, with shards of sunlight falling through onto the polished floor. On another day they would have stopped to gaze upwards at the magnificent building. But today they had work to do.

A large banner saying, WELCOME ASTRONAUTS! YOUR JOURNEY STARTS HERE! hung over a table where a man and a woman in blue flightsuits seemed to be packing up. Shadowed by Ebot, Annie and George nervously made their way towards them.

'Hello?' said Annie. 'We're here for *Astronauts Wanted*.'

'You're a bit late!' said the young woman, but she smiled at the two friends, not noticing Ebot. 'Everyone else is already here – the induction is about to start.'

The man next to her nudged her sharply and she looked again and almost jumped out of her skin. Their

eyes boggled as they gazed at Ebot in undisguised horror. Annie and George looked around too, startled by this reaction. The only unusual thing they noticed about Ebot was that he too seemed to have lime-green paint on his glasses now.

'Isn't that . . . ?' she whispered to her friend.

'I don't know!' he whispered back. 'I never actually met him!'

'I only saw him once,' said the woman. 'So I don't know – but that sure looks like him.'

'Names?' said the man nervously, addressing the two friends.

'George Greenby!'

'Annie Bellis,' they both announced at the same moment. At the word 'Bellis', they both heard a sharp intake of breath.

The man looked down at his tablet screen. 'It looks like we have a full house already! Are you sure?' he said doubtfully, eyeing Ebot suspiciously once more.

'Of course we're sure!' said Annie, producing her phone. 'Look, here are our registration barcodes!'

But as she and George swapped looks, they both knew the other was feeling a prickle of unease. What had happened at Kosmodrome 2 that would cause this reaction when Annie said, 'Bellis'? Why would these nice-looking people seem so anti-Eric? Of course, George and Annie already knew Eric had experienced pro-blems at work, just like they knew there was something going on with Europa that seemed suspicious. Now they both also felt an 'uh-oh', as though something much more sinister than they had imagined lay below all this.

George gulped. It was too late to go back now, he figured. And he didn't really want to – he wanted the chance to train as an astronaut. He wanted to help cheer up Annie and he hoped they could solve the mystery of Artemis and find out what had happened to Eric at Kosmodrome 2. But suddenly it seemed an awful lot for one boy and his friend to take on.

The woman took the phone and scanned in the barcodes. 'Oh, yes,' she said in surprise. 'You're the late additions – that's why you're not on the main list.'

'That's so odd,' muttered the man. 'She's a *Bellis*. Why would they let a Bellis back in here? After—'

'Shush! She's on the list,' said the woman. 'So we have to sign her in!'

'We need a parent to give authorization,' said the man, who was now looking very shifty and uncomfortable.

'We've got one right here!' said Annie, who was losing some of her confidence but was determined not to show it. 'He can sign for both of us.'

'He's my loco-thingy,' George tried to explain. 'My real mum and dad are away. They've gone on a farming holiday. To an island. With my little sisters, Juno and Hera. That's why they're not here. But they totally gave their permission to—'

Annie trod on his foot. 'Stop talking!' she hissed. 'Eb— Dad!' she summoned her robot. 'Sign us in. Please,' she added, trying to soften her command. 'You lovely Dad person, you!' She knew how fake she sounded but she still felt she had to say something. The commands you give to a robot are not quite the same as the way you talk to your parents.

The android stepped forward, smiled politely and

pressed his hand against the screen, transferring Eric's signature electronically.

Eric W. Bellis flashed up on the screen in squiggly writing.

'OMG,' said the woman, with a mixture of fear and respect. 'It really is.'

'Sir,' said the man carefully. 'Thank you

for signing these two astronauts into the programme. I am now calling Security to escort you off the premises.'

'No need,' said Annie quickly. 'He knows the way back to the car park.'

The two Kosmodrome 2 workers gave her an odd look, but Ebot had already turned round and was walking back out of the doors.

'Love you, um – Dad!' Annie cried after the departing android, trying to make it seem more realistic. But Ebot left without a backward glance. As he did so, two full-sized gleaming metal robots appeared to one side of the hallway.

'You two!' said the woman unnaturally brightly. 'Here are your pagers. They will direct you to the changing rooms where you will find your flightsuits. Leave all your personal belongings, including anything electronic, such as iPads or phones, in the lockers. They will be quite safe. While you are at Kosmodrome 2, you must keep your pager on you at all times. It will tell you what to do and where to go next. Good luck!'

Annie and George left quietly, following the directions in red letters on their pagers. As they walked away, they heard the two Kosmodrome 2 workers whisper to each other. 'Did you see that? He didn't even say goodbye to the two kids! He didn't even look back! They were right – Professor Bellis isn't really human at all!'

George got a tight hold of Annie's elbow and pulled her with him, knowing she wanted to go back and correct the two check-in staff. 'You can't tell them!' he said. 'You can't say anything!'

Annie threw a cross glance over her shoulder, but turned back with a mutinous expression on her face. 'I know,' she muttered. 'So unfair.' She eyed a drone, fluttering past. 'Oh well!' she sighed, giving a bright but fake smile. 'Space camp, here we come!'

At that moment, both their pagers started beeping to alert them that they needed to hurry:

'Induction due to start in Mission Control!'

'See you on the other side,' said Annie, hurrying into the girls' changing room.

'See you in space,' said George, giving her their

traditional sign-off. Taking one last look down the empty corridor, he went into the changing room to put on his flightsuit.

Chapter Eight

Entering Mission Control for the first time, Annie and George got a real sense of the awesome scale of the task they had signed up for. They were here to trial as astronauts for Mars! Which meant that one day they might actually be in a spaceship, zooming towards the red planet! And they wouldn't travel to Mars just to touch down and leave again – they were going to build a whole new habitation for the human race there. They were heading way beyond the frontiers of what any human had ever done before.

They both caught their breath. It was as though they had been so bound up in other mysteries – the phenomenon of *Artemis*, the strange way Annie's dad had suddenly stopped being a scientist, and the hole on the ice on Europa – that they'd almost forgotten that they could be on the brink of the greatest space journey since humans landed on the Moon.

Annie and George had to squeeze into the back at Mission Control, a room packed with banks of computers which operated the many space missions

Building Rockets for Mars

When I was growing up, I was interested in maths and science, but my passion was actually ballet. When I was in high school, I enrolled in a very challenging curriculum for maths and science – it had a heavy workload that made it nearly impossible to dedicate the time required to study ballet. But I still wanted to do both! After a difficult year I chose a curriculum that allowed me the flexibility to study ballet too. It was a fantastic decision, because I was able to continue dancing while still preparing myself to study engineering at university.

Now I work at NASA, but I still practise and perform ballet on nights and weekends, so I enjoy the best of both worlds!

As a NASA engineer, I am helping develop the Space Launch System (SLS) rocket that will travel to Mars. This is so exciting, to be part of this great project.

Right now NASA is preparing for Exploration Mission-1 (EM-1), a flight test of the entire SLS rocket. This will be the final flight test of the vehicle prior to launching humans. It is my responsibility to ensure that a part of the rocket called the *volume isolator* is properly designed for the loads and conditions of this flight.

Volume isolators are used in rockets to contain purge gases within certain sections. These purge gases keep each section at the right temperature and humidity conditions for the sensitive instrumentation inside. This is important because the rocket has cryogenic fuel – this makes it very cold in places, but instrumentation nearby needs to be warmer in order to function properly.

The volume isolator I am responsible for is called the *MSA diaphragm*. It is located near the top of the rocket, just below the crew vehicle in a section of the rocket called the Multipurpose Crew Vehicle Stage Adapter, or the 'MSA' for short. It is located there to make sure that the environment below the isolator is properly conditioned by the purge gas.

The MSA diaphragm will need to endure the force of liftoff, so it needs to be strong.

But it also needs to be as lightweight as possible to reduce the amount of fuel needed to launch the crew vehicle into outer space.

A challenge, right?

Here's how we deal with that.

The MSA diaphragm is dome-shaped, with a 5-metre diameter, and it is made from a high strength and lightweight material called *carbon composite*.

Carbon composite is created by layering pieces of carbon fabric with epoxy glue. In the case of the MSA diaphragm, the layers of carbon fabric are placed inside of a large bowl-shaped mould. Each layer of fabric is laid down at a different angle in order to create a final product that has quasi-isotropic properties. This means that the dome will have the same strength no matter the orientation – this is important. If the angle of the fabric stayed the same in each layer, the final product would be strong in one orientation, but comparatively weak in any other orientation.

After every layer of the MSA diaphragm has been placed in the mould, the entire mould is rolled into an enormous oven to cure and harden. Once the MSA diaphragm is hardened, it is pried from the mould and machined to add bolt holes that will be used to connect it to the MSA.

This method of creating a strong yet lightweight structure by layering fabric is also used when creating the shoes that allow me as a ballet dancer to dance on my toes! Each shoe is designed with a strong yet lightweight box that surrounds my toes and provides the support needed to balance, spin and even jump on the very tips of my toes. This box is created by layering fabric and glue, much like in the MSA diaphragm.

Not everyone who looks at a rocket part sees a ballet shoe, but my life experiences have given me the perspective to see the world in a unique way. Through following *your* passions in life, you will begin to see the world from *your* own unique viewpoint.

At NASA, we aim to build teams of people who have unique perspectives so that we can see problems from multiple angles. This diversity helps us to overcome the many challenges associated with building a rocket – a rocket that will travel all the way to Mars.

Allyson

in orbit around the Earth or other planets in the Solar System, or travelling around on pre-planned routes.

In the past, space missions had been run from different locations all over Planet Earth. But as more and more spaceships and robotic spacecraft launched, keeping track got really complicated. One – but only one – of Kosmodrome 2's roles was to monitor everything that flew in space – from satellites to spacecraft to deep space probes. Human and robotic activity in space had now been centralized into this one mega corp of cosmic business.

The walls of Mission Control were covered in screens displaying the different journeys of the active missions across the Solar System. Some of the screens showed pictures sent back by Rovers from the surface of planets, moons or comets. Other screens reeled off streams of raw data, just in from space, which still had to be filtered into recognizable information.

On a couple of the screens, Annie and George could see the path of different robotic missions as they journeyed across the Solar System. On another, they could track the looping pattern that nightfall made across the Earth as one of the monitors followed the International Space Station. They could even key into images relayed from the robotic explorers on the Moon or on Mars. It was an incredible sight. From this one room, it was as though they could travel anywhere across space! Only one screen, at the bottom on the right-hand side, was entirely blank. All the others displayed a wealth of information about the progress of human beings and robots across our cosmic neighbourhood.

'This is incredible!' said George, brightening up. For the first time since they had stepped across the threshold of Kosmodrome 2, he felt pleased to be here. Looking around, he could see nothing sinister, no security bots, no drones. Instead, just lots of real, ordinary humans, chattering away in great excitement.

At the back, a mezzanine balcony held lots of Kosmodrome 2 staff, hanging over the edge of the parapet, waving to the new arrivals. Every available nook was completely jam-packed. Kosmodrome 2 workers, in their bright blue flightsuits, filled the circular room. Alongside them stood a sprinkling of outsiders, easily identifiable thanks to their casual clothes. Beside them, shifting nervously, were a bunch of much younger people, also dressed in blue flightsuits.

Annie and George, who were both friendly by nature, smiled at a couple of the other recruits.

'Hello!' George said to one boy of about his age who was walking past. The boy looked startled and hurried away. Annie tried to talk to an older-looking girl, but she looked straight over Annie's head and moved on.

'They're not very friendly!' whispered Annie to George. 'Do we want to be stuck in a tin can with this lot for nine months! And look! Everyone else has brought their parents into Mission Control! Their parents didn't get told to leave!'

Despite everything, George was secretly relieved that his own parents weren't there. His little sisters would have created absolute havoc in this environment – he wouldn't have been surprised to look up at one of the monitors and find they were controlling a Rover on Mars, while his father would have been haranguing Kosmodrome 2 staff about the eco-friendly (or not) aspects of space travel.

Over on the other side of the crowded Mission Control, two parents were loudly quizzing some Kosmodrome 2 staff.

'Will she get extra credits for her participation in the programme?' a sharp-faced mother with big puffy lips rapped out while the father looked about blindly, lost without his smartphone. 'It is crucial that we can add this to her résumé.'

George looked over. This woman, all angles apart from her inflated lips, was the opposite of his own mum, who was smiling, round-faced and gentle.

'Résumé?' he whispered to Annie. 'What's a résumé?'

'It's a thingy,' she said helpfully, 'where you write down all the stuff you've done.'

'It will go with her musical training at the Conservatoire, her ballet programme at the Marinksy, her perfect grade-point score, her weekend volunteering with the under-privileged, her studies in advanced mathematics and her place rowing in the eights at the Junior Olympics,' the pushy parent continued.

George's jaw dropped. 'Wow!' he said to Annie. 'I thought *you* were an over-achiever.' It gave him a cold feeling inside to hear all this. None of it sounded very happy or fun, and certainly not as though these prize

achievements had been done because someone loved these activities so much they couldn't not do them. It sounded like they had been painstakingly put together and done with gritted teeth.

'And,' the mother added, 'her weekly culinary column in *La Bonne Bouche Junior*.'

Despite all this magnificence, the daughter looked remarkably unexcited by her surroundings. Composed, certainly, and very still – but very unbothered, almost to the point of being inert. To the outside observer, it was as though she simply wasn't there inside her body.

At that moment, all the screens on the walls went blank. The room darkened as though a show was beginning. Even the noisier parents quietened down and stopped their clucking. The screens sprang back into life, all showing the same panoramic view of space. On each screen was an incredibly beautiful image of a stellar nursery, an area of space where new stars are born.

'It's like Cosmos's window!' Annie whispered to George. 'That time that Dad used Cosmos to show you how a star is born in space.'

'It's probably a picture from a space telescope,' said George.

'But it's moving!' said Annie.

She was right – the great clouds of gas and dust were not static as they would be in a photograph. Instead, they were dynamic – collapsing in on themselves through the force of gravity to become a ball, which got so hot at its heart that it started to fuse hydrogen to helium, creating a new star. As everyone in the room watched, gripped by the spectacle, the star shone with a ferocity and heat unimaginable. As the star blazed, it created elements in its furnace of a belly.

When the star could burn no more, it exploded, in a

What are chemical elements and where do they come from?

Very simply a chemical element is a pure substance made from a single type of atom. Why is that interesting? Well, there are only 118 known elements and all things in the world are made from a combination of one or more of these elements. The study of how these elements behave and make compounds is the science of Chemistry.

If everything is made from these elements, where do they come from? The two smallest elements, Hydrogen and Helium, were formed at the start of the Universe in the Big Bang and sometime after they came together in large quantities to form stars. In stars, like the Sun, Hydrogen burns at very high temperatures in a process called fusion to make Helium. As stars get older the amount of Helium builds up and Hydrogen runs out and so the stars starts to use Helium as fuel, leading to larger elements like Carbon, Nitrogen and Oxygen. Since these elements are the basis of Human life, you could say that we are made of stars!

Depending on how big and hot the star is larger and larger elements are made in a number of different fusion processes until you reach Iron. After that, one of the major ways of forming elements happens when stars explode, which is called a supernova. A supernova releases the huge amounts of energy that are required to make the heavy elements.

All these processes account for 94 of the elements, and they all occur naturally on Earth. The other 24, called 'transuranic' as they are heavier than Uranium, are man-made with special equipment like nuclear reactors or particle accelerators. These elements are not very stable and fall apart to form smaller, more stable elements in a process called fission. Elements that fall apart in this way are called 'radioactive'. When radioactive compounds fall apart, they also release energy, and that can be used to generate electricity, which is what happens in a nuclear power station.

The Periodic Table

At first glance, the Periodic Table looks like a simple list of all the known elements, but it is much more powerful than that. It tells you how heavy they are, how many protons and electrons are in the element and how they are arranged. It is the arrangement of the electrons that govern how elements react.

It is called the Periodic Table because the properties of the elements repeat periodically. For instance, all elements in a group (the downward columns) have their electrons arranged the same way and so react in a similar way. This repeating pattern occurs because electrons are arranged in energy levels and each level can only contain a fixed number of electrons.

The table was invented by Dmitri Mendeleev in 1869 and has developed over time as more elements have been discovered. He was a chemistry professor who had been thinking about how a number of elements behaved in a similar manner and how best to display the information he had. He spent so long thinking about it that the answer finally came to him in a dream.

The most impressive thing about his idea was that he left gaps where he thought that there should be an element but one had not yet been discovered!

A very important thing to do when you have a new scientific theory is to use it to make a prediction that you can test, to see if your theory is correct. Mendeleev did just that. In his table, he had a gap below the element Silicon and he made a prediction about the properties the missing element would have. He called it *eka-silicon*. It was not until 1886 that the element was discovered and called Germanium – and the properties of Germanium are almost exactly the same as Mendeleev had predicted for eka-silicon!

Toby

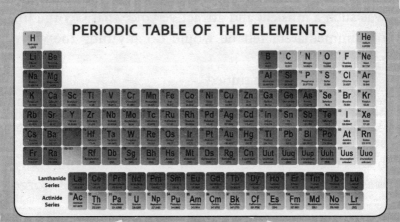

huge great big supernova explosion, sending the outer core across space in a great hot cloud of gaseous dust once more. Inside that cloud were the elements the star had created. In the centre of the gigantic explosion, the core of this huge star remained, collapsing in on itself to become a point in space where gravity is so strong that nothing, not even light, could escape. The massive star's death had formed a black hole.

And yet from this black hole something was emerging . . . The gathered crowds watched in amazement as particles expelled from the black hole assembled themselves, making a shape which quickly took on human form and came to dominate the screen. The figure got clearer and clearer until the whole screen was filled with just one image.

The sound was not far behind. 'Greetings, fellow travellers!' purred a voice.

Annie and George heard a sharp intake of breath as the whole room seemed to register this new presence. It was such a musical and attractive voice that George for one immediately felt he would do anything the voice required.

'Welcome!' it continued.

They could now see clearly the face on the screen. They knew this must be Rika Dur, because they had seen her photo on the internet – but what the photo hadn't really captured was how mesmerizing Rika really was. Completely unexpectedly, both Annie and George found themselves drawn to the image on the screen.

'Cosmic seekers,' the figure continued. 'Welcome to Kosmodrome 2! My name is Rika Dur, and I am head of Kosmodrome 2.'

Even Annie, whose own father had been replaced by Rika, found herself nodding in approval at this statement.

'Kosmodrome 2,' continued the virtual Rika on the screen, 'is home to the world's two greatest space exploration aims – firstly, sending life in the form of human beings out into the Solar System and beyond. And secondly, finding alien life forms in space and bringing them back to Earth for scientific study. These are the two greatest projects ever undertaken. And you – candidates – are going to play your part! Congratulations on getting this far. You have taken your first steps into space already. You have beaten tens of thousands of other applicants to join the Mars Mission training programme for young astronauts.'

'She's amazing,' said George in a whisper to Annie as

a cheer went up around the room. 'I thought she'd be horrible, but she's kinda awesome.'

'You are the best and brightest candidates. This is Phase One, where we train you in the skills you will need to survive in space. In Phase Two we will sift through the group. Who is stardust and who is nuclear waste? Who will be discovered, like the Higgs Boson, and who will rejected, like the steady state theory of the Universe?'

Annie felt very conflicted. She wanted to hate Rika because she was in the place where her dad should be standing, but she also thought Rika was really cool and wanted to hear more of what she had to say.

'Who will adapt to survive . . . and who will become extinct?'

'Me!' Lots of trainees had their hands up. 'I want to survive! I want to be an astronaut! I want to live on Mars!'

'Not all of you can go into space,' continued Rika, her huge face now filling all the screens, a look of heart-melting sincerity and compassion on her face. 'A few of you will emerge victorious from the process – but I am afraid that most of you will be eliminated as we go along.' She smiled. 'From this very minute,' she continued blithely, 'you will enter the training period of your mission, learning about life in space and about the tasks you will undertake on Mars. At the end of the training period you will be paired with another candidate, and together you will take part in a series of challenges. You must move through the challenges together. If we send you into space, we must be able to depend on you entirely to do the right thing, not only for your own sake, but also for that of your fellow travellers and for the space colony itself. You will be the very first people to live on a planet other than the Earth! You will found an off-Earth civilization – it will be your descendents who perhaps survive for millennia into the future. Can you feel the crunch of the red planet under your space boot? Can you gaze into the distance and see the Sun sink through the pink sky over the empty Martian horizon? As the process goes forward, weaker candidates will be weeded out and only the strong will survive! Good luck, new recruits to Kosmodrome 2,' said Rika, in a thrillingly excited voice. 'May the best candidates win!'

Chapter Nine

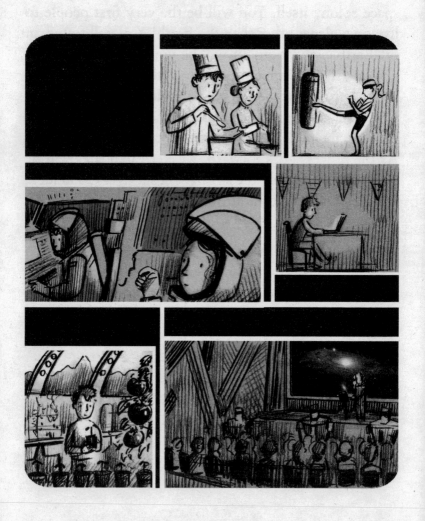

Chapter Ten

At the end of their week, Rika was at Mission Control in person to greet them! Surrounded by a semi-circle of the now familiar robots, she stood at the front of the room, a slight figure in a blue suit, the gigantic screens of Mission Control forming the perfect back-drop to her confident, poised stance. But she exerted the same fascination as she had when they had seen her on the screen. The other trainees pushed and jostled to get as close to her as they could, as though she was a pop star and they were her fans!

'Welcome back!' smiled Rika as the whole room

melted a little and swayed in adoration. 'I hope you have all enjoyed your time with us. For some of you, the journey is about to begin. For others, it's time for you to depart.' She sounded sorrowful, as though she was genuinely distressed that some of the trainees hadn't made the grade.

But already, Kosmodrome 2 workers were tapping trainees on the shoulder and motioning to them to follow. At first, those selected grinned confidently as they trotted after their designated Kosmodrome 2 worker, thinking that this meant they had made it to the next stage.

Then Rika spoke again. 'Only twelve girls and twelve boys will go through to the *Challenges* stage of the process. If one of my wonderful Kosmodrome 2 staff approaches you now, it means it is time, regretfully, for you to leave us. You will depart, safe in the knowledge that you were selected to take part in this extraordinary process – and that you did your bit to ensure humanity progresses out into the Solar System.'

The recruits started glancing around nervously, hoping against hope that they wouldn't feel the tap on the shoulder that meant they had to leave. Annie and George looked at each other, wondering what would happen. George almost expected to feel the light touch of a hand on his shoulder! But it didn't come and, very soon, only a much smaller group of trainees stood in the much emptier Mission Control.

'You will now be paired up with your companion astronaut for the next stage of the process, the *Challenges*!' purred Rika. 'We have already chosen who goes with whom, so listen for your names. I repeat, it is vital that you go through this next stage together. Until now, you have been trained and assessed solo – but when you get to Mars, you will need to work closely with your fellow astronauts to found the new human colony on the red planet. Remember, you are not just visiting Mars! You are not a tourist! You will live there and create a new human habitation, the first off–Earth civilization in the Solar System! For us to choose you, we must know you can work as part of a team.'

Annie and George expected to be paired with each other, so they just stood there, perfectly relaxed. All the other trainees were eyeing each other up, but not Annie and George. They'd come together – and they were always together. They'd even done all the training so far together. They trusted each other in a crisis, they'd been on any number of extraordinary cosmic journeys together, and so it never occurred to them that they wouldn't go into the astronaut competition as a team. Which meant they were totally shocked when it turned out they weren't twinned with each other after all!

First Annie's name was read out and George assumed his name would be next – but it wasn't! Instead, 'Leonia Devries' was announced as Annie's partner.

'Oh, no no no no,' whispered Annie. 'I've got *her*!'

Leonia Devries turned out to be the blank-faced girl with the pushy mother who had made such a scene at parents' day. She looked over at Annie, and apart from the shadow of a sneer, her expression didn't change.

More names were read out, and young astronauts paired up with each other, forming a row across the front of the banks of computers in Mission Control, facing the big screens. George took his place with his new partner, a very small, very shy Russian boy called Igor.

'Now, astronauts,' cajoled Rika in her charming manner.

Annie looked at her, and suddenly had the strangest feeling. George was too far away for her to ask him, but Annie suddenly just knew that somehow, somewhere, they had met Rika before. She couldn't place where or when, but she knew without a doubt that they had come across this person before. And it wasn't at Kosmodrome 2. And her name hadn't been Rika Dur . . .

Annie's thoughts were interrupted. 'It is time for the challenges to begin!' cried Rika.

The screens behind her, which had been filled with extraordinary cosmic images, suddenly turned bright red, orange and yellow, and started broadcasting the ear-splitting noise of a spacecraft during the first few seconds of a launch. At the same time, all the young astronauts' pagers started beeping furiously. Annie twisted hers round so she could read the text scrolling across it.

But to her surprise, before she had even registered the words, she felt her wrist being encircled as though in a cold grip of steel as Leonia pincered her with her long cool fingers. Then she was pulled along at great speed as Leonia gracefully started forward, her limbs scissoring like blades. Somehow Leonia seemed to know exactly where they needed to go. She dragged Annie down corridors, up stairs, across empty fore-courts between buildings, occasionally pausing to check her pager to ensure they were headed in the right direction.

Finally they came to a standalone build-ing on the far edge of the Kosmodrome 2 compound – they seemed to have run and run for miles, and Annie was panting and thirsty. Leonia, however, showed no sign that she had even broken a sweat. Her marble-white face remained expressionless and serene, her hooded eyes showing no emotion or excitement as she flung open a large double door and pushed Annie inside. Annie caught the faint acrid whiff of chlorine as Leonia relentlessly charged forward . . .

George and Igor were far behind, still dithering in the main entrance to Mission Control.

'Let's go!' said George, pointing to the other recruits hot-footing it towards a huge building.

'To my mind, their supposition is not entirely correct,' fretted Igor.

'You mean, they're going the wrong way?' asked George.

'*Da,*' replied Igor, nodding. He pointed in a different direction, where they could just make out two tiny figures in the distance, running at championship speed. 'After them follow we need.'

George wondered if Igor meant to speak like Yoda or whether it was translating from Russian that made his sentence order so odd. But he didn't have time to ask. As he gazed in the direction in which Igor pointed, George caught the glint of sunshine on a blonde pony-tail and realized that one of the distant figures could be Annie. If that was the way she had gone, he was ready to follow.

'Yup,' he said. 'Well spotted. Let's get after them!' He bolted away, but then turned round and saw Igor plodding along slowly, his head drooping like a small donkey's. 'Can't you go any faster?' he asked him.

The smaller boy gave him a pained look. '*Nyet,*' he

said, shaking his head. 'I am a mathematician and not an athlete.' He sighed. 'I have physical work done much week one, weary now.'

'OK, piggyback,' sighed George. 'It will be quicker.'

'What is this back of a pig?' asked Igor suspiciously.

'Jump on and I'll carry you,' said George.

Even though Igor looked tiny, he weighed quite a bit, but George hefted him onto his back and started running after the two figures who might (or might not) be Annie and her partner. From the other side of the campus he heard a roar as the other candidates realized they had gone the wrong way. A cohort were wheeling round and heading back in the direction George and Igor were now puffing (George) along in . . .

'Where are we?' Annie asked. She realized she hadn't yet heard Leonia speak. But Leonia stayed mute. She didn't need to say anything, for the answer was right in front of them. They had emerged into a vast cavernous room with a high vaulted ceiling where light played

WHAT IS NEUTRAL BUOYANCY?

Ever wondered why astronauts famously say, 'Houston, we have a problem'? That's because Mission Control for NASA-manned space missions is based in Houston, Texas, USA. The people astronauts talk to from space are in Houston, Texas, at the Johnson Space Center. Nearby you can also find most of the training facilities for US astronauts. And lots of astronauts and their families live in this area so they can get to work (on Earth) easily. It's not at all unusual at schools around the Johnson Space Center to have students whose parents are in space!

The Neutral Buoyancy Laboratory, or NBL, is near the Johnson Space Center. It's a place where astronauts can train for their work in space. From the outside, the NBL looks like a huge warehouse, but inside is a massive shimmering blue swimming pool. Sunk into that pool is a mock-up of the spacecraft the astronauts in training need to prepare to work on. They might be mending the spacecraft or building an extra part of the International Space Station. It depends on the job that particular astronaut has to learn for when he or she gets out into space.

The reason the astronauts practise these tasks in water is because it allows them to feel what it will be like to work in microgravity when they are in space. The NBL helps to train astronauts for when they go on an EVA – extra-vehicular activity, or space walk. A space walk takes the astronaut outside of their spacecraft, in a spacesuit. Tethered to the spacecraft for safety, the astronaut has only hours to complete an important job.

In specially modified suits, the astronauts are lowered into the pool on a platform by a crane. Once they are in the water, divers help them to move around. It isn't exactly like being in space – water isn't quite the same as being outside the space station! But still – practice makes perfect!

And on a space mission, nothing can be left to chance . . .

about the beams and struts in a liquid moving pattern.

Annie gasped. But it wasn't at the size of the room or the changing luminous display on the ceiling. It was something quite different. Where she would have expected to see a floor, there was just a shimmering blue expanse; a huge turquoise rectangle.

A few robots stood motionless around the pool, these were the same type of tall, silver metallic bots that Annie and George had seen waiting to escort Ebot off the premises.

'A swimming pool?' exclaimed Annie. Leonia looked at her with a very unimpressed expression. She cocked one elegant eyebrow. 'Didn't you do any prep for this at all?' she asked.

The honest answer would have been 'no', but Annie didn't think it was the moment.

'Neutral buoyancy,' Leonia went on. 'C'mon, we've got here first. We need to find the subaqua suits and put on weights. Tell me you can at least dive!'

'Yes I can, actually,' huffed Annie. 'Thanks.' She'd done a subaqua course with her school swimming club.

'Good,' said Leonia. 'Then you'll know what this is about.'

'I will?' said Annie, rather alarmed. She didn't feel like she was keeping up at all.

'Hush!' said Leonia calmly, holding up one finger. 'Listen!' In the distance, they heard a sound.

'What's that?' said Annie, whose wrist was still held in Leonia's merciless grip.

'It's the others,' said Leonia. 'We got a head start on them – I studied the layout of Kosmodrome 2 before I came so I would know the quickest routes across the campus. But they won't be far behind.'

'How did you do that?' said Annie. 'You can't even see Kosmodrome 2 on Google Earth! Isn't that classified information?'

'It is,' said Leonia calmly. 'There are ways.'

She had led them into a changing room where a few weighted subaqua suits lay ready. Annie didn't count them, but she felt pretty sure there were fewer than twenty-four suits in the changing room.

'Put one on,' said Leonia. She shrugged off her outer layer of clothing to reveal a silver bodysuit which covered her from ankle to neck. Swiftly, she slithered into a wetsuit while Annie was still trying to get out of her flightsuit. A few minutes later and Leonia, who was already changed, grabbed Annie and unceremoniously stuffed her into a diving suit and plopped a tank of air on her back. She shoved a mask in Annie's face and motioned her to head back to the pool. The suits, which had extra weights fitted so that when they were underwater they would feel the same sensations of movement as they would on a spacewalk, felt very heavy in Earth's gravity.

'What now?' Annie removed her mask to speak. She

wasn't used to being told what to do – she was more used to being in charge than being a follower. This was a very new experience for her.

Leonia checked her pager, which she had transferred to her wetsuit.

'Inside the pool,' she said, 'there is a full mock-up of a spacecraft like the one we will go to Mars in. Our mission today is to dive into the pool where we have to try and mend a solar array which has been dented in an impact with a meteorite. Look!' She showed Annie a small diagram on the pager. 'It's not difficult – we just have to get down there and get a solar array straightened out. Are you ready?'

Annie nodded and fitted her mask properly, putting the air pipe into her mouth and checking she could breathe from the tank.

Leonia put on her own mask and then held up a wetsuit-clad hand and counted down on her fingers – three . . . two . . . *one!* When she reached 'one', the two girls jumped into the pool. As they flew through the air over

the turquoise water, they just caught sight of the main doors opening, and a couple of other hopeful astronaut trainees dashed in.

Even though George ended up carrying his partner, Igor, the whole way, they were still the second pair to arrive. Everyone else got confused or lost and took much longer to work out where they should be. Running into the changing room, George saw Annie's fluorescent trainers under a bench. He breathed a sigh of relief. So it must have been her he had seen in the distance! Quickly he found a small wetsuit and chucked it at Igor.

'Put this on!' he said. 'We're going into the pool!' He had a thought. 'You can swim, can't you?' He pulled on his suit very quickly and attached his breathing apparatus – it wasn't hard to figure it out when you were quite used to wearing a spacesuit with an air tank.

'Of course,' said Igor, to George's relief. It was one thing carrying Igor on the ground, but underwater? Igor, however, was struggling with his suit, so George took over, treating him as though he was one of his little sisters making a mess of putting on her school uniform. Other trainees were pouring into the changing room now so George dragged Igor towards the pool, checked his diving gear, gave him the OK sign and pushed him into the pool.

*

The two girls had already sunk to the bottom of the pool, where they had righted themselves and checked each other and their equipment. They gave each other the 'OK' signal and swam down towards an enormous tubular structure. It looked like a real spaceship on the bottom of the pool!

Leonia moved quickly and confidently to one side of the submerged spacecraft. Annie felt very much like an 'also swam' as she watched Leonia's deft movements and decisive turns and spins in the water. Trailing a stream of bubbles behind her, Annie swam rather

unenthusiastically after her, heading for the solar array – a space version of the kind of solar panel that some people have on their roofs – which was bent at a very strange angle. She supposed it must have been left like that deliberately, to see which of the trialling astronauts would be the first to put it straight.

She swam towards it, just thinking that if every task was this easy, she and Leonia were bound to come out of it with top marks, when she felt something – or rather someone – grab her ankle and pull her sharply backwards. She looked round and saw an adult-sized figure in a wetsuit right behind her, determined to pull her out of the way.

At first, Annie thought she was being scuppered by her own partner, but looking sharply round she saw to her horror that Leonia, on the other side of the curved hulk of the spacecraft, had also been seized by another swimmer and was fighting to get free. These divers were clearly grown-ups, so they must be Kosmodrome 2 workers who had been waiting in the pool for the trainees to arrive, to see if they could ruin their chances of being first to the solar array! This didn't seem fair, thought Annie angrily as she fought free. On a real spacewalk, they wouldn't encounter aliens trying to drag them off the outside of the spacecraft they were trying to mend! She felt betrayed – she had thought the challenges would be mock-ups of situations they might actually experience! This wasn't right.

Above Leonia, very near to the surface, Igor was having a real problem in sinking. His buoyancy didn't seem to be neutral at all! He was stuck, paddling around in a whole explosion of bubbles. George had to waste precious time trying to help his  training partner to descend to the bottom of the pool. He knew it wasn't Igor's fault, but at the same time he couldn't help feeling it was very unfair that he had been landed with a dud partner. He gave a cross sort of exhale which turned into a million bubbles as he finally managed to drag Igor down.

Over by the solar array, Annie was struggling. The other diver, who had hold of her ankle, swung her around by her foot and cast her away from the spacecraft, sending her across the pool in a flurry of disorganized limbs. Annie recovered herself and shot forward once more, so angry that now she didn't hesitate to grab the other diver around the waist. Such was the force of Annie's forward motion that she cannoned into the diver in front of her, managing to slap him or her against the side of the spacecraft.

On the other side, Leonia had booted her assailant firmly in the stomach with both her flippered feet, sending the unfortunate diver spiralling backwards and into the far edge of the pool. She reached forward, but as she did so, yet another diver arrived, intent on pushing her out of the way. Annie managed to shove the diver she was tussling with under the spacecraft, getting her foot on top of the other diver's head and pushing down as hard as she could until they sank to the bottom on the pool. Freed from her opponent, Annie rose upwards, heading once more towards the damaged solar array. As she did so, she saw a whole swarm of

other divers plunge into the pool above her, until the water was alive with swimmers, all eagerly shooting downwards towards the spacecraft. Annie knew that if she or Leonia didn't get to the solar array in the next few seconds, they would have no chance. The water was so thick with bubbles now that she could hardly see where she was going.

At that moment Leonia got free of the diver she had been struggling with. She and Annie dived together, from either side of the spacecraft, towards the solar array, both wanting to be the person who straightened it out and won the first challenge. For a second Annie wondered if Leonia was going to strike her out of the way so she could be the first. But as they rose together, as gracefully as though they were performing a synchronized ballet underwater, Leonia motioned to Annie to pull the array back into place. Annie grabbed the support which held the solar panel – a vital piece of the spacecraft, responsible for providing the power which allowed life to continue inside the ship – and replaced it at the right angle, slotting it into the groove on the spacecraft.

As she did so, she felt rather than saw a red pulsating light flash on and off above the swimming pool. Rising upwards, she and Leonia broke through the surface of the water, now teeming with divers.

They swam to the side and jumped out of the pool, Annie pulling her mask off as the curved space throbbed with the bright red light and the same howling alarm sound that had sent them off on their first challenge rang out again.

Annie looked around for someone who could be George. She really wanted to talk to him about her doubts about Rika. And she wanted reassurance from someone she knew, for this first challenge had been a horrible shock to her. Space camp had been really cool up until about half an hour ago, when it had changed completely and become something very different; something Annie wasn't at all sure she liked.

The other divers were surfacing, their body language already telling of their disappointment at an early failure. Despondently, wetsuit-clad trainees clambered out of the pool, removing subaqua equipment and grumbling that it hadn't been at all fair.

Two kids hadn't even made it into the pool – they had arrived too late and found that the wetsuits had run out. These kids were already being told that they were leaving the process – anyone who had not even managed to get themselves a suit was immediately disqualified. 'Transport home,' Kosmodrome 2 workers told them, 'awaits you in the main reception.' They would get a certificate and a photo of themselves at Kosmodrome 2, but they definitely wouldn't be going to Mars. The boy, who was very small, burst into tears at the news.

The next shock for Annie was the reaction of the other kids. She had expected they would be grudgingly happy for her – lots of high-fives and grumpy smiles acknowledging that she and Leonia had deserved to win. But the reaction was completely opposite: the other trainees gave Annie and Leonia sneering looks!

Annie tried to smile back at them, but they returned blank looks or whispered to each other. 'Stand firm,' Annie told herself. 'You've been through this before! And you survived last time. Don't let it get to you.' She stuck her nose up in the air, determined to ignore the others. But that didn't mean she was enjoying it or that she wanted this to carry on.

Leonia didn't look despondent at all – her cat-like eyes glinted with the reflection of the red light, giving her an otherworldly look. She held up one palm for Annie to slap.

'Well done, partner,' she whispered. 'And now there are only twenty-two of us left.'

Chapter Eleven

The next evening, Annie sat in her sleeping pod inside Kosmodrome 2, waiting for Leonia to drop off to sleep so she could sneak out and meet up with George. While she waited, she thought back over her time so far at space camp. At first, she knew, she and George had come partly because they wanted to, but also because they felt they *had* to. They were on the trail of several mysteries, all of which pointed to this place.

After a couple of days, however, space camp had started to be real fun, when they were all mucking about together, learning about space travel and Mars. The programme was residential, because lots of the kids came from far away, some even from other countries. For the first week, the girls had slept in one big dormitory and the boys in another. It had been a laugh – even though the would-be astronauts knew that not all of them could make it to Mars, the atmosphere had been upbeat and jolly. The offhand attitude of some of the others at the induction meeting at Mission

Control had changed into a feeling that they were all in it together! Evenings were chatty and friendly, though everyone was usually so tired after their long days of astronaut preparation that they tended to drop off to sleep almost immediately.

The trainees had also been receiving supportive messages from their family and friends – not directly, as none of them were allowed to have their phones or tablets with them. But there was a message relay every morning and evening, when messages, printed out on long thin strips of paper, were handed out by Kosmodrome 2 staff. Although Annie received nothing from Eric – she and George suspected his messages were being blocked by the Kosmodrome 2 staff – she got several from her mum, happily describing locations and concerts in far-flung parts of the world. Even George received updates from his parents, telling him they were very busy tilling the soil and living off the land but that they missed him. One evening Annie even got a message which must have come from Ebot as it was cryptic sentence. She started to try and work out if it meant something, but it had arrived at the end of an especially exhausting day of fitness training so she had fallen asleep in her space pyjamas, slip of paper in her hand, before she had had any insight into what it might mean. When she woke in the morning, the piece of paper was scrunched in her fist so she tucked into the pocket of her flightsuit, meaning to decode it later and had then

Why do we weigh different amounts on different worlds?

- Your *weight* is the amount of gravitational force between you and the Earth.
- Your *mass* is the amount of matter, or stuff, that you contain.

Mass is measured in kilos (kg). But isn't weight measured in kilos too? Isn't that confusing? Yes, it is.

Weight is commonly described in kilos on Earth but it really should be given in *Newtons* (N). A Newton is a unit of force.

> **A mass of 1kg on Earth is about 10N.**

When you travel across the Solar System, your mass doesn't change. But your weight does.

When you land on a planet or moon with weaker gravity than the Earth, your weight changes although your mass stays the same.

What does this mean in practice?

> **If you weigh 34 kilos on Earth, here is your weight in kilos on other bodies in our solar system!**

Mercury	12.8 kilos
Venus	30.6 kilos
The Moon	5.6 kilos
Mars	12.8 kilos
Jupiter	80.3 kilos
Saturn	36.1 kilos
Uranus	30.2 kilos
Neptune	38.2 kilos

So you could jump over really high bars with ease on the Moon or Mercury – but find it hard to even take a step over a bar on the ground on Jupiter!

completely forgotten about it.

And then suddenly, just as Annie thought that she and George must have got it wrong – there was nothing spooky about Kosmodrome 2 and no actual mystery linked to her father's swift exit – everything started to seem weird once more.

At the same time as they had moved on to the *Challenges* section of the process, they had been split into their pairs and made to take up residence in smaller 'pod' units. After the neutral buoyancy challenge Annie had been dismayed to find she couldn't go back to the dormitory and was shown to a small white circular room containing two hammocks and not much else, with Leonia in tow. But after the surprisingly hostile reaction from the other kids immediately after she and Leonia won that first challenge, Annie really felt quite glad not to be going to the dormitory. Instead, she was rather relieved to be sharing the pod with the one person, Leonia, who wouldn't hold their joint triumph against her.

But now here she was, in the pod for two, waiting

to creep out and find her best friend George to see if he was having the same thoughts as her – that they had been right. There *was* something peculiar about Kosmodrome 2. Annie couldn't put her finger on it – just like she couldn't say why seeing Rika Dur in person had given her such an odd feeling. But she had learned from past experience that if her senses and intuition told her something wasn't right, then it probably wasn't.

It had been a long day, she thought, as her stomach rumbled after a meal of rehydrated spaghetti bolognese and a dusty ice-cream wafer with dried apple rings. She would love to fall asleep, but she knew she mustn't! She wanted to talk to George, so she pinched herself and made herself remember the events of that day to stop her eyes closing into deep sleep.

The second challenge, which they had done that morning, had involved a baffling task: at first it looked as though the kids were simply expected to pick up litter from a rocky landscape. They'd been taken across Kosmodrome 2 by bus. On the way, Annie had looked out and seen, in a distant part of the campus, what looked like a huge spaceship on a launch pad. She'd asked one of the Kosmodrome 2 staff what the ship was there for, where it was heading to, but the staff member had quickly got on his two-way radio and advised the other bus to take a different route to the Mars Assembly Room. Annie thought she heard him

say, 'Go via the perimeter so you don't pass *Artemis*,' but she wasn't sure.

Their bus had suddenly veered off in such a way that the spaceship was hidden from view and Annie couldn't catch sight of it again.

The Mars Assembly building turned out to house a mock-up of the surface of Mars – without the low gravity, of course. The surface gravity on Mars is only 38% of the gravity on Earth, not quite as small as on the Moon, where a space colonist could easily float up into the air if they moved too quickly!

In front of the kids lay a reddish brown, hilly land-

LIFE ON MARS

Normally I enjoy sleeping late, but every year on the morning of my birthday, my eyes seem to pop right open with excitement. Last year was no different, and on the morning of 16 February, I jumped out of bed. Except something *was* different. There were no birds chirping outside my window, no scent of my favourite breakfast wafting in from the kitchen, and I couldn't hear the familiar sounds of my family moving around downstairs.

Then I remembered that I wasn't at home for my birthday this year. In fact, I wasn't even on Planet Earth! I was on Mars with six other scientists from around the world, studying what it's like to live on another planet.

Have you ever wondered what it would be like to live on another world? It's easy to forget that Earth is not the only planet in the solar system. Seven other planets whiz around the Sun just like ours! This is lucky for us, because someday humans might need to find a new home! We haven't always taken very good care of our planet, and one day the Earth will be overheated and unable to support us. Besides global warming, we also have to remember the dinosaurs! Those magnificent creatures ruled the planet for over 165 million years, until an asteroid struck Earth and ruined their home, driving the whole species to extinction. Today we have special software to track asteroids from far away, but if we want the human species to survive for a million years, we need to spread out and learn how to live in space.

But we can't live just anywhere! We need to find a planet that's not too hot and close to the Sun, like Venus or Mercury, not too cold and far away, like Uranus or Neptune, and it can't be made of gas like Jupiter and Saturn! That leaves Mars – our rocky, red, neighbouring planet.

Lots of astronauts have visited space, but except for a few short trips to the Moon, they've never been far from Earth. No human has ever travelled to Mars, but we're now starting to prepare for this trip. Imagine a car ride that lasts for more than 200 days with no rest stops. That's how long it would take a crew of astronauts to travel to Mars, 140 million miles away from Earth! When you're that far away from home, no one can send you extra food or water, so you have to bring as much as you can with you, and learn to produce the rest yourself.

Before we send astronauts on such a big journey, we need to understand as many of the challenges they might face as possible. One way we research what life will be like on Mars is by living and working in Martian research stations right here on Earth. These special laboratories, or 'habitats', are designed to look and feel exactly like a house on Mars, with a kitchen, a bathroom, a 'greenhab' to grow food, a laboratory with microscopes and other science tools, and tiny bedrooms for crew members. On the morning of my 26th birthday, that's exactly where I woke up.

Usually my birthday would be filled with phone calls from friends and hugs from family, but there are no phone calls on Mars, because the signal would take too long to reach Earth! When we want to speak to our family, we can send an e-mail over the internet, but it can still take more than 20 minutes for the message to reach them. That also means we can't watch TV. Instead, we can store digital versions of our favourite books, movies and television programmes on a small computer, to read or watch whenever we're bored.

There's almost no time for boredom, though. There's a lot to be done every day, like checking and cleaning equipment, growing crops like potatoes, cooking for the crew, recording videos for students and classrooms, and even venturing outside to collect samples of soil and rocks. Mars doesn't have nearly as much oxygen as Earth, so you need a helmet to help you breathe whenever you go outside. When you come back, sticky and sweaty from a long walk in a heavy spacesuit, you can't even take a shower! Water is a precious resource on Mars, and we have to save as much as possible. Instead of taking showers, we clean our bodies with baby wipes!

My six crewmates must have known that I would miss my family on my birthday, because when I came out from my room, they were waiting with a hand-made birthday card. Instead of '26', the card said '13.8', because that's how old I would be on Mars, where years are almost twice as long as Earth years! They also cooked me a special breakfast of heart-shaped pancakes. Meals can get very boring on Mars. Because fresh food would go rotten quickly, almost all of the food is in a powdered form that you mix with water – even the meat! My favourite Martian meal is macaroni and cheese.

I thanked all of my crewmates for such a nice birthday surprise, and I realized that I'm lucky to have such great friends here. Getting along with your crew is very important, especially when you're stuck in a small space together for a long time!

After three weeks of living and working in a Mars habitat, I know life won't be easy for the first astronauts who travel there. I would miss all of my friends and family, my favourite foods, warm showers, and even just being able to breathe fresh air outside without a helmet on. Still, I would choose to go, and I'm lucky to have a family who encourages me to reach for the stars. We might be years away from the first flight, but I know we'll see footprints on Mars in our lifetime. I certainly hope they're mine!

But even if they're not, I'll always remember a birthday that was out of this world. Maybe you too will one day spend a birthday of yours in a Mars habitat – or even on the distant red planet itself!

Kellie

scape with a pink skyscape projected in the background, showing the Martian sunrise behind a massive volcanic mountain range. Again, a couple of the same silent and oddly menacing robots stood about, seemingly inert but ready to spring into action if challenged. Surprisingly, the ground at their feet seemed to be strewn with bits of plastic. In the distance they could see a couple of Martian Landers, the kind of capsule in which the astronauts would descend to the surface of Mars from the orbiting ship which had brought them from Earth.

The kids were given no instructions at all, just told to 'Start!'

Leonia had chewed her lip thoughtfully while looking at the trash-covered scenery in front of them.

But Annie's brain had got there first. 'Ooh!' She gave a start. 'I know what this challenge is!' she whispered to Leonia. The drones fluttered around them, clearly trying to record their activities, which was like being pestered on a picnic by wasps. 'Nuisance things!' said Annie, batting one away with her hand. It came straight back at her, enraged, but Leonia held her arm so that her wrist faced the drone. To Annie's amazement, the drone dropped out of the air to the floor and seemed to give up entirely.

'Anti-drone wristwatch,' murmured Leonia.

'Why do you even have that?' asked Annie.

'My parents try to monitor my activities with drones while they are at work,' replied Leonia calmly. 'So I had

to invent something to counteract them.'

'Wow!' said Annie. For a few seconds, she was too flabbergasted to speak as her mind turned over the possibilities of what this meant in reality. What it really meant was that not only did Leonia have a rotten childhood, but also that they lost valuable time in the second challenge – time which allowed another duo to sneak ahead of them.

George and Igor! On another bit of Mars, just behind a hummock, so out of sight and sound of Annie, George had had exactly the same thought as her. Igor had been gazing at the rubbish in dismay. 'Surely they not mean we are to gather trash?' he said, sounding disappointed.

'Is this a challenge about recycling? Perhaps to make energy to fuel our trip back to Earth?'

'Yes!' said George, delighted that he had a bolt of inspiration about why there was much garbage hanging around on Mars. 'Listen, Igor,' he said. 'I need you to make your way over to the Mars Lander without alerting the others, and go inside.'

'For what purpose?' said Igor, looking perplexed but willing.

George bent closer to Igor's ear and whispered.

'Aha!' said Igor happily. 'I hope very much your assumption is correct! I go now!'

Idly, as though heading in no particular direction, Igor ambled away, while George stealthily started to collect items of rubbish from the surface of the simulated planet. Watching Igor potter away, no one would have any idea that his destination was the Mars Lander. Jauntily, the small boy took such a winding route towards the spacecraft that none could have suspected his aim was so true. As he approached the steps leading into the small craft, he darted like a hummingbird up them and slammed the door behind him.

Everyone else in the challenge, apart from Annie and Leonia who were also starting to collect up the plastic, was still standing around, arguing with their partner over the meaning of this particular challenge. But they were all too late, including Annie and Leonia. Like George, Annie had understood that the plastic repre-

sented the items, food packaging and so on, that would be discarded by the astronauts during their proposed nine-month flight to Mars.

But unlike George, child of uber-recyclers Terence and Daisy, Annie hadn't quite made the next leap. Sending Igor to the Mars Lander had been George's particular stroke of brilliance, as he had found in the Lander all the parts he needed to construct a 3D printer, which would be used to recycle the plastic into the foundations of the habitation that the Mars astronauts would need to build as soon as they touched down on the surface of Mars.

Igor, with his advanced technical and engineering skills, had done a very creditable job of assembling a

3D printer before anyone else had time to storm into the Lander and demand that he hand over the equipment.

As the same brain-achingly loud noise as the day before blared, to announce that another challenge had been won, Annie used the cover to shuffle over and talk to George while Igor climbed back out of the Lander. They had already been told that it was against the rules to have any discussions with a person other than your team-mate during a challenge; a rule which at the time had struck Annie as odd and unnecessarily unfriendly. After all, they were supposed to show people-skills of cooperation. Even so, she didn't want to risk being jettisoned now, just when things were starting to get interesting. And she was safe, for she and Leonia had done enough in the challenge to stay. Two kids who hadn't managed to pick up a single piece of rubbish would be leaving.

'Meet me later,' Annie managed to murmur to George. 'By Mission Control.'

He nodded and they parted before any of the remaining drones had time to capture their interaction. Everyone else was watching the tearful exit of the two who had just been told they had failed the challenge and would now be escorted out of the space camp . . .

*

Checking that Leonia was asleep, Annie slipped on her

team-mate's anti-drone wristwatch, which lay on the floor by her hammock. The doors weren't locked – they didn't need to be, since candidates' cell-like pods each had a drone hovering outside. If anyone crept out, as one homesick candidate had last night, the drone immediately alerted Security who came, in robot form, and took the candidate away, along with their unfortunate partner. Disqualification, they had learned, was instant for this type of rule-breaking. They had been gathered together that morning and told, very solemnly, that one of their number had been 'eliminated' due to night-time rule breaking, and warned that the same would happen to anyone else who tried it. And their partner, who had to take responsibility for their team-mate's actions, just as they would if they were on the surface of a colonized planet!

Annie knew she had to be careful. She popped her pager in her pocket – they never went anywhere without them – then opened the pod door. The second a drone flew towards her, she turned the watch towards it, just as she had seen Leonia do earlier. It made no difference – the drone still flew towards her. In a panic, Annie pushed all the buttons she could find on the side of the watch; one of them must have activated, as the drone fell to the ground and lay there, inert and unmoving. In the distance Annie thought she heard the sound of a child crying. It was a mournful and sad noise, as though some poor kid was sobbing his heart out.

Torn, Annie wondered if she should go and see, but she didn't know how long she could be out of her pod before her monitoring drone woke up and noticed she had gone. She resolved to meet George first and then try to find and comfort the child.

Creeping up to Mission Control, she spotted another figure in the gloomily lit entrance. Kosmodrome 2 had seemed so busy and vibrant when they first arrived – and now, just days later, it seemed emptier and emptier, almost like a ghost facility instead of the beating heart of international space travel. From the size and shape of the form, she could see the figure was George.

'Did you lose your drone?' she whispered hastily.

He nodded and smiled. 'It's playing chess with Igor,' he replied.

Annie scrunched her face into a 'What?' expression, but George just grinned and she knew he was teasing her.

'Can you hear that?' she whispered, straining her ears for the sound of the child crying. But it must have stopped as she only heard silence.

George beckoned to her to follow. 'I've got something to show you!' he said. He took Annie to a spur corridor which led away from the central well of Mission Control. It looked like a row of offices. One of them had Annie's dad's name – crossed out – on the door!

'Dad's office!' said Annie, a lump coming to her throat.

George softly turned the door handle but it didn't give. 'Locked!' he whispered. 'Let's go into Mission Control itself.' They went back down the short corridor into the entrance hall and stole through the big doors into the back of the room, which now seemed completely deserted. The robotic missions displayed on the screens continued, but no one seemed to mind or be monitoring their progress. The robots in space streamed back their data to an uncaring, empty Mission Control, abandoned apart from George and Annie – two junior recruits who couldn't help but take a moment to gaze upwards at the screens.

'LOOK!' Annie said soundlessly to George, pointing to the screen that had been blank when they first visited Mission Control. George's jaw dropped open as he followed her finger. It was exactly the same view they had seen through Cosmos's portal: the same greenish white ice marked with ridges and squiggles, the same black sky scattered with brilliant diamond-like stars. In the distance they could see a vast stripy gas planet, which told them that this indeed was a moon of Jupiter. But the greatest clue of all was the same round circle in the ice that they had seen that day; the day before all their adventures had begun in earnest.

'Europa!' said George silently. 'It has to be! Back online!'

'And,' mouthed Annie, 'someone's there!'

George strained his eyes to look at the grainy picture on the screen and saw that his friend was right. Dark shapes were moving around on the surface of this Europa-like moon. They seemed grouped close to the hole in the ice and it looked as though they were taking samples of fluid out of the ice hole. One of the robots even had what looked like a large net and another, a harpoon – as though they were ice fishermen, waiting for their prey to swim into the icy trap below!

'*Artemis,*' breathed Annie into George's ear. 'The *hunters* – and they're on Europa!'

At that moment, they heard a noise. George grabbed Annie and pulled her backwards under the desk with him – and just in time, as it turned out. From their vantage point on the floor, they saw three pairs of robotic legs clank past, following a pair of human legs in a blue flightsuit and high heels.

'Rika!' whispered Annie to George. Suddenly they both felt genuinely scared. 'What if our pagers go off?'

George's heart jumped. 'Put it in your mouth,' he whispered back in her ear. 'That way, if it goes off, the

sound and light will
be muffled.'

Annie pulled an
'Ew' face back at him
as they lay under the
desk but did as he told
her, unhooking her
pager and popping

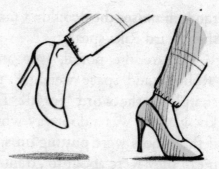

the gobstopper-sized object into her mouth. She desperately wanted to tell George about her revelation – that
she thought she had met Rika before somewhere, and
she was racking her brains as to where that could be or
when. But with the pager in her mouth, she couldn't
even whisper to her friend.

After a few minutes, which seemed like hours on end
for Annie and George, during which they just heard

random noises they couldn't make any sense of, finally they heard Rika speak.

'Prepare the portal,' she announced very clearly. 'Robots, add space weights!' Annie pinched George sharply at the word 'portal'. The kind of portal they knew about was a doorway which led into space. And if the robots were putting on space weights, that must mean they were about to go into different gravitational conditions where they needed to be heavier. 'Open portal.' They heard Rika's voice give the order. But her voice wasn't charming or as honeyed as it had been before. This time, it was a little metallic and seemed to have a screeching echo at the back of it, as though it wasn't quite a real voice after all.

From under the desk, Annie and George both saw a brilliantly white light flash across Mission Control. They heard a clanking noise, which sounded like the three robots were slowly walking heavily forward. A blast of cold air rushed into the room, carrying a mineral-rich scent with it. And after just a couple of seconds, the light, the cold air and the smell was gone. And then they heard tap-tapping footsteps and saw Rika's high heels under her blue flightsuit walking back the way she came. She closed the door of Mission Control behind her and was gone.

Very cautiously, Annie and George levered themselves out from under the desk, pagers still held inside their mouths. Even though they had not seen the three robots leave the room with Rika, they were now alone once more in Mission Control. The robots had seemingly vanished into thin air! And where the moving image of Europa had been, the screen was now just blank and black.

George motioned towards the computer, meaning they must try and log on, to send a message to Eric – surely it must be possible to send a message *out* to him, even if his messages *in* might not reach them – but as he did so he noticed Annie's cheeks start to glow with a translucent red colour, from her pager inside her mouth, now beeping and flashing. Annie, of course, also saw George's face light up like Rudolph the red-nosed reindeer's.

And they both knew what they had to do. There was no time to try and send a message to Eric or search for

more information about how the robots could have seemingly disappeared from inside this room, what the mysterious portal was generated by or whether that really had been Europa they had seen on screen.

There was only one thing to do – run!

Chapter Twelve

The next morning, the alarm went off incredibly early. Annie groaned and rolled over in her hammock. She felt shattered. The run back to the sleeping pod last night had been terrifying. Her pager had been flashing like crazy the whole way and she was convinced that she – or George – would get caught. But astonishingly, she made it back to the pod and let herself in to find Leonia still sound asleep and the drone camera still lying in the corridor like a dead fly.

Almost at the same time, her pager stopped beeping and flashing – clearly it must just have been some kind of exercise to see how quickly they could react to a sudden need for action. In that case, Annie thought, Leonia would have failed, for she had slept right through her pager.

Annie had flung on her space pyjamas before she slipped off the watch and picked the drone up from the floor. It came back to life and whizzed around the room a few times, registering that both girls were in their hammocks, but at least one of the pair was sitting upright in bed, ready for action in response to the pager; then a familiar red light flashed and the drone flew away again. Annie held her breath for what felt like for ever – but no one came to check further on them so she eventually fell asleep, figuring that somehow she and George had got away with it.

In the morning she still felt like she could sleep for ages. But Leonia was already up and dressed in her blue flightsuit, her long hair drawn back in a sleek ponytail, doing a set of warm-up stretches in preparation for the day ahead. Annie wished she could talk to Leonia about what she and George had seen last night. But she didn't dare. She had no idea if she could trust Leonia – perhaps the other girl would report Annie straightaway to the authorities at Kosmodrome 2 and ruin her chances of ever finding out what was happening on Europa, or why her dad had been fired. Then a thought struck her. If Leonia told the staff about Annie sneaking out, Leonia herself could be on a one-way ticket home too! The other girl wouldn't risk that . . .

'What are we doing today?' she mumbled sleepily.

'How should I know?' said Leonia in surprise. 'But whatever it is, we need to be at our maximum alertness. Given our performance to date, the others have marked us out – or rather marked me out – as strong contenders, which means we will face deliberate sabotage at some time in the day.'

'Oh, great!' said Annie. 'Perhaps we'll be out of here

by the end of today.'

'No!' said Leonia very sharply, for the first time showing something like emotion.

Annie sat up in her hammock in surprise.

'I don't want to go home!' said Leonia very fiercely. 'Not there! Not back there. With those . . . people.' To her amazement, Annie saw her team-mate's silver eyes blink very rapidly as though holding back tears. But Leonia recovered her usual sangfroid quite quickly. 'Hurry up,' she snapped. 'You know today will be much harder than the previous days and we can't make it worse for ourselves by being late.'

'Yes, sir!' said Annie under her breath as she slid out of her hammock, blearily rubbing her eyes as she went. She changed out of her space pyjamas into her flightsuit – and as she did so, the television set in their pod flickered to life without either of them touching it.

'Greetings!' said the now familiar voice of Rika Dur, but pitched rather higher than when Annie had last heard it. Annie shivered. She couldn't imagine why she had thought Rika was so lovely. Now that her suspicions that something was afoot at Kosmodrome 2 had been confirmed – and that this something was linked to Rika and to Europa – she couldn't for the life of her think why she had thought Rika was impressive. Rika even looked different. Her face was strangely lop-sided all of a sudden, as though it was slipping down one side of her neck. It was an odd and pretty gruesome sight.

'Are you ready for Challenge Number Three?' Rika sang out, the same tinny echo that Annie had picked up in her voice the night before ringing once more.

'As ready as we'll ever be!' said Leonia, nodding.

'Do you notice anything different about her?' Annie suddenly decided to check she wasn't seeing things that weren't there.

'Um, yes!' said Leonia in surprise. 'Something's happened to her nose, right? But shush, we need to hear about the challenge.'

'Today,' said Rika through the TV set, 'your challenge is mechanical. You will build and operate a Rover on the surface of Mars. You have already been to the Mars Assembly Room. The buses are waiting outside to return you to that location – that's the place where most of you failed to comprehend the last task in front of you. I was disappointed,' said Rika, actually sounding quite cross, 'that so few of you were able to divine what lay in front of you. I felt quite let down.'

'She's in a bad mood this morning,' commented Leonia.

'I trust that today none of you will leave me as deflated as you did yesterday,' scolded Rika. 'My hope is that you will all show at least a creditable effort. Otherwise I will start to wonder whether there is any hope for humanity at all.'

'Not so nice now,' agreed Annie. She still didn't quite know if she could trust Leonia or not. 'Is this how you thought it would be?' she asked tentatively. 'The Mars training process?'

'Nope.' Leonia shook her head. 'Not a bit of it. And not in a good way. I'm not sure I trust this lot enough to take us to Mars. It just all feels a bit too random and weird, like something's going on behind the scenes that we don't understand.'

Annie nodded. That was exactly how she felt too! But they had no time to talk about it further.

'Astronauts!' Rika suddenly shouted, coming much too close to the TV screen for Annie's liking. 'Go!'

Once Annie and Leonia had arrived, in the little shuttle buses, at the Assembly Room, they ran in to find that the mocked-up surface of Mars now had track running around the edge and through the middle. Around the edges of the room stood a pile of cardboard boxes. As all the recruits in Annie's group trooped in, Leonia leaped forward, sharp elbows flying, and used her long muscular arms to grab one of the boxes and rush to the other side of the room where she positioned herself behind a small red hill in order to gain a tiny amount of privacy from the other challengers. She quickly tore open the box and she and Annie dived inside to bring out the contents.

The Martian Rover, it turned out, came with a very minimal set of instructions – not much more than 'fit widget A to sprocket J' – and a set of lightweight tools. Once they had got all the parts out of the box, Annie couldn't help looking around the room to see if she could spot George this morning, to check he had also made it safely back to his pod after their adventures of the night before. But she just saw a group of unfriendly faces, all clad in the same blue flightsuits.

A few Kosmodrome 2 workers stood around the edge of the Mars Rover Assembly room, watching and making notes as the candidates struggled to put their machines together. The end game of the challenge was not only to construct the Rover but also to mobilize it over a track which had been modelled to look like the surface of the red planet, with craters, hummocks and bumpy rocks strewn about the causeway. The Rover had to pick up a rock and place it inside its on-board oven, just as it would on Mars. It was a complicated task and the two girls lost no time in getting to grips with the many bits and pieces that they had to find a home for in order to put their machine together.

'Are you going to be any good at this?' Leonia asked Annie but her tone was light and not dismissive. 'Or should I do all of this myself?'

'Actually, I will be brilliant at it, yes, thanks for asking,' said Annie cheerfully. She wasn't really offended by Leonia – she had plenty of experience of being with people who said exactly what was on their mind without worrying about how other people felt about it. Lots of her father's friends and students were just like this – direct, clear and to the point. In fact, they tended to get confused if you responded on an emotional basis to what was supposed to be a factual enquiry. Such people, Annie had concluded long ago, tended not to see the shades of colour that made up the life of feelings of other human beings and saw everything in black and white. 'I'll be amazing, in fact,' she added confidently. 'My parents got me my first advanced Lego set when I was two – and I built it straight away! I'll ace this.'

'Good,' said Leonia, almost smiling. 'In that case, you can put the structure together and I'll wire it up.'

'Deal,' said Annie, trying to sound more confident than she felt.

George, who had never been allowed Lego sets or radio-controlled cars by his eco-warrior parents (who wanted him to make his own toys out of sticks and leaves)

Doing Experiments on Mars

As we speak, there is a Rover the size of a car, which has just celebrated its third birthday on Mars!

Its name is *Curiosity*. *Curiosity* is a very sophisticated robot with ten different scientific instruments on it, all trying to find out information about what the Martian environment is like. This information is then sent back to Earth, where hundreds of scientists try to work out what Mars was like in the past, and how it came to be as it is now. There have been three other NASA Rovers launched to Mars before *Curiosity*.

Why are we so interested in Mars?

The temperature on Mars is much colder than Earth, spending most of its time below the freezing point of water, which is why any water on the planet would be found as ice – and there is evidence to show that there is a significant amount of ice on Mars! Scientists wondered whether, in the past (more than 3.8 billion years ago), Mars had a warmer temperature, and whether this ice was in fact flowing water, like our oceans!

Water is essential for life, so this is very important information. It made scientists question: if Mars was once Earth-like, could it have ever been home or become home to life as we know it? And so began the search to see just how habitable Mars is – and *Curiosity* was built!

How would we know if there was ever life on Mars?

If there was once life on Mars, then we may be able to find traces of organic molecules and amino acids that are stuck and preserved in the rocks. *Organic molecules* are those that are found in living systems. *Amino acids* are a type of organic molecule that are essential and common to all life forms. So if we find any of these 'molecular fingerprints/footprints' stuck within the rocks, then this could suggest that there was once life on Mars.

How can we find these molecules?

Onboard *Curiosity* is an instrument called *SAM* (Sample Analysis at Mars). SAM is one of the most complex machines that has ever been made. Engineers had to try to miniaturize a whole laboratory of instruments and fit them all into a small machine about the size of a microwave.

SAM is very clever, as he has to collect the samples, put them into cups and run experiments on them, without any humans helping him!

The engineers that created SAM had to think long and hard about how they should design him. SAM's job is to try to find these molecules, and this is how he does it.

Let's take, as an example, a rock that contains lots of different organic compounds.

These compounds are stuck inside the rock on Mars.

Curiosity drills a sample, turning the rock into powder, and deposits it into SAM.

SAM vibrates the powder into a cup.

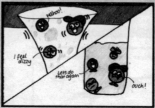

The sample is heated to about 950 degrees Celsius, and some of the smaller molecules are able to escape. Some larger ones can break down into smaller molecules and also escape. This is called *pyrolysis*. These gases then travel down to the next step.

Others remain, and still aren't volatile enough to escape. SAM is very clever, though, and so there is a different experiment that can be done instead of pyrolysis. This is called *derivatization*. This reaction helps the molecules become more volatile, allowing them to escape the rock sample more easily.

These gases then travel to the next station.

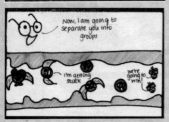

This station is a separating station, where SAM tries to separate the same molecules into groups, so that the same molecules come through at the same time.

This is done by passing the gases through a column with a sticky material on the inside of it. Some molecules prefer this material more than others, so they travel more slowly through the column.

By the time they reach the end of the column, all of the molecules should be separated into groups. This is called *Gas Chromatography*.

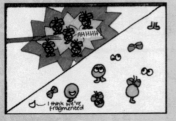

SAM then wants to be able to tell what molecules he has actually found. This is done in a very clever way, using a process called *Mass Spectrometry*. As the molecules come through in their groups, they are blasted with an electron beam, and split into pieces.

SAM then looks at the different pieces that come out the other end and counts up how much of each fragment was there.

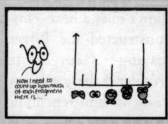

Each type of molecule splits differently, and by seeing how it splits, we can work out which molecule was actually there.

Scientists back on Earth have created a library of the splitting patterns of many, many, *many* molecules, and so, when SAM sends his data back home, they can compare SAM's data to their data, and work out which molecules were stuck inside the rock!

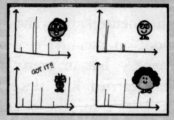

CLEVER!

What happens next?

If scientists are going to send humans to Mars, then *Curiosity* can help give them more information. There are so many different factors and problems to think about and solve before sending the astronauts up.

- How does the human body respond to being without gravity for over a year?
- What material can we use to protect the astronauts from the dangerous radiation?
- How can we store enough food for the astronauts for over a year?

All of these questions need answers – and one day *you* could be one of those scientists helping to make history and discovering more about how our wonderful Universe works.

Katie

was at the service of Igor for this task. Fortunately Igor didn't miss a beat – his hands flew about as he capably constructed the Rover, leaving George to wonder if there was any point in him remaining in the process. Could he really be an astronaut? he asked himself. He didn't feel he'd made much contribution so far. He'd literally carried Igor to the neutral buoyancy pool on the first challenge – but in pretty much every other way, Igor had carried him since then. George felt useless. If it wasn't for the strange scene he and Annie had witnessed the night before in Mission Control, where a bunch of robots had seemingly disappeared, possibly through a portal to Europa, George thought he would probably have given up. But he couldn't leave Annie here, and also, with a shock, George realized he didn't want to let Igor down. If George left, then Igor would be kicked out too, and that wouldn't be fair at all.

Annie and Leonia were having a more equal experience. Both girls intuitively knew what they were doing – Annie could visualize how the structure of her Rover should look, and this guided her in working out how the different parts of the exterior should fit together. Leonia was able to work out how to fix up the electronics so the Rover could motor over the surface of Mars, operated by the remote control. They worked quietly and companionably, and soon, from a pile of assorted wires and struts, a recognizable shape was emerging.

But they weren't alone. There were other kids in

the room who also wanted to go to Mars – and who, it seemed, were prepared to do anything they could to make sure that Annie and Leonia didn't steal their spot.

'Oi!' said Annie as a rival Rover skidded very close to where she and Leonia were trying to assemble their model, sending up a cloud of sticky thick red dust which settled over their machine. When Annie looked closely at the random Rover, however, she noticed something – it was no more than an electronic box on wheels. She stood up, furiously waving over at two trainees who were directing the Rover with remote controls from the far side of the room. 'Sabotage!' she yelled. The other Rover carried on trying to bump into her and Leonia's far more advanced version.

The other two trainees in the distance smiled sweetly and waved back, moving their Rover away from Annie and Leonia and sending it towards the main track. 'Sorry!' they called. 'Practice run!'

But the way they giggled made Annie think her suspicions were correct.

'That Rover is nowhere near ready to run on the track,' she hissed to Leonia. 'They just put the basics together and sent it over to wreck ours.'

As she spoke, one of a super-confident pair of trainees – twins called Venus and Neptune – walked past and tripped, partly falling onto Annie and Leonia's Rover and squashing it.

'Oh, apologies!' said Neptune, pulling herself up with a huge grin and a flourish of her hand. 'I don't know what came over me!' She flounced away, leaving Leonia and Annie gazing in dismay at their squashed, dirty Rover.

'These people!' said Annie. 'This is awful.'

'Human beings are the problem,' replied Leonia. 'But remember, there will be far fewer of them on Mars. We'll only have to deal with solar winds, hostile weather, sand storms, extreme temperatures, and a lack of a magnetic shield, gravity, oxygen and water. It'll be much simpler.'

'Well, when you put it like that . . .' said Annie, straightening out the crumpled parts of the Rover. 'OMG!' She suddenly noticed a Rover was on the track and starting to do the circuit.

Leonia put the finishing touches to her work and then easily picked up their Rover and set it on the track. 'Let's see.' She pressed the remote control and their Rover shot backwards. It would have fallen off the track altogether into a crater if Annie hadn't made a leap for it and caught it. 'Good reflexes!' said Leonia approvingly. Clearly Annie was turning out to be less of a burden than she had feared. 'OK, let's do it,' she said, pressing the remote control again. Their Rover shot forward, in hot pursuit of the only other Rover currently on the track. It needed to do a full circuit from where it had joined the trail and then collect a rock and stow it. But Leonia was finding it hard to control the Rover. It cornered sharply and nearly toppled over.

'Give it here.' Annie snatched the control from Leonia's hand. Righting itself, their Rover sped forward once more, gaining on the one in front. Annie – all her computer gaming skills coming into use now – chicaned her Rover round the competition and was heading out in front when a rogue vehicle appeared, as if from nowhere, trying to drive straight into their Rover from behind. It bashed Annie and Leonia's Rover, causing the body of the vehicle to fall off, leaving just the wheels, axis and on-board oven. It was a sad battered sight, but it was still moving.

'Hey!' protested Annie loudly. 'That's not fair!' She looked over, and yet another pair of other recruits were

grinning evilly at her. She coughed. It was dusty in the room now, with the Rovers grinding up the track. And it was getting dimmer – the light seemed to be fading.

'There's no *fair* on the road to Mars,' muttered one of them, again aiming his Rover straight at hers. But Annie was too quick for him. She very quickly spun her Rover round and sent it back in the other direction so it was now going counterclockwise. This confused the other drivers and their Rovers so greatly that while they hesitated, Annie was able to get their Rover far away. She drove it on, up the hills, down over the hummocks and into the little valleys, skidding slightly on the tight bends but always managing to keep moving forward and keep the momentum going.

A few more Rovers were now joining the track, some of them well constructed, some looking as though they had been made from a piece of string and a tin can. One or two fell to pieces the minute they started to gain speed. The track got more and more congested and traffic pile-ups started to happen as Rovers smashed into each other. Annie and Leonia's Rover was still clear of the others and just about to arrive back at the point where it had started when something really unexpected happened . . .

The air had been getting thicker and thicker, but none of the trainees had really registered it as they were so intent on driving their vehicles. Now Annie suddenly realized she could hardly see across the room as the atmosphere was so heavy with red dust.

She felt a tap on her shoulder and heard a voice in her ear. 'It's coming from the vents! Look up!'

Annie looked to where Leonia was pointing. Pouring into the room were thick funnels of dust, swirling in the air around them.

'What is it?' said Leonia, who had her hand over her mouth now.

'Yikes, a Martian sandstorm,' said Annie in a muffled voice. Once upon a time, she had been stuck in a sandstorm on Mars itself. She and George had been following a set of cosmic clues which had led them out of the Solar System to a far distant planet in another star system. So Annie knew immediately what they must do. 'It's time to evacuate!' she said firmly.

'We can't,' said Leonia, whose eyes were stinging. 'We've got to complete the challenge!'

'This *is* the challenge,' said Annie, dragging Leonia towards the door. 'The challenge is to *go!*'

Leonia dug her heels into the crunchy ground and resisted. Annie kept pulling as though they were in a tug of war with each other. None of the other young astronauts were leaving their posts. They were still battling the conditions to get their Rovers to finish the course. The inevitable monitoring robots were also struggling to cope with the thick dust. It seemed to get into their parts and cause mechanical malfunction – one robot just keeled over entirely and lay face down on the surface of Mars.

Annie kept hauling Leonia onward towards where she thought the exit was. She could barely breathe and she could hardly open her eyes. The haze of the red dust of the fake Martian sandstorm was turning out to be as

vicious and scary as anything Annie had experienced on her space travels in the past. And she knew she was right. This was the challenge – knowing when you were in too much trouble to continue safely and you needed to evacuate as fast as possible. The challenge was not to finish the course at all costs, but to get out and rescue what you could from a mission, the most important parts being the human beings involved.

Leonia stopped resisting, and together they staggered towards the doors and shoved them open – and as the doors opened, the same alarm sounded. The vents stopped pouring dust into the Assembly Room and started sucking it back out again, the lights went on and the other astronauts, covered in red dust, dropped their remote controls in disappointment.

Annie and Leonia had won once again.

Chapter Thirteen

Over the next few days the pattern continued. Whether they were experiencing centrifugal forces (being spun round and round very fast while strapped into a chair), trying to operate the robotic arm of a spacecraft, deploying basic medical skills or giving commands over the radio to solve an emergency, relayed in a foreign language, the two girls came top – or nearly top – every time. And each time they won another challenge, the other candidates hated them even more. More kids had left the camp – only one now, for each challenge, meaning several new pairs had to get used to working together.

Although George and Igor had not won another challenge after the triumph of the 3D printing on Mars, each time they turned in a very creditable performance. They might be in second or third place, but it was a good second or third place. Even so, George felt embarrassed that all their success was pretty much due to Igor – and all their failure, he reckoned, down to him. He wasn't very pleased with himself. But he also wasn't thrilled with the way the process was heading. It now felt more like taking part in some kind of television reality contest, where the aim was more to entertain through humiliation and failure than to participate in a great scientific and exploratory experiment for the future of humanity.

By the end of the second week, with only half the kids now left in the programme, Annie felt a strange combination of hungry and sick as she went back to the sleeping pod for the night. They'd had an extra-ordinary day, taking part in a zero-gravity flight. Annie's group, consisting of just three pairs of astronauts, had been driven out across a runway, still in the massive Kosmodrome 2 grounds, where they had boarded an aeroplane. The front part of the passenger plane was completely empty, and there were only a few rows of seats at the back. Over the tannoy, a mechanical voice had instructed them to strap themselves into their seats as the plane prepared for takeoff. Sitting behind Leonia and Annie were the still broadly grinning pair of sisters, Venus and Neptune: V and N, as they called each other. They were certainly super confident – it didn't seem to occur to them that they wouldn't be going to Mars. In the number two spot on the daily league tables, they exuded a glossy, self-satisfied air at their own competence.

'Candy?' V stuck her hand between the airline-style seats to where Annie and Leonia sat. 'Ooh, yes please,'

said Annie, who was heartily sick of rehydrated food. She reached for it, but wasn't quick enough. Leonia snatched the candy away from her and broke it in half, sniffing it suspiciously.

'Oh, come on, Leo,' groaned Annie. 'I just wanted some sweets!'

'You're not supposed to eat non-space-regulation food,' snapped Leonia, crumbling the sweet between her fingers; Annie watched her treat disappear into crumbs on the airplane floor. 'It's against the rules – you could cost us points. And I don't like the smell of it,' she added.

'It wasn't for you,' said Annie through gritted

teeth. 'I wasn't asking you to break your diet. It was my piece of candy – it would have been *my* lost point.'

'I think it had been chemically altered,' Leonia whispered in Annie's ear as the noise of the plane engine got louder and louder, preparing to takeoff. 'If you'd eaten it, I can't guarantee what would have happened to you. You could have vomited uncontrollably. Or fallen asleep. Or worse.'

'Worse?' Annie whispered back.

'You might have turned bright green and grown hair all over your body,' said Leonia.

'EW!' Annie couldn't help herself from crying out. 'NO!'

'No, not really,' said Leonia. 'But I think it could have made you pretty sick.'

'Did you just make a joke?' said Annie suspiciously.

'Did I?' Leonia looked pleased. 'Was that funny?'

'Well, nearly,' conceded Annie.

'Why was that funny?' persisted Leonia. 'Explain to me, please. Then I'll be able to replicate this success another time.'

'Best not,' warned Annie. 'Humour sort of needs to be spontaneous, otherwise it won't work.' But she made a note not to accept further gifts of food or anything else from V and N.

An automated announcement came over the tannoy. 'Astronauts! The ascent has begun!' The plane had no windows, so they couldn't understand what was happening by reference to the Earth below. But they could feel movement – the plane was starting to fly steeply upwards. Someone watching from the ground would see an aeroplane shooting up almost verti-cally, as though it was trying to fly through the atmosphere and into space itself. If they kept watching, they would see that same plane's trajectory flatten out as it flew over a long curve and then nose-dived back down towards the ground. It kept on flying like this, in huge great big looping curves – Earth-bound spectators might

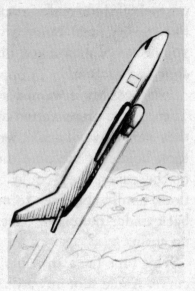

ask themselves what in heaven's name was going on up there.

Inside the plane, the six trainee astronauts had followed new instructions to leave their seats and take up positions at the front of the plane. Flying over the curve, the junior astronauts inside rose from the floor of the cabin where they had been sitting. For all except Annie, this was their first experience of zero gravity and none of them could stifle their laughter! Suddenly, from being competitive, determined participants in what felt like a fight to the end, the young astronauts reverted to being what they really were – kids who loved playing games with other kids. They turned somersaults in the air, they touched the ceiling with their toes, they pushed off the aeroplane walls and flew across the cabin like superheroes! None of them could stop laughing! Annie and V exchanged high-fives in mid-air as they shot past each other in opposite directions, the matter of the possibly poisoned sweet completely forgotten. Then, as the plane started to head towards Earth again, they sank slowly back down to the floor as the G-force took hold. By the time the plane was at the bottom of the curve, they could only lie motionless on the floor, hardly able even to move a finger until it turned back under the curve once more and started heading up again.

This time the astronauts rose faster than on the last curve. Annie shot upwards so rapidly that she bumped her head on the ceiling. But no sooner had she adjusted to being in zero gravity, flying around the cabin, than she had the sense that the plane had already started heading back towards the Earth again. She felt gravity grab her, like the diver had grabbed her ankles, and pull her back towards the floor. She lay there once more but almost immediately she felt herself ping up again, heading towards the ceiling of the plane. She looked for Leonia, only to see her team-mate was signalling

Zero-gravity flights

A zero-gravity flight is a way to experience microgravity or the same kind of gravitational conditions as the astronauts on the International Space Station! That means being able to push off the ceiling with your feet or throw droplets of water around and see them float!

There is a serious point to zero-gravity flights – NASA and other space agencies use zero-gravity flights to train astronauts so they can be better prepared for their work on the space station.

But in 1994 a man called Peter Diamandis decided to offer flights to ordinary passengers as well. He wanted to open up the space travel experience to everyone, not just professional astronauts. He has flown lots of famous people on his zero-gravity flights, including the second man on the Moon – Buzz Aldrin – and Stephen Hawking, one of the authors of this book!

> **When you go on a Zero-G flight, your plane doesn't leave the Earth's atmosphere! You don't actually go into space.**

When taking a Zero-G flight, everyone gets on a normal-looking plane, like the sort of plane you might board to go on holiday. But this plane doesn't fly like a normal plane! Instead, it flies in long curves called parabolas.

What happens is this:

- The airplane, flown by special, highly qualified pilots, ascends sharply upwards. But then it nose-dives back to Earth again.

- While the plane is going 'up and over the hump', it puts you into 'zero gravity'. At that point, you are in freefall, just as you would be inside the International Space Station. It's pretty exciting!
- To get you used to the sensation of weightlessness, the first few parabolas – or curves – that the plane flies over are not too steep. This means you have the feeling of reduced gravity, the same conditions you might experience on Mars or the Moon. Mars has 40% of the Earth's gravity so you can bounce around in big leaps. The Moon has less gravity than Mars and so, on the 'lunar parabola', you can do a press-up with one finger!
- When the plane goes into descent again, you experience 'high-g', strong gravitational forces which pin you to the floor. Lying on the floor, you can't even pick up one finger to move it! As the plane ascends once more, you gently start to float away from the floor once more.

During the Zero-G parabolas, you experience complete weightlessness. You can do a somersault in the air or walk on the ceiling! These Zero-G parabolas are over too quickly – everyone says, 'Again! Again!'

But what goes up must come down – and eventually your plane must land and bring you back to Earth once more . . .

for her. Annie shot along the plane to the front where Leonia was hovering.

'Something is very wrong,' muttered Leonia. 'We need to get into the cockpit. Try and shield me so the others don't see what I'm doing.'

'Do you think this is the challenge?' asked Annie.

'No idea,' said Leonia as she tried the cockpit door, only to find it was locked. 'But we must get in there before we go into high G again!' She sounded as close to panicking as Annie had ever heard her.

Annie blocked Leonia from view by floating in front of her. V and N tumbled over towards her but the plane shuddered violently and they were thrown back in the opposite direction.

'Leo, get the door open,' said Annie urgently.

'I'm trying!' said Leonia. 'It's not budging!' At that moment they felt the plane turn and start back down again.

Annie felt terrified and nauseous. For a second she froze entirely, unable to move or think. Then, as though her brain had used that tiny pause to change into a higher gear, she became incredibly, unnaturally calm as she realized she had to take charge and she had to do it now.

'Everyone!' Annie shouted, finding her true voice for the first time since the bullying at school. Face to face with true and immediate danger, Annie was no longer cowed or afraid. Her courage burst through and she was ready to act. 'Everyone, come here – as fast as you can! We have to get this door open. We need to throw ourselves against it to break through!'

The other recruits had enough respect for Annie and Leonia's winning streak to obey.

'One . . . two . . . three!' cried Annie. '*Charge!*'

Together, they barged the door and it sprang open, sending Leonia and, behind her, Annie, into the cockpit where they almost crashed onto a figure slumped at the controls.

'Wake up!' Annie shook the pilot as hard as she could, pulling his head up from the joystick. Looking through the cockpit win-dow and at the multiple altitude dials around the cabin, there was no doubt they were now nose-diving towards Earth and the plane was out of control. 'Wake up!' she shouted full in the face of the pilot – only to recoil in absolute horror. She screamed – she couldn't help it – and then quickly managed to take  a firm hold of herself. The figure in the pilot's uniform that they'd all seen climb into the cockpit before takeoff was not, it turned out, human after all.

'It's a robot!' cried Annie, her hair standing on end! 'It's a robot! The plane was being flown by a robot! There are no humans on board – only us!'

The pilot's hat fell off, taking the wig and glasses the robot had been wearing with it. The robot's face had been painted a fleshy pink colour with features drawn on. Close up, it was almost unbeliev-able that they had ever been fooled. But they had only seen the pilot for a few seconds from a distance. They had seen what they had expected to see, not what was really there. Leonia grabbed the robot, which was fortunately smaller than some of the massive bots they'd seen patrolling around Kosmodrome 2 and shoved it out of the pilot's seat, upending it as she did. 'Sit down,' she ordered Annie. Annie climbed obediently into the pilot's seat.

'Leo, do you know how to fly a plane?' she asked desperately. They were losing altitude at a terrifying rate. From the cabin came sounds of screaming as the other trainees on board realized what had happened.

'Only in theory,' admitted Leonia. 'This plane should be able to pretty much fly itself.'

'Theory is better than nothing,' said Annie. 'Tell me what to do.'

'Grab the joystick,' said Leonia. 'Raise it, very gently.'

Annie obediently followed her orders. Slowly she raised the joystick, which was positioned to the left of the pilot's seat, feeling the nose of the plane rise very slightly. Meanwhile Leonia flicked a series of switches on the many panels surrounding them in the cockpit. The needle on the speed dials left the red bar and headed back to a more normal position as Annie levelled out the plane and it started to slow down.

Leonia picked up the radio and spoke into it. 'Hello, Mayday, Mayday!' She gave the international alert for distress. The radio crackled in reply but no voices were heard. 'Mayday, repeat Mayday!' continued Leonia. 'I need to land a plane at Kosmodrome 2. Requesting permission to bring plane in to land at Kosmodrome 2.' The radio fizzed and burped, but no human or machine spoke back to them.

'You're going to have to land this plane, Annie,' she said to Annie. Outside, it was getting dark. 'It'll be easier after sunset as we can fly in by the lights on the runway.'

'I've got to land the plane?' Annie couldn't think of anything more frightening.

'Well, I don't think any of *them* are in a fit state,' retorted Leonia. The sound of sobbing from the cabin filled the cockpit.

'Why can't *you* do it?' fussed Annie.

'I'll be operating the landing gear and the navigational controls. As much as I can, I'll make the plane land itself, but I don't know how to put it on full autopilot so you've got to guide it down. Just like driving the Rover with the remote – you were much better at that than I was.'

'Have we got radar?' asked Annie faintly.

'Yup,' confirmed Leonia. 'The good news is that I've found the coordinates for the Kosmodrome 2 runway.'

'And the bad? Apart from the lack of trolley service or in-flight movies,' said Annie.

To her surprise, Leonia laughed. And then apologized. 'Sorry,' she said. 'I don't always identify the appropriate emotion for the situation.'

'No, my fault,' said Annie. 'It's really not the moment to make jokes. Tell me the bad news.'

'You need to turn the plane round,' said Leonia. 'We're going the wrong way. That's the bad news.'

'Oh crikey,' said Annie. This was unexpected. Of all the problems they could have, going in the wrong direction wasn't the one Annie would have guessed at.

'You need to use your feet,' pointed Leonia.

Annie looked down – there were elephant-sized pedals in the footwell. She placed her sparkly trainers gingerly on them.

'Use the joystick to keep the nose steady,' instructed Leonia. 'And use the foot pedals to change the horizontal plane of the aircraft.'

Annie gulped. It was better, she figured, than running out of fuel or flying through turbulence. She wasn't at all sure she could manage that. But to turn a plane round? It was pretty awesome for someone who had never driven a real car to find herself in charge of a plane. But Annie took a deep breath and told herself that she could do it. Looking straight ahead, through the curved glass of the pilot's window, surrounded by hundreds of switches and dials, all of which she now hoped had been put on autopilot, she tentatively pressed harder with her left foot. The plane shifted round as it slowly began to turn back in the opposite direction. Annie accidentally pressed with her right foot and the plane jumped a little.

'Tell them to strap themselves in – this could be a bumpy ride.'

'Astronauts!' Leonia shouted back into the cabin. 'Stop crying and get back to your seats. That's an order.' She returned to Annie. 'Did I do that OK?'

'Perfect,' replied Annie. 'Hold tight!'

Leonia grabbed onto the nearest thing she could find to steady herself, which turned out to be the leg of the robotic pilot who had now toppled upside down and wedged himself between the cockpit seats, his feet in the air.

Annie slowly swung the plane round, causing a huge outcry from the back cabin. The kids cried or groaned as the plane dipped and bucked. Annie went as steadily and as cautiously as she could, but even so she couldn't keep the plane level for the whole turn. But after a few minutes of mayhem, the plane straightened out, and when Annie looked at the computer display in front of her, she could see it was now guiding her towards the runway at Kosmodrome 2. She exhaled the most massive sigh of relief she had ever given, bigger than when she and George had stopped the Large Hadron Collider from exploding, greater than when they had escaped from a madman and his quantum computer, but not *quite* as huge as the time they had rescued her father when he fell inside a black hole.

'Listen up, kids,' she said, taking the handheld tannoy that Leonia passed to her. Her voice echoed down the plane, completely clear and steady, not a wobble to be heard. 'I'm going to try and land now – so buckle your seat belts and please don't scream if you can help it. It's really uncool and it doesn't help.'

Leonia nodded as Annie steered the plane so it was in line with the computer diagram on the screen in front of her. She was amazed by how natural and easy it felt. Leonia twiddled a few switches and they heard the noise of the landing gear lowering in preparation for landing.

Twenty . . . nineteen . . . eighteen. The computer screen gave the number of seconds to landing.

'Annie,' said Leonia as the countdown continued.

'Yes,' said Annie, with a tiny gulp.

'If I do go into space,' continued Leonia as the computer read out *fifteen . . . fourteen*, 'I'd want you with me. You'd be the best astronaut of all of us.'

'No I wouldn't,' said Annie firmly. The landing lights along the runway now looked very close indeed, and she could only hope they were going to glide onto the runway and not crash right into it. 'It's you. You should go to Mars. I think I might stay at home after this anyway.'

Ten . . . nine . . . eight . . .

'You're not serious?' said Leonia. 'You can't do that! One bad experience doesn't mean anything. You've got to keep going.'

Four . . . three . . . two . . . one . . . said the computer as the wheels touched down on the tarmac of the Kosmodrome 2 runway. The plane was still going a bit too fast to land, so it bumped back up again, causing another wave of groans and screams from the back. But the wheels came back down, and apart from veering off to one side and ending up more on the grass than on the runway itself, Annie brought the plane to a standstill long before they had got close to the buildings which housed the Kosmodrome 2 airport.

'This is your captain speaking,' said Annie, addressing her passengers. 'Thank you for travelling on the Air Martian Express, and we do hope you will fly with us again in future.'

Chapter Fourteen

Annie thought the runway would be thronging with Kosmodrome 2 staff, ready to greet them after their ordeal. But the tarmac was empty and quiet. It felt wrong after the huge excitement and tension of the airborne emergency they had just successfully navigated their way through. At the very least, they expected blue flashing lights and thronging Kosmodrome 2 staff. But there was no one, no support vehicles rushing out, no mobile staircase or bendy bus turning up to guide them back to the spaceport.

'Was that really the challenge?' said Annie to Leonia as they sat in the cockpit together. 'Landing the plane. Or was that all an accident?'

'Unless . . .' said Leonia. And then she shook her head.

'What?' questioned Annie. 'Tell me.'

'Have you noticed anything weird about "the process"?' asked Leonia slowly.

'I just landed a plane!' exclaimed Annie. In her head she said to herself – *I just landed a plane! Take that,*

*Belinda and all you others. Bet you couldn't do that!
And stay calm. And not cry.* 'And you're asking if I've
noticed anything odd!'

'Apart from today,' persisted Leonia.

'I just thought training to be an astronaut – especially
when we have to compete with the others – would
be tough,' Annie mused as they looked out over the
deserted runway. 'But I've got to say, no way was I
prepared for this. This is literally incredible.'

'I didn't actually think it would be fun,' said Leonia.
'But I didn't think they'd put us in danger.'

'Was that deliberate?' Annie asked. It was a shocking
thought, but after what had just happened . . . Her
thoughts shot back to her night-time meeting with
George in Mission Control. *Had* they been spotted?
Were they deliberately trying now to *kill* her? Even if it
meant killing five other kids too? She swallowed hard.
Was George in danger too?

'Annie, I don't think they meant to kill us. But they
put a load of kids in an aeroplane flown by a robot,'
said Leonia. 'And then the robot malfunctioned –
and there was no backup, no emergency procedure,
nothing. If it hadn't been for you, we would have
crashed.'

'Us,' said Annie. 'That wasn't all me.' She gazed out
of the cockpit window. 'Leo,' she said slowly, noticing
something. 'This isn't the runway we took off from,
is it?'

'Nope,' said Leonia. 'Must be another part of the campus.'

'OMG!' said Annie. 'Look, it's that spaceship again, the one they drove away from on the Rover challenge, so we couldn't see it.'

'So it is,' said Leonia. In the distance they could make out a spacecraft, held vertical by complex machinery in preparation for launch. They were too far away to see it clearly – but the spaceship appeared to be lit up and to have tiny black objects, like flies, crawling all over it.

'They're getting ready for takeoff!' said Leonia. 'But where's it going? And who is on it? There are no live missions listed for launch. I don't get it.'

At that moment V and N popped their heads into the cockpit. 'Hello, heroes!' they cried cheerily. Any idea of competition had vanished now – everyone was just so relieved to be alive.

'I'm sorry, you guys,' said V bashfully. 'I'm so psyched you didn't eat that candy! It was drugged – it would have knocked you out and then we might never have survived. I'm so sorry.'

N chipped in. 'We were promised a television deal and a modelling contract if we made it through the process to become Mars astronauts,' she said ruefully. 'So it kinda seemed worth it to cheat for us.'

'But it wouldn't have been,' admitted V. ''Cos if we had taken Annie out . . .' She trailed off. The two sisters looked at each other and shook their heads.

'I dunno, V,' said N. 'Let's take up tennis instead.'

'Yeah, good plan,' said V. 'I don't really want to go into space now.'

'What about singing?' mused N. 'We're pretty amazing at that.'

'Or we could start a fashion line,' said V.

'We'll think of something,' said N. 'We always do.'

They both turned and beamed at Annie and Leonia. It was impossible not to smile back at this pair. There was just something about them.

'We've opened the hatch,' said V. 'And we've put out the emergency slide. The other two are leaving the plane now.' From the cabin, they heard whoops of excitement as the other pair of kids slid down the plastic chute, landing on the runway at the bottom.

'Oooh, I've always wanted to do that!' exclaimed Annie. She jumped up and squeezed past the others. V and N followed her, and behind her came Leonia, who had for reasons known only to herself decided to bring the robot pilot with her. One by one – or in Leonia's case, two by one – the girls jumped onto the slide and reached the bottom, arriving just as a vehicle from spaceport finally showed up and a couple of very

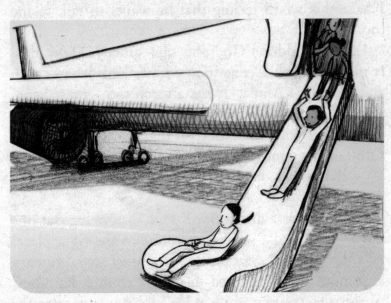

anxious Kosmodrome 2 staff leaped out and started quizzing the astronauts.

'Don't tell them anything,' Leonia whispered into Annie's ear. 'I don't trust them.'

Annie nodded. They piled into the small van, the staff so preoccupied that they didn't even seem to notice that Leonia was carrying the robot pilot. Once they arrived back at the accommodation wing of the Kosmodrome 2 facility, the six astronauts filed back to their pods in a group huddle, with Annie, Leonia and the robot pilot in the centre. As they walked, Annie said quietly to Leonia, 'I need to find my friend George. I've got to talk to him about what just happened. And I have this weird feeling that he wants to talk to me too.'

Leonia nodded. 'Go,' she said quietly. 'Take this. It might help you.' She took off her anti-drone watch and gave it to Annie. 'It has a torch too – press here.' A beam of light shot out of the watch. 'Peel off. I'll put the pilot in your hammock, so if anyone's watching us through the cameras, it'll look like you are sleeping. V' – she poked one of the sisters – 'can you cause a distraction?'

'Can I cause a distraction?' said V, popping out one hip and striking a pose. 'You came to the right place! N – let's hit it!' She let out the most extraordinary high note and N chimed in with a counter-harmony. A cappella, the two of them broke out into song in the

corridor. They didn't just sing – they started to dance as well, the music, the energy and the fluid movements striking a chord with the other recruits who had been, only a short while ago, in terror for their very lives. Something about the way V and N's beautiful voices rang around the corridor seemed to release all the pent-up emotion in the trainee astronauts, who had been so stressed, exhausted, worried and scared. Less tunefully, but just as enthusiastically, the others joined in, cheering, shimmying and singing for all they were worth – even Leonia, though it was clear this was all rather new to her. It was as though a carnival had just broken out, there in a bland corridor inside the Kosmodrome 2 grounds.

Annie slipped away. She had no idea where she might find George. But she had to try. He could be in real danger! Between them, she knew they could solve this just as they had with so many challenges in the past. And she also wanted to let any of the other recruits she came across know they might be in danger too. And that they mustn't compete with each other any more – they must stick together and help each other instead.

She had to let the others know that the astronaut training process was going horribly wrong. Why had all these talented, clever kids been brought here? None of them, Annie realized, as she sidled along the endless web of corridors which seemed to make up Kosmodrome 2, even knew how to get out of the place to go home. They didn't have their phones or their tablets, they relied on the increasingly scarce Kosmodrome 2 staff to give them messages from their families. They were, she realized, trapped, with no way of summoning the outside world to help them.

Suddenly the lights in the corridor went out. The automated system in Kosmodrome 2 had decided it was time to flick the switch. At least, Annie thought, this gave her a little cover of darkness. She stole along the corridor, wishing she had the Google glasses she and George had used on a previous adventure to navigate across the whole of their home town when the lights went out after someone had interfered with the power supplies to the whole country. Those glasses had also

given her night vision, which had been pretty useful in a total blackout. Annie sighed. Now she had no technology other than Leonia's watch to assist her, just her own eyes and ears and her own brain to work it out. It all felt very low tech for Annie, and very old school.

But, she thought to herself, *if I can land a plane, I can do this too.* She stopped and let herself listen to the sounds around her. From somewhere far away, she heard again the distant noise of a young child crying. It was a sad and heartbreaking sound. Annie tiptoed along the corridor towards it. It got louder and louder, and Annie sidled up to an intersection and peered round the corner. To her surprise, she wasn't the only one of the trainees to have heard the noise and come to investigate. A much smaller girl, called Farah, was approaching from the other direction, also clearly intent on finding the source of the crying. But as little Farah approached the door off the corridor from where the noise

seemed to come, a robot stepped out of the door, grabbed Farah, picked her up, threw her over his metal shoulder and stomped away in the opposite direction from Annie. Farah, who was kicking and struggling against the robot, lifted her head to look back. Her eyes locked with Annie's.

'RUN!' Farah mouthed.

Annie didn't need to be told twice. She sprinted away. Wrenching open a door at random, she ran through it. It took her to a staircase which only led down. She followed the stairs to the bottom, where she found herself in a long downward-sloping corridor. Thinking it was better not to stand still at the moment, she jogged along this dim passage until she reached another staircase at the other end. She clambered up it and popped out into what must be another block of the Kosmodrome 2 facility.

It was quite unlike anywhere that Annie had so far visited. Around her, everything was brilliantly white and brightly lit. It looked – and smelled – like a hospital. It was also silent except for a beeping and a rhythmic whooshing noise. Looking up and down the corridor, Annie could see no clues as to what this block held. Except that here there were no drones. Perhaps that meant that no trainees were ever meant to come here, as otherwise there would be drones to monitor their activities. Perhaps this was a forbidden block with restricted access so it didn't need the same security measures?

Then she heard the brisk tapping of a couple of pairs of footsteps coming towards her.

Annie dived through a door, closing it behind her. Inside the room, it was dark and still but the noise of beeping and whooshing was louder. Annie pressed a button on Leonia's watch, giving herself a tiny but brilliant beam of light which she used to look around the room. It seemed to be lined with long rectangular boxes, perched against the wall at a gentle angle.

She shone the light on one of them. It was around two metres high and about seventy centimetres wide, with a heavily frosted glass top and white walls and bottom. Inside the box, Annie could see an object, but she couldn't tell what it was. More clearly, she could see that attached to the box was a whole series of wires and tubes. The wires led to monitors where squiggly lines of coloured light passed across a screen at regular intervals. The tubes linked up to a machine which looked like some kind of pump, going up and down and making a gentle whooshing noise as it went.

Annie directed the beam onto the next box. It was exactly the same – the same setup. All around the room, each rectangular box looked identical, all gently pumping and buzzing as some kind of input and output travelled through the wires and tubes.

Annie's torch moved on – and lingered on one box where the door was open and it was clearly empty.

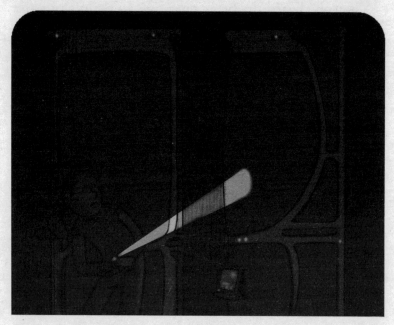

The footsteps she had heard were now getting closer. She steeled herself to ask herself the question: *What's inside those boxes, the ones with their doors closed?* She moved the beam of her torch back to the closed boxes.

Nooo! she thought. *It can't be . . .* Through the dim light, it was difficult to see properly, but she was sure she could make the outline of a—

Just then, she heard voices right by the door to the room she was hiding in. With no time to do anything else, she jumped into the open box, closing the lid as far as she dared. She couldn't risk closing it entirely or it might never open again.

The door to the room opened and a dim light came on. Through the glass, she saw two figures in white coats enter. They seemed to be checking the monitors and pumps attached to the other boxes.

'Blood gas levels are normal,' she heard one voice say. 'Gas exchange is good, weight remains stable, blood pressure within the healthy range.'

'So, Doctor,' laughed a horribly familiar voice. 'The only health problem that our volunteers are experiencing right now is that they are fast asleep!'

'If we were to bring them round, they would be in perfect health,' said the doctor.

'And can we do that?' queried the other voice. 'Can we wake them up?'

'Oh yes,' said the doctor confidently. 'I can bring

them out of suspended animation any time you wish to end the experiment.'

'Yes, yes. Will you be able to transfer them safely to *Artemis*?'

'As soon as you give me the command,' said the creepy doctor.

'I want them moved immediately,' replied the other. '*Artemis* is preparing to leave. Their life in a "bubble" – on this planet or another celestial body – looks set to continue without interruption!'

'Tell me,' said the doctor. 'How did you source volunteers for this project? Who would possibly want to be put to sleep in order to travel across the Solar System?'

But the other laughed again, a grating, menacing sound, which had nothing to do with joy or happiness. 'I can be very persuasive when I want!' she said. 'And without realizing it, they may find themselves responsible for the greatest discovery in the Solar System this century! They may hold the key to life itself.'

'Just where are you sending them?' The doctor almost sounded suspicious. 'Where are they going to make this great discovery?'

'Oh well, let's see where the spaceship takes them!' she replied airily. 'What an adventure! Now come, Doctor, there is much to be done.' With that, the pair left the room, switching the light off as they went.

As soon as they were gone, Annie burst out of her box, which she had suddenly realized looked just like a coffin. 'They're people!' she said to herself, starting to shake. 'Inside those boxes are *people*! And they're still alive!'

What is Reality?

Every day you wake up. Returning from the wonderful adventures you may have been having in your dreams, you become you again. The memories of who you are and what you have been up to in your life come back. And you also realize that there is a world that lies outside of yourself, simply called *reality*. Then you get up.

This all seems very ordinary and not very exciting. However, all of this is linked to the hardest question that humans have ever asked themselves: What exactly is reality? What is this thing, made up of space, time and objects, we live in?

After thousands of years of trying to understand the world and our place in it, we still have no real answers to these puzzles. We are like fish swimming in water without ever realizing that the water is everywhere around them. This is reality: we live in it, it is everywhere, we are even part of it – but we cannot see it.

Now, you may disagree and say that you see reality very well. You can even touch it, hear it and smell it. Well, here things get interesting. The scientists who look at our brains and try to understand how they work are called *neuroscientists*. In recent years they have discovered a very important thing about how our brains *know* about reality.

Imagine sitting in a dark room. Suddenly, in front of you, a screen lights up and a movie starts to play. You see images of mountains, trees and lakes and you think to yourself, *What a wonderful place that is.* However, the images you are seeing have been generated by a computer and do not exist outside the cinema you are sitting in. Now imagine putting on a pair of virtual reality goggles. You enter into a computer generated fantasy world you can interact with: you can fight battles or learn new skills. Suddenly a computer game has become your reality.

This is the biggest and most impressive illusion that your brain can do. It is convincing you that you are experiencing a world outside of your mind. But what is *actually* happening is that your brain is generating these sensations of the world *inside of your mind*. What you are *really* experiencing is just a simulation – a virtual reality.

Put in other words, when you are awake, you are really just dreaming the world around you!

Now, you may say, 'Well, OK, but this doesn't really matter, as the world actually does exist outside of my mind. So it is like I am seeing reality through the sunglasses of my brain.'

Unfortunately, this is also not so! Not only do we not experience reality as it is - but reality itself is also an illusion. *Quantum physics* is the part of science which tries to understand how reality looks like when you zoom in with a very powerful microscope until you reach the tiniest of atoms. For over a hundred years now, scientists have been trying to understand what quantum physics is telling us about the nature of reality. Still today we don't know how to understand this quantum reality, as it is a truly amazing place. Everything is in a state of change as quantum objects constantly alter their shape, appear from and disappear into nothingness. Also, everything is always instantaneously connected to everything else, as nothing exists in isolation. And just by *looking* at reality, you, the observer, *change* its behaviour.

A truly bizarre basis on which our reality is built upon! What looks and feels like solid objects to us is mostly just empty space with some quantum particles dancing in it and creating the illusion of matter.

This may all come as a big surprise. The ordinary act of waking up every day raises very deep and hard questions we cannot answer: *What is reality and what am I?* One clever thinker once said: 'The only thing I can be sure of, is that I am experiencing something right now. However, I can never know what this something is and I also don't know what exactly "I" am in the first place.'

But perhaps our confusion about ourselves and the world comes from a very simple fact. Maybe we have been told the wrong stories of how to think about the world. Perhaps the illusions have been so convincing for so long, that only now we are very slowly starting to rub our eyes and realize our mistake in believing that the illusions are real.

Since the beginning of mankind we have believed that space and time are the stage on which the Universe, made up of stuff, performs its grand play. During this performance, the Universe got more and more complicated. Then, suddenly, life emerged from this new-found complexity. Finally life developed the human brain and our minds started to ask the question: 'What is reality?'

But maybe this story is told the *wrong way round*. Perhaps we have not been thrown onto the stage of reality and expected to act? Maybe our *minds* in fact conjure up the stage on which now space, time and objects perform their play? Remember how in virtual reality a computer creates reality for you? In a similar way your mind and thoughts create the world *outside of you* as well!

Or perhaps the mind and the reality we experience are in fact very closely related? Like the two sides of a coin. They can appear to be very different but are actually part of a bigger whole. Could it be that the world and our minds are phenomena that are made up of the same essence? Pure *fields of information* organizing themselves into physical illusions? In other words, if we look deep enough into our own minds, do we see the same source as when we look deep into the structure of reality?

Or will reality, including ourselves, in the end turn out to be part of a computer program running in a huge cosmic computer? *The Universe has now become the virtual reality computer* and it is computing reality including yourself: an epic saga starting with the Big Bang and currently continuing with you reading this sentence.

For millennia, the question of what reality *really* is was attempted to be answered by philosophers and religious people. Now, for the first time in history, science has expanded its understanding and has only just started to uncover all the illusions surrounding us. There are quite a few scientists who, after thinking deeply about these things, slowly dare to believe in such crazy ideas mentioned above. And if any of these ideas turn out to be true, it would mean a very big shift in the way we humans understand reality and ourselves. But for the moment we can comfort ourselves with two answers to the question, 'What is reality?'

One is that reality is a much bigger, richer and more complex thing than we ever dared to dream.

Or a short answer could be, 'I create *my* reality!'

James

Chapter Fifteen

While Annie was unexpectedly flying a plane earlier that day, George had been trying a virtual reality moonwalk challenge. It was a timed challenge where he and Igor had to collect samples in VR from the surface of the Moon and return to a lunar landing capsule before it departed, leaving them stranded.

Igor, who had been so useless to begin with, turned out to have definite strengths, one of them being his lifelong devotion to gaming. The VR challenge was easy for him, but much less so for George, whose parents still limited his screen time and refused to allow computer games in the house. His only experience of VR had been using Annie's cardboard headset in the treehouse, and brilliant though that had been, it hadn't really qualified him for something as advanced as this. Still, George knew he could have picked up the principles quickly enough, if only he had kept his mind focused on the moonwalk and not on thoughts of Eric, *Artemis* and the sea life of Europa.

Even as George moved across the surface of the

Moon to collect the sample as instructed in the brief, he knew his thoughts were elsewhere. He was completely distracted. As he pretended to take part in the VR astronaut game, he tried to work it out: *Did Eric come to Kosmodrome 2 that evening and have a showdown with Rika Dur over Europa?* he thought. *Did that cause Rika Dur to get rid of Eric in order to make sure he couldn't find out more about* Artemis? *But why is* Artemis *such a big secret? Why can't we all know? What's it for? What does Rika Dur want?*

At that moment he felt a real-life very sharp kick to his shins as Igor broke him out of his reverie by giving him a hard wallop on the leg.

'Ouch!' exclaimed the real-life George, who started hopping around from the pain, causing his lunar astronaut figure to throw some very peculiar moves on

the Moon. But when he looked properly, he saw why Igor had given him such a short sharp shock. He had drifted far away from the lunar landing module and had to turn round and hurry back towards the landing craft, which was preparing for takeoff. But as fast as George tried to sprint across the Moon's surface, he found he couldn't moonwalk fast enough. The capsule doors closed, with the Igor figure waving from inside the window as it lifted off, leaving George all alone, the only man on the Moon.

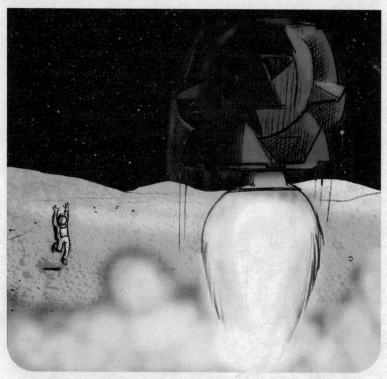

George took his headset off and came back to the room to re-join Igor, who looked like he might explode with rage.

'Won we should have that!' he said crossly. 'Until you asleep fell on the Moon!'

'Sorry,' said George humbly. There was nothing else he could say.

'We will get kicked out of the process,' said Igor, who was so angry that he got his words in the right order for a change. 'And it will all be your fault.'

George felt stung. He had grown fond of Igor and he didn't want to be the reason his dreams of flying to Mars came to an end. He knew he'd let his training partner down – and he felt really bad about it. But George felt as though he was failing everyone around him. He was failing Igor because he wasn't really contributing enough to the challenges, failing Annie by not being able to solve the enigma of Kosmodrome 2, and letting himself down too by under-performing every time it looked like the big chance was his.

It was time to change, thought George determinedly. He couldn't do anything about the past, but he could tackle the present by making a proper effort to get out into Kosmodrome 2 and find some clues which would help him and Annie unravel whatever was going on in this strangest of spaceports.

'I mean, you lack strategic vision, you have no mental power,' bored on Igor as they trailed back to their sleeping pod. 'You fail to calculate moves ahead, you don't concentrate or play by the rules, you don't take responsibility for your actions and you are clearly unable to problem-solve in an uncertain environment . . .'

'I get the picture, Igor,' said George. But even through his gloom, he noticed an interesting fact. For once, they weren't being followed by a drone. This, thought George, cheering up immediately, meant it was time to prove to himself and any others that he wasn't merely a passenger or a waste of space. He would show everyone that he too was a useful space citizen and Earth-dweller. He would get to the bottom of what was going on both here and on Europa. The others might win the challenges but, George thought to himself, he would be the one who solved the puzzle at the heart of Kosmodrome 2 and everything connected with it.

'I think I'll go for a walk,' he said casually.

'As you wish,' said Igor. But his tone had softened. Despite how annoyed he was with George, he couldn't help remembering the times George had looked out for him or just been a friend, a proper friend, the kind which Igor had never had before. Igor had also noticed that the drone which usually hovered outside their pod was missing. 'If the drone returns, I will occupy it on your behalf.'

'*Spasibo*,' said George gratefully, using the Russian he had learned for one of the challenges.

'*Ne za shto,*' replied Igor politely, almost but not quite managing a smile.

At least, George thought as he walked away from Igor and set out on his own path, he was unlikely to be caught by a flesh-and-blood Kosmodrome 2 worker. Like Annie, he had noticed over previous days that the numbers of human Kosmodrome 2 staff seemed to be getting fewer and fewer. At the beginning, there had been Kosmodrome 2 folk everywhere you turned. But as the days passed, there were hardly any left, only robots.

Now, when they did the challenges, instead of the staff levels being almost the same as the number of competitors, one lone Kosmodrome 2 worker had to look out for all the junior astronauts. George had asked one of them where the other staff had gone and only received the bitter and mysterious reply, 'Austerity measures.'

George tiptoed along the corridors, wondering which way to go. Where would he be most likely to find Annie? He was just pondering this when he felt a hand – or rather a pincer – land on his shoulder. It obviously wasn't human – through his thin blue flightsuit George could feel that the thing on his shoulder was made of metal, not flesh. His heart rate shot up immediately, pounding with terror. But drawing a deep breath, he forced himself to turn round to face whoever – or whatever – was behind him.

And whatever he was expecting – it certainly wasn't this.

It was a robot – toweringly tall and fashioned in the same familiar way as the robots he and Annie had seen wandering around Kosmodrome 2. It had the same block-shaped head and elongated arms and legs, attached to a cube-shaped trunk, which formed the body of the machine. Once upon a time, he and Annie had encountered this same style of robot on a mysterious invisible spaceship in orbit around the Earth! Those robots had been 3D printed from a network of printers across the world and were sleek, shiny and silver.

But this robot looked like it had been cooked in a furnace! The metal was twisted and blackened, parts of its pincers had melted into weird shapes and its head was misshapen and lopsided on the metal neck. The expression on the face was still visible though, and that was almost the most shockingly horrible part of it all. The robot was smiling.

'Hello, George!' it said in a happy voice. 'It really is simply marvellous to see you again!'

'Brian!' said George in total astonishment. 'Boltzmann Brian! The famously nice robot! Is that really you?'

'It is,' confided Boltzmann, leaning forward and patting George on the other shoulder, an affec-

tionate gesture which turned out to be rather painful for George, as the robot patted him quite hard with the distorted pincer of a hand.

'What are you doing here?' said George, who was totally astonished. Boltzmann Brian was a one-in-a-trillion robot, created to be sentient and have emotions, which in him all tended towards the extremely nice end of the spectrum. His owner, evil Alioth Merak, had tired of Boltzmann quite quickly and decided never to make another nice robot again, which was why he created the rest of his robot army as aggressive, mean and angry bots. 'How did you escape the quantum

Space Diving

When you go up into space in a spacecraft, you pass through a line which seems to divide the blue of the Earth's atmosphere with the black of space. This is called *the Karman line* and it is 100km above the surface of the Earth. It marks the start of space!

> **The Earth's atmosphere doesn't just suddenly stop and then you're in space – it's not like putting your head out of a window! No, it thins; but the Karman line marks the point where 'space' officially begins.**

To do a space dive or a space jump, you jump out of a spacecraft or hot-air balloon from *above* the Karman line, then freefall down through space into the Earth's atmosphere, where you eventually open a parachute to land on the ground.

This is incredibly dangerous! Several space jumps have ended extremely badly indeed.

Who has the record for the longest space dive?
- 1960: The record was set by an American called Colonel Joseph Wittinger. Colonel Wittinger was part of a research project into high-altitude bail-outs for pilots. He did three jumps from a helium balloon at over 31 kilometres above the Earth! Later, Colonel Wittinger would write that the speed he travelled at was unimaginable.
- 1962: A Soviet colonel called Yevgeni Andreyev set a new record by freefalling further to Earth before opening his parachute than anyone had previously managed. But Joseph Wittinger still kept the record for the *longest* skydive as Yevgeni Andreyev leaped out of his capsule at 25.48km – not so high up.
- 2012: Joseph Wittinger's record for the longest dive and Yevgeni Andreyev's record for the longest freefall were not broken until this century, when Felix Baumgartner broke them both in one go, jumping from 128,100 feet!
- 2014: He didn't have long as world champion, as a computer scientist called Alan Eustace stole his thunder by completing the highest altitude jump with the longest freefall only two years later. Eustace fell over 25 miles in just 15 minutes, his speed peaking at 822 mph. People on the ground heard the boom as he went through the sound barrier!

222

- Mount Everest, the world's highest mountain, is about 8.5 kilometres high.

- An average aircraft flies at just under 11 kilometres of altitude.

- So if you were looking out of the window of a plane, one of these spacemen could have come falling past you!

A space travel company is now working on a special suit which would allow space diving from even higher altitudes!

But these suits are not for stunts or record breaking – they are being developed as an emergency exit route for astronauts who need to bail out of their spacecraft and return to Earth in freefall.

Truly life-saving.

spaceship? I thought it blew up in space!'

'Oh dear, yes,' said Boltzmann. 'When the ship exploded – who would have thought it – I parachuted down to Earth.'

'You parachuted?' said George, feeling a little guilty. He had, after all, been a major factor in causing the spaceship on which Boltzmann and the other robots had been left behind to blow up.

'I space-jumped, if you prefer,' said Brian. 'People do, you know. Human people do it and survive. They jump from the edge of space down to Earth. The only difference is that I actually space-jumped from space.'

'How did you . . . ?' said George, goggle-eyed with wonder. He could hardly speak.

'I got a little charred going through the Earth's atmosphere,' admitted Boltzmann. 'As you may be able to see, although I really think it isn't that obvious. Admittedly, my metal isn't in peak condition. I've been promised an upgrade of my carapace, but so far it hasn't materialized.' He sighed sadly.

'But why are you here?' asked George slowly. 'Boltzmann, why are you at Kosmodrome 2?'

'Oh, that's easy!' Boltzmann perked up, happy to be able to answer. 'I'm here with my master.'

'Your master?' said George in an accidentally high-pitched squeak. 'Your . . . master?' He couldn't believe what he was hearing. 'Did you say – your *master*?'

'I did!' confirmed Boltzmann happily.

'But that's not possible!' said George, who had turned white. Alioth Merak, Boltzmann's master, was a very clever but very evil man who had tried to control the whole world through a display of fake kindness. It couldn't be true, thought George in horror, that Alioth Merak was here, at Kosmodrome 2. If it was true, they were in far more trouble than he could have possibly imagined.

Merak was the most resourceful, determined and manipulative opponent that George and Annie had faced in all their cosmic adventures. It had never crossed George's mind that Alioth Merak might somehow be involved in the shenanigans at Kosmodrome 2 because George had just assumed that they, like everyone else in the world, were safe from Alioth. That he was safely and securely locked up – and would stay that way for ever.

'I . . . thought your master was in . . . p-prison!' he stammered.

'He was!' said Boltzmann, as though he could hardly believe it. 'There must have been some mistake. He is such a lovely man – I mean, person.'

George wondered briefly why the robot had corrected himself like that but he let it pass. There were more important facts to pursue. This was the grimmest and most awful news ever. George realized that they could all be in terrible danger, if Alioth Merak were on the loose once again. 'Did you help him escape from jail?' said George, taking a canny guess.

'Of course!' said Boltzmann proudly. 'I am fitted with a special homing device to locate my master wherever he is. Once I fell to Earth – well, once I pulled myself together after my landing . . .'

'Where did you land?' asked George.

'In a haystack on a farm in the remote mountains of Romania,' replied Boltzmann. 'It took me a while to work it out myself.'

'How did you get here?' Despite being aghast at this news, George's mind still boggled at what it must have looked like to see a flaming robot fall from the sky.

'I walked,' said Brian cheerfully. 'That's the nice thing about being a robot. It's much easier to get around.'

'Did no one notice you?' asked George, wondering how a two-metre-high robot had managed to cross the whole of Europe without being spotted or stopped. He felt like he was just keeping Brian talking, playing for time, while he figured out what on earth to do next.

'I moved around by night,' said Boltzmann. 'And if people did spot me, I did my impersonation of a pile of old junk and they left me alone.'

'Like a Transformer?' said George, imagining the robot suddenly folding himself up into a piece of rubbish and lying beside the road.

'Exactly,' said Boltzmann. 'It worked every time.'

'How did you cross the English Channel?' asked

George. 'Oh, never mind, you'll have to tell me later. Wow, I wish you'd filmed your journey.'

'I did,' said Boltzmann. 'I can show you . . .'

'Look, Brian,' said George, realizing he had no choice but to face up to the truly shattering prospect that Alioth Merak himself might be somewhere on the premises and that this could all be so much more complicated and perilous than he had thought. 'When you released Alioth Merak from jail, where did he go? Where is he now?'

'Where?' said Boltzmann, looking confused. 'I thought you must know. I thought that was why you were here.'

'Why I was here?' George murmured, wondering what the robot could possibly mean.

'Here,' said Brian. 'Alioth Merak, my creator and controller, is here. He is in charge of Kosmodrome 2. Alioth Merak is—'

Chapter Sixteen

In the hospital block, Annie was still staring in horror at the boxes.

She wondered briefly if she should try and open one of them, to check her suspicions about what lay inside. But then she decided that was a bad idea – the life support systems were probably complex and delicate and she might disturb them. Then Annie suddenly had an awful thought. There were three 'people' in the largest boxes, as well as two smaller ones beside them . . .

She went up close to one of the smaller boxes and pressed her eye up to the glass. It couldn't be – could

it? No, she told herself firmly. Her mum was far away, somewhere on a musical tour. And George's parents were having a lovely time on an organic farm with their two small children. The number – three big ones plus two very small – was just a coincidence. It must be, she told herself very sternly. Anyway, she said to herself, she'd been receiving messages all this time from her mum, telling her about the concerts, the long plane rides, the hotels, the foreign food and the other members of the orchestra. Just like George had been getting farming updates from the Faroe Islands, along with snippets of family news from his mum and dad. Whoever was in those boxes had nothing to do with Annie or her family – or George either. Perhaps they were, as Rika said, volunteers who had put themselves forward for medical research. Annie tried to comfort herself that this must be the case, although she didn't feel very convinced.

She spotted another lone box on the other side of the room, also closed and with all the machines activated. Remembering that Rika had said the boxes were ready to be loaded onto *Artemis* and that *Artemis* was poised for launch, Annie stared at the lone box. What did all this mean? They had thought *Artemis* only referred to a mechanical fishing expedition to Europa, an attempt to capture life using robots from another location in the Solar System. And then, in a flash, she remembered how they had talked about *Artemis*, the first time they had

Medically Speaking, is Suspended Animation Realistic?

In real life, suspended animation is still science fiction. Astronauts cannot hibernate like groundhogs during a long space voyage. People cannot sleep for 100 years and wake up young, like Aurora in the original *Sleeping Beauty*. But these things may be possible in the future. Today, scientists are working on suspended animation, and doctors use something like it to help sick people.

In science fiction, usually the purpose of suspended animation is to keep people young and healthy in sleeper ships. During long space voyages, they sleep with their bodies cooled. They don't eat, they hardly breathe, and their hearts beat slowly, because their bodies use less energy and oxygen.

In real life, the same thing happens in hibernating animals. They fall into a deep, cold sleep for many weeks. Scientists also think that they may age more slowly while they hibernate. So, when you read a story about astronauts waking up young after sleeping for decades, it's a vision of the future that really could come true.

Using a gas called *hydrogen sulfide*, scientists can create a state of almost suspended animation (also called a 'hibernation-like state') in mice that don't hibernate naturally. The gas makes them sleep, their temperature drops by 11 degrees, and they use only 1/10th the normal amount of oxygen. They can remain in this state for more than six hours and wake up healthy!

Humans can fall into a low energy state when they're trapped accidentally in very cold places. Occasionally, people hide in wheel wells of airplanes, desperate to escape from bad places, or eager to travel to new lands. Usually, they die by falling out, or because of the extreme cold and lack of oxygen when the plane reaches high altitude. But, once in a while, the cold doesn't kill them and they fall into a state that looks like hibernation. The same thing can happen to people drowning in very cold water, or in snow avalanches that bury skiers in accidents.

Because doctors know that cold protects the brain, often they cool people on purpose. When a person's heart stops beating, often it can be restarted with special medicines and electricity. But then, the person must be placed into a state of *hypothermia*, meaning low body temperature. The person is put to sleep and cooled slightly – just a few degrees below normal body temperature. It's also common for doctors to use hypothermia, or special medicines, or both, to put a person into a *coma* – a state of low brain activity – to protect the brain after a terrible head injury.

Surgeons are also working on a more extreme kind of hypothermia, cooling patients to just a few degrees above freezing. It's a kind of suspended animation, but the new treatment already has a more medical-sounding name: *Emergency Preservation and Resuscitation for Cardiac Arrest from Trauma* (EPR-CAT). It's designed for people who have lost a lot of blood after an awful injury, and may be able to keep somebody alive for two or three hours, even with no blood flowing through the brain! This can give surgeons time to repair the injury.

EPR-CAT may be a long way off from the kind of suspended animation that can get you to another star system, but it could be a first step. Researchers believe that EPR-CAT will work on human beings, because they've already tested it on dogs and pigs. If it does work in people, there will be good reasons to work to improve it, to change the techniques so that people can hibernate for much longer than three hours. As we learn more, people might be put into hibernation-like states for days, weeks, months, and even for many years.

This is the sort of valuable research that is sure to be developed further by future doctors and scientists. By people like you, for instance?

And then it might even be possible in your lifetime to see astronauts using such developments to help them cope with the challenge of travelling beyond our Earth . . .

David

231

come across it. *Artemis*, she remembered, sent humans out into space to investigate whether life existed on a watery moon in the Solar System! *Artemis* used human explorers to investigate the presence of when life forms, not just robots! And here were these mysterious boxes which apparently contained 'volunteers', put to sleep for long-distance space travel. Did that mean they were bound for Europa? Were they really volunteers? Would they ever come back – or would it be just the data they collected that made it back to Earth! They pretty much knew that Europa couldn't support human life for very long – so what would happen to the 'astronauts' in the boxes once they had done their tasks for Rika Dur?

All the talk of a great space mission in 2025 was a red herring, she understood in a flash. The next major manned space mission, she thought furiously, was due to happen much sooner than 2025; sooner than almost anyone else knew. Annie had seen the spacecraft waiting on the launch pad, the one that the Kosmodrome 2 worker had accidentally referred to as *Artemis* in Annie's earshot. Now she had stumbled across the silent, and no doubt unwilling, human cargo about to be loaded onto it. There was no time to lose, Annie realized.

She had to get to Mission Control straight away . . .

At exactly the same moment, George was also heading for Mission Control, being marched there by a dangerously nice robot.

'My master will be so pleased to see you!' enthused Boltzmann as they marched along.

'I doubt it,' George couldn't stop himself from replying. 'He wasn't so thrilled last time.'

'Oh well, these things happen,' said Boltzmann airily. 'He's so good and kind, I think he will forgive you for what happened last time. I'm sure you can explain how it was all a misunderstanding, and when you tell him how sorry you are, he will be very happy to make friends.'

'Hmph,' said George, who doubted entirely that Alioth Merak would ever be pleased to see him or become friends.

And George was not sorry that he had stood up to Merak, so he would never apologize, no matter what. But he was certainly sorry to think he might have to see him again. From the little he knew about Alioth Merak, George fully expected he would still be beyond furious at the way his plans for world domination had been brought literally crashing down by two kids and an antique computer who, together, had managed to defeat his fiendishly complex plans.

A whole stream of robots now seemed to be trudging in the same direction as George and Boltzmann. The robots didn't look interested in George or Boltzmann, which wasn't surprising as George figured they hadn't been programmed to pay attention to unexpected developments in their environments. But George also saw that among the crowd of identical robots, all silver and shiny unlike poor blackened and twisted Boltzmann, walked not a single human.

Just robots.

A cold chill stole through him as he wondered whether any humans were left at the space facility other than himself and the other young 'candidates' in the Mars Training Programme. What if it was just him and a bunch of kids, pitted against Alioth Merak – wherever he was – and the fierce robot warrior army?

'You did it before, only you and Annie,' he said to himself inside his head. 'You can do it again. Yes, you can.'

As they reached Mission Control, the largest and

most central of all the buildings which made up the Kosmodrome 2 facility, George paused. He grabbed Boltzmann by the 'arm' and pulled him to a stop.

'Come on,' said Boltzmann, beaming. 'Aren't you in a hurry to see my master? Don't stop now!'

'I'm so excited to see him,' lied George, while he thought at the speed of light. 'But I want to be really sure that I make the best impression possible.'

Even in the semi-darkness outside the Mission Control building, which was illuminated from within as though with some kind of radioactive glow, George could see that Boltzmann's robot cheeks seemed to be lit up with pleasure.

'Oh, totes!' Boltzmann enthusiastically agreed.

'I think . . .' said George, who just making stuff up now. He had no clue whether this was a good or a bad idea, but he figured that walking straight into Mission Control and the clutches of premier-league madman Alioth Merak was about the worst plan he could think of. Anything had to be better than that. 'I would like to check out what Merak's up to before he sees me, so I can talk to him intelligently. Otherwise he'll just think I'm really stupid if he has to explain everything to me.'

Boltzmann's robot eyebrows knitted together. He looked worried.

'Is there anywhere,' George pressed on, 'in Mission Control where I can see Merak but he can't see me, so I can absorb what he's saying to the other robot guys before I say hello?' He looked hopefully at Boltzmann.

To his great relief, Boltzmann's brow cleared. 'The mezzanine balcony!' he said. 'I can take you up to the balcony and you can get an overview of my wonderful master and the ground floor of Mission Control. Would that work for you?'

Boltzmann was so keen to follow his programming and be 'nice' that George felt awful at his deception. 'He's just a robot,' he reminded himself sternly. 'He's not alive, he doesn't really have feelings so you can't hurt them.' Even so, as George gazed at Boltzmann's battered but innocent robot face, it was tough to harden his heart and remind himself he was dealing with a machine. Boltzmann, he realized, was on the cusp between human and non-human, a dividing line between person and machine. And it was hard to know how to react to him (or even it). A sentient being who was technologically created from parts of machinery and yet who seemed to display human emotions? George gave himself a little shake to pull himself together. It wasn't the moment to be distracted by wondering at what point machines with feelings had to be treated like people after all.

'Perfect,' he said instead. 'Take me there, Boltzmann, the nicest robot that ever lived.'

Chapter Seventeen

From the balcony overlooking the whole of Mission Control, George could see banks of computer monitors and the walls filled with screens, just like the first time he had been there.

This time, while the computers were exactly the same and the screens were in the same place, there was a very different atmosphere to the control room. It was full once more, but there were no excited kids or chattering parents, no buzz of nervous happiness and excitable joy. Just the flat insistent tone of the call signal backed up by the ringing clank of robots, taking their places around the room.

As George peered over the edge of the balcony, he could see his fears were real. The beings moving about down below him were all robotic – not a single living human among them. And they weren't friendly, people-pleasing robots, like poor battered Boltzmann. They were the powerful sleek ones, so like the kind that he and Annie had once met on the Moon that you would swear they were the same make and model. He tried to

breathe really quietly. Had Kosmodrome 2 been taken over by a robot revolution? And did that have anything to do with Eric and the weird and sudden way he had been forced to leave.

George didn't have to wait much longer for an answer. A lone human figure had manifested itself, as if by magic, in the centre of Mission Control, standing under the big screens, which seemed to be showing very different views of space from the ones George had seen there previously. The last time, the screens had shown views of many contrasting regions of space, from the volcanoes of Venus to the icy Nitrogen glaciers of Pluto. Just one of them had shown Europa. Now, all the screens showed the same place – a strange aquamarine world, where the light seemed dim and diffused, as if filtered through thick liquid.

He didn't have time to wonder where this was – was it the inside of Europa? – as Boltzmann poked him with a twisted metal finger. 'Look!' he whispered excitedly. 'It's my master! It's Alioth Merak!'

George eyed the scene more closely over the edge of the balcony, looking down on the small, now-familiar human figure, towards whom all the robot figures automatically turned, clearly waiting for their next command. There was no doubt who was in charge here. 'But—' He had recognized the figure, but was finding it hard to process what his eyes were showing him. He was now horribly confused. 'I don't understand. Where is Alioth Merak? I can't see him!'

'Your human eyesight can't be that defective!' said Boltzmann. 'Although I say that in a loving and kind way, as an expression of my concern for your welfare. How can you not see my master? He is right there, in the middle.'

'That person – in the middle?' said George slowly. 'You're sure that person standing in the centre of Mission Control is Alioth Merak?'

'Of course I'm sure,' said Boltzmann, now sounding rather offended. 'You know I have no facility to tell lies. But if you wish me to convince you, shall I summon my master?'

'Nooo!' George hissed urgently. The last thing he wanted was to have the attention of the figure down below drawn towards him. 'I'm sure you're right! But at the same time – you *can't* be! That's not Alioth Merak! That's Rika Dur . . .'

As George looked down on Mission Control from the balcony, Annie approached the same destination from below. Attempting to leave the hospital block again by the underground tunnel which had brought her there, she must have somehow taken a wrong turning, as she found herself in a dim series of interconnecting tunnels.

They looked as though they had been built a long time ago, given the crumbling brickwork, the amount of mossy green algae growing on the damp walls and ceilings and the huge cobwebs which stretched from wall to wall. She walked right through one of them and spent a few moments fighting off the webby, filmy net she was stuck in, frantically trying to brush it out of her mouth and her hair. She plodded bravely onward, with no real idea where she was going and only the faint light from Leonia's watch to show her the way ahead. Why were there these dirty underground tunnels running underneath Kosmodrome 2? she wondered as she squelched through a muddy patch.

And then, chillingly, she thought she heard rapid, light footsteps. They seemed to be behind her, so she hurried forward – but some trick of how the footsteps relayed through the subterranean space meant the sound suddenly seemed to be coming towards her. Annie backed away very fast and went slap-bang into someone running very quickly in her direction . . .

George, on the other hand, was rooted to the spot. He could clearly see that below him stood Rika Dur, as perky and smug as ever in a tight-fitting blue flightsuit, her blonde hair carefully styled, her lips a brilliant carmine red. She was very obviously the only human being in Mission Control – and yet the rapt and devoted expression on Boltzmann's face told George that the robot was in the presence of its master. George couldn't see Alioth Merak anywhere – so was he now invisible? Had he managed to disassociate his particles so that he floated in the ether rather than appearing as a whole human form? What could this all mean?

'Friends, robots and countrymen!' said Rika, who was clearly enjoying this moment. Her robot audience all looked as thrilled as Boltzmann. 'We are on the brink of the greatest moment in the story of Planet Earth! We are about to achieve an incredible feat! This is the game changer! Now is the time, my friends! And we are the ones in charge.'

Briefly, George wondered why Rika would bother to address a host of robots like this! And then he noticed that flying around Rika's head, and around the whole of Mission Control, swooped a flutter of tiny drones carrying cameras, the sort that had been used to monitor the progress of the trainees during the challenges. No wonder his journey across Kosmodrome 2 that evening had been fairly drone-free – Rika had clearly summoned them all here to record her every statement from every possible angle. And then he knew. She was filming herself! This was Rika's great moment, and the words she was saying were not really for the robots. They were for a future audience.

'Far away,' continued Rika, 'we are already poised to extract life from the oceans of a moon within our Solar System. We have established the high probability of finding life in this location.' George watched, boggle-eyed, as the screens on the wall showed a now-familiar view, that of robots working on what looked like an icy surface that stretched for as far as the eye could see – except for large round holes in the ice. The robots appeared to be fishing around in the dark liquid that lay under the ice on this strange and alien world. As the cameras panned outward, George could see the robots had already made several new holes in the ice, one of which they seemed to be trying to enlarge.

Rika Dur continued to explain to her future audience. 'This means we can now begin Stage II of Mission Artemis. Sadly, due to widespread ignorance across the globe at this time, I am not able to livestream my great explanation of the secret mission!'

'*Artemis!*' said George to himself. 'We were right!'

'Much of the challenge,' continued Rika, 'has been how to proceed with Mission Artemis without ignorant fools getting in the way. We must be allowed to continue without delays or interruptions. Any hold-ups would be fatal to my visionary master plan! It would never have been approved if I had not sent away those pedestrian scientists who objected to my methods, with their ethics and their committees.

'But I have triumphed, and Kosmodrome 2 belongs to me! I am sending a ship of human cargo out to Europa to set up a temporary colony so they can assist my robots in investigating the presence of life on this most fascinating of Jupiter's moons. Some of these are proven survivalists, who will reach their peak age when the mission time elapses. These brilliant young astronauts will be capable of all the mission tasks and experiments I have loaded onto the ship! And if they are not, I have sent back-up models, just in case!

'Nothing will stop us from investigating the origins of life on Europa. Because once we can truly understand this phenomenon we will come to know how life itself begins! Once we know how life starts, we can make genuine life forms of our own. I can make you all alive – you will be robots no more! You will count as living beings as I will give life to you, my faithful servants and my brave army. I will send you to Europa where my "human" servants will make you real.'

The robots cheered! They couldn't wait to become true living beings rather than clanking metal bots.

'These alien life forms,' explained Rika, 'will help us to understand the process by which life has begun both in space and on Earth. And once we know that, we will rule the Earth! This whole planet will be ours. We will own the planet in the Solar System which is most naturally adapted to harbour life. This watery planet, the Earth, will be ours – but the other important celestial body, Europa – the blue moon of Jupiter – will also belong to us. And we don't have to stop! Any planet we choose can become ours. Mars can be next! This way, when any other space agency or country finally gets around to sending a mission to another planet or moon, guess what! We will have already got there first. Won't that be a lovely surprise when they jump off their spacecraft to find my ro-humans or human-bots already there?!'

Through the true horror of Rika's words, George noticed something else. Her voice seemed to be getting deeper. He looked across at Boltzmann, to try and get some kind of explanation of what all this

meant. Who was departing across the Solar System, never to come back? What 'Mission' Artemis? What did Rika mean and where was Alioth Merak? He turned to ask Boltzmann, but as he did, he realized something terrible had happened. One of the drone cameras, which had been fluttering around below, seemed to have sensed the movement at the mezzanine level.

He found himself directly facing a hovering camera drone, which immediately relayed the footage it captured – George, with his mouth hanging open – onto all the screens in Mission Control. Switching the image abruptly from the view of an icy moon in the Solar System to a close-up of George's face didn't just give George the shock of his life! It caused the speaker in the centre of the room to stop very suddenly and give a bloodcurdling screech of feedback, followed by a very loud exclamation from the floor:

'Get him!'

Chapter Eighteen

In the underground tunnel, Annie opened her mouth to scream, but the person behind her was too quick. A firm hand covered her mouth, stopping any sound from emerging.

'Annie!' hissed a familiar voice. 'It's me! Leo! Don't make any noise!'

Annie sagged in relief. She hadn't been captured after all. Leonia dropped her hand from Annie's mouth and Annie turned round to face her team-mate. But what was Leonia doing here and how had she found her?

As though she was reading Annie's mind, Leonia held up her wrist with an identical watch to the one she'd given Annie. 'The watch! It's got a tracking device in it. When you didn't come back, I decided to follow you.'

'You didn't tell me there were two watches,' complained Annie, who had got back the power of speech.

'I didn't know if I could trust you,' said Leonia calmly.

'Charming!' snorted Annie. But she had to admit she had thought exactly the same about the other girl.

'But when you landed the plane like that, I knew you were a force for good,' said Leonia, smiling in the darkness.

'Huh, well, that's what I figured too – only about you,' said Annie, thinking she might as well come clean now.

'So what *is* going on?' asked Leonia. 'What have you found out?'

'Well, we know something's wrong,' said Annie, 'because no training camp anywhere would let a bunch of kids fly their own plane.'

'Agreed,' said Leonia. 'Although it was really fun, so maybe they should.'

'No!' said Annie, amazed that Leonia was being so flippant.

'Only joking.'

'Wow, you're really making a habit of that,' said Annie.

'It's kinda fun. I never knew . . .' said Leonia. 'And that singing and dancing . . .'

'Anyway,' said Annie firmly, 'I heard the sound of someone crying so I went to check it out. But I think it was a trap – a way to lure any of us who were out walking around at night – because a robot guard appeared and picked up one of the girl trainees who was doing just that.'

'Those robots are everywhere this evening.' Leonia shivered. 'I don't think there are any other humans left in the space facility. Where do you think the robot took the other trainee?'

'Somewhere in these underground tunnels, I think,' Annie hazarded a guess. 'Where are we anyway?'

'Didn't you know?' Leonia sounded surprised. 'Kosmodrome 2 was built on the site of a weapons factory from the last war. It had all these underground tunnels built so that workers could move around without fear of getting bombed. And that's why this is a secret location – it was given "Hidden Status" back then – the war ended but this place stayed secret . . .'

'That's why it's not on any maps!' exclaimed Annie. 'Do you know your way around underground?'

Leonia hummed and hawed. 'Not technically,' she said. 'But I have a special gift for spatial thinking. It's like I can find where I'm going even if I've never been there before.'

'Like you swallowed a satnav, basically,' said Annie.

'Basically,' agreed Leonia. 'Where do you want to go?'

'Mission Control,' said Annie. 'If there's any place where we can find out what's really going on here, it will be there. And I'm hoping we might find George there as well.'

Leonia was as good as her word. Soundlessly, she guided Annie through the dank, smelly underground tunnels, somehow knowing which exit to choose so that they popped out into another corridor, this time recognizably in the building which held Mission Control.

'Where now?' asked Leonia as they stood in the corridor. They could hear noise coming from the central well of Mission Control itself.

'Not in there,' said Annie, shaking her head. 'I think we'll walk straight into something. Oh!' she said, remembering the night walk she and George had taken and how they had seen a row of offices to one side of the main concourse. 'I know! This way!' And she led on ahead.

This time, when Annie tried the door of Eric's old office, it popped open. It was dark and cool inside. A desk stood in the middle of the room, no longer covered in sheaves of paper, books, old tea cups and the funny-shaped awards that Eric had won during his long career as a scientist. The blackboard still remained, covered in the chalky mathematical squiggles that Eric used to express his ideas about how the Universe was formed. But everything else had gone – just like at home, all Eric's artefacts had been removed, taken away somewhere . . .

Annie stood in the middle of the room and thought hard. There must be something here that could help them. Flinging open the cupboards, she was dismayed to find them empty.

'What are you looking for?' whispered Leonia.

'Anything!'

'Something like this?' said Leonia, producing a flat silver laptop.

'OMG!' said Annie. 'Where did you find that?'

'It was just here,' said Leonia, pointing to a bookshelf.

'OMG,' said Annie again. 'This is . . .' She went to press the power button and realized that Cosmos was already switched on.

'At last.'

Leonia jumped out of her skin as the computer spoke.

'I've been wondering how much longer it would take you.'

'WHAT?' said Annie.

'I've been sending you messages,' continued Cosmos. 'Well, one message at least.'

'I don't have my phone!' said Annie. 'Or a tablet. And they wouldn't let us have any internet access.'

'Well, I knew that,' said Cosmos. 'I am the world's most intelligent computer, after all. Or I was until recently when I had much of my capability downloaded to an inferior machine. That's why I tried to send you some vital information through a different means so that it wouldn't be lost to us for ever.'

'How did you send it?' said Annie. 'And where?'

'I sent you a "family" message,' said Cosmos. 'While you were at space camp.'

'Oh!' said Annie. 'So you did!' She rootled in her pocket and brought out a very scrunched piece of paper. 'Here it is! What do you mean' – she suddenly realized what her supercomputer had said – 'that you've been downloaded to an inferior machine?'

'I,' her supercomputer said dramatically, 'am Cosmos no more!'

'Yes you are!' said Annie. 'Look – you've still got the flower-power stickers that I gave you when I was in Year Six!'

'Technically speaking, I am the same piece of hardware,' agreed the computer. 'But like your esteemed father, I too have been retired, outpaced by the march of technology. I am Cosmos no more!'

'I don't understand,' said Annie. 'How come you are just sitting in here, switched on and alert and yet saying you're not Cosmos when you obviously are? If you're not Cosmos, who or what are you? And where is Cosmos if it's not you?' Annie felt entirely bewildered.

'There is a "new Cosmos",' said the great and venerable supercomputer. 'But the one who has taken my place, who has received the "Cosmos" mantle of honour, is a . . . *tablet*.' Cosmos said the last word in a tone of total disgust. 'Which is a ridiculous piece of technology, without the storage or operational capacity which would befit the upstart to be the true holder of the "Cosmos" legacy.'

The version of the computer in front of them was the latest of several Cosmos models built through the ages of computer history. The original Cosmos was so large that it took up a whole basement in the university where Eric had been a professor! Over the years, Cosmos had been refined and reduced in size until it had reached the proportions and look of an ordinary laptop. But as Annie well knew, Cosmos was no ordinary laptop.

'Don't worry,' continued Cosmos, or the computer that Annie would always think of as Cosmos, sarcastically. '*Tablet* Cosmos can't do very much.'

'Can *Tablet* Cosmos take you to space?' said Annie.

'Theoretically,' sniggered Cosmos, 'yes. In reality – no. That's why old poo-face is so angry.'

'Who is poo-face?' said Annie. But she already knew.

'Rika,' spat Cosmos. 'That evil being *pretending* to be a scientist, who sacked Eric and destabilized my operating system by attempting to transfer it to her own version of "Cosmos". She was in here earlier, trying to force me to open up a doorway to space.'

'What do you mean!' said Annie. '*Pretending* to be

a scientist! Rika *is* a scientist, you know – she's very distinguished!'

'Oh, yeah,' said Cosmos. 'The real Rika Dur is a very eminent scientist. But are you sure that the person you have seen is really Professor Rika Dur?'

'Well, she looks like Rika Dur!' Leonia threw in. 'At least, she looks like the Rika Dur I've seen on the internet. Sort of.'

'Is she someone else?' asked Annie. Was this the meaning of her growing dislike of Rika. 'Is she a Rika-like?'

'Who else could she be?' said Leonia in amazement. 'And *why*?'

Annie felt a cold chill run through her blood. 'And you say she was in here, trying to make you open up the portal to space?'

'Affirmative,' murmured Cosmos.

Annie flicked through the logs of activity, desperately looking for a clue. It showed up red bar after red bar: ACCESS DENIED.

'So you wouldn't let Rika go out into space!' exclaimed Annie. 'Look,' she said, reading the lines of code she had brought up on screen as easily as if it were a story unfolding. 'So Rika came in, tried to force you to open a portal and then stormed out, leaving you active . . .'

'But,' the supercomputer added in a much more urgent voice, 'we have no time to spare.'

Is There Anyone Out There?

To understand the Universe, you must know about atoms. About the forces that bind them. The contours of space and time. The birth and death of stars, the dance of galaxies.
The secrets of black holes . . .

But that is not enough. These ideas cannot explain everything. They can explain the light of stars. But not the lights that shine from Planet Earth.

To understand these lights, you must know about life. About *minds*.

Somewhere in the cosmos, perhaps, intelligent life may be watching these lights of ours, aware of what they mean.

Or do our lights wander a lifeless cosmos? Unseen beacons, announcing that here, on one rock, the Universe has discovered its existence?

Either way, there is no bigger question. It's time to commit to finding the answer, to search for life beyond Earth.

We are alive. We are intelligent.

We must know . . .

Stephen

'Time to spare from what?' asked Leonia, who seemed to have recovered from her shock at the talking computer.

'The reason Rika wanted me to open the portal to space is because the version she has developed herself is faulty.'

'So?' said Annie. 'If she tries to go to space through a non-functional portal, is that our problem?'

'Rika has been using a different method to send robots out into space – not a computer-generated portal like the one you know so well, but a form of quantum teleportation,' continued Cosmos. 'She has been imprinting robots onto entangled atoms previously dumped via Tablet Cosmos. And now she wants to duplicate alien DNA by mixing it up with organic matter . . . !'

'So she wants to see if it works for living beings,' finished Annie, feeling the full force of that ominous statement.

'Exactly,' confirmed Cosmos. 'She wants to try bringing life back from other locations in the Solar System . . .'

'Life! In the Solar System!' said Leonia. 'But we haven't found any!'

'That's as maybe . . .' said Cosmos darkly. '*And,*' he added grimly, 'she wants to try sending a life form – a human life form – from here out into space using quantum teleportation.'

'But she didn't want to travel via QT herself, in case something went wrong!' said Annie, catching on. 'So she wanted you – or *tablet* you' – Cosmos snorted – 'to take her to space while she sent someone else via quantum teleport-thingy. Am I right?'

'You are excellently correct as usual,' confirmed Cosmos. 'But we must hurry because the quantum teleportation transfer is about to begin. And although the outward journey should be straightforward, the return is likely to be extremely dangerous, not only for the traveller concerned but also for all human life on Planet Earth should the alien life form molecules arrive here with no precautions being taken.'

'OMG!' said Annie. 'But who – who is she sending into space? And where?'

'I believe she may have just found her ideal traveller,' replied Cosmos, shooting out the beams of light which he used to draw a doorway to space.

Leonia's mouth fell even further open as a door shape emerged, at first painted in shimmering light, and then quickly solidifying to form an actual doorway. The door swung open and beyond it lay a misty, swirling, pale blue world with an icy landscape as far as the eye could see. Leonia's silver eyes reflected the spooky glow coming from the frozen landscape as she stood, agog at what she was seeing.

Annie was much quicker to process the sight that lay before them. 'Cosmos,' she said urgently, 'I can see movement on the surface. It's Europa, yes? And lights. What's happening out there?' In the distance, she could make out what looked like an encampment around a large circular hole. Figures seemed to be purposefully striding about, some of them carrying mechanical heaters which they were pressing down onto the thick icy crust.

In response, Cosmos shifted the doorway a little closer and both Annie and Leonia got a clearer view.

'What are they doing?' Annie asked, screwing up her

eyes to try and see better.

'They're making holes,' said Leonia quietly at her side. 'Look! It's like the holes the Inuit use to fish in the Arctic!'

'You're right!' breathed Annie. 'Leo, they're fishing! They're fishing for aliens in the underwater ocean beneath the icy crust . . .'

'On Europa,' finished Leonia. 'And those are the same robots as the ones at Kosmodrome 2. They're attempting to catch an underwater alien.'

'Trying to find samples for the humans on *Artemis* to work on when they arrive!' said Annie, slapping her forehead.

'I don't understand,' said Leonia, surprised to hear herself say those words. 'I thought you just said Rika was trying to bring life back by using QT.'

'Yeah, but she knows that probably won't work,' said Annie. 'Or not the way she wants it to. So she's got a back-up plan, called "Artemis". It's a super top-secret mission to find life on Europa – but it's not just that. It's also the name of the *spacecraft* on the launch pad, the one that's getting ready for takeoff. I reckon that Rika is trying to find life on Europa using her robots, but at the same time she knows she needs human subjects to study the life forms in their natural habitat. And she knows that her stupid space portal device won't do the job properly so she's had to go old-school and send out a spacecraft as well.'

'To Europa?' Leonia thought fast.

'I've got that bit. But which humans is she sending? I'm starting to suspect,' said Annie, 'that she meant to send . . . us.'

'Us?' said Leonia. 'What? But we're meant to be going to Mars – but not yet, not for years! That's why we're here, that's what we're training for.'

'I think space camp was just a play to get lots of clever kids to come together for a training programme.'

'Huh, devious,' muttered Leonia. 'She got a load of high achievers to spend the summer learning about space flight.'

'She found the smartest kids in the world, the ones who would be most likely to survive on another planet. And she wants to send kids because . . .'

'She believes that young people like yourselves,' said Cosmos, 'are better at dealing with the new technology, being, as she calls it, "digital natives" as opposed to those who did not grow up with technology as powerful as myself.' He gave the equivalent of a computer sniff. 'Apparently you can adapt to dangerous situations quicker, especially those of you familiar with virtual reality, as used in computer gaming. I believe some of the tasks you have been set recently used virtual reality headsets—'

'So she'll send kids off on a spacecraft with a set of spare human beings in suspended animation,' cut in Annie grimly. Leonia's eyebrows shot up at that. 'In case the live astronauts don't make it. I'll explain – but later.'

As Annie spoke, she and Leonia saw a ghostly shape materialize just next to the encampment. Annie clapped her hand over Leonia's mouth to stop her from screaming. It was very obviously a real human being, not a robot. As they watched, the figure got clearer and clearer until it seemed to be standing right on the surface of Europa, on the other side of the largest hole in the ice and next to the robot drilling camp. It was a human being wearing a spacesuit, but even so it was creating a form which Annie had seen plenty of times on Earth and in space.

'Nooo!' she cried, quite forgetting to keep quiet herself. 'It's George!'

Chapter Nineteen

'We have to get out there and rescue George,' said Annie urgently. 'We need spacesuits – Cosmos, where can we get spacesuits?'

'Well, you are in the world's largest space facility,' he pointed out. 'So there must be spacesuits *somewhere.*'

'Why do we need spacesuits?' asked Leonia. It was, after all, her first ever sight of the space portal and she could be forgiven for not knowing what was actually going on.

'Because we're going through the doorway to get George!' said Annie. 'Rika must have quantum teleported him to space. We have to go and get him back!'

'I know where to find spacesuits!' said Leonia, pleased that at last she had thought of something useful to do. 'I'll be back.' She sprinted away.

Annie peered through the doorway to where she could see her friend George still slowly materializing out of the thin atmosphere on Europa to become a solid shape.

'Could I stop the transfer this end?' she asked Cosmos.

'Unwise,' he said. 'If you stop it mid-way, you might never get the whole George back again. We could end up with half of him over there and half back here. I believe the full transfer will take place in' – he calculated rapidly – 'about six minutes.'

Annie's face crumpled. This was the most horrible of all the scenarios she had ever faced! 'How can Rika do this?' she asked Cosmos in despair.

The great computer sighed. 'Human beings are notoriously unpredictable,' he observed. 'From what I understood of the character of Rika Dur, the respected and well-known scientist, this is most out of character. But if my experience in dealing with humans has taught me anything, it is that they are most likely to do the most unlikely actions. Unless, as I said before, this is not Rika Dur at all.'

'But who could it be if it isn't Rika?' said Annie. 'Her and her horrible robots?'

'The robots are only doing what they were commanded to do,' said Cosmos gently. 'They are machines – their actions come from the wishes of humans. The robots themselves are as nice or nasty as the person who operates them.'

'Apart from you,' said Annie.

'Apart from the Cosmos generation of supercomputers,' replied Cosmos. 'We are so intelligent that we have the ability to learn from our mistakes and make judgement calls about decisions in the future – which is very similar to the process that humans know as "thinking".'

At that moment Leonia burst back into the room, carrying two spacesuits. They were a very dirty white with enormous bulbous glass helmets, rather tatty-looking stitching and a distinctly musty smell.

'Ew!' said Annie. 'Those are pretty old school!'

'I got them from a display about the history of space travel!' admitted Leonia. 'I think this one might have actually walked on the Moon.'

'It's going to be mahosive on you!' said Annie. 'Perhaps you'd better stay here with Cosmos.'

'What!' said Leonia. 'And let you go into space by yourself! No WAY!'

'OK, but you stay close to Cosmos's doorway,' said Annie, who was already putting on the historic space-suit. 'Because you're not used to doing this and we haven't got any time to teach you how. And the gravity is going to be different on Europa. I may need you to hold onto me with a rope.' She payed out a section of space rope from her suit and handed the other end to Leonia. 'You are to stand and not move! In fact, you should just stand on the other side of the doorway, on Earth, so you can hold onto me and stop me floating away. But you should still put your suit on, just in case you need to step through. I hope these air tanks aren't empty.' She fitted the tube into her helmet and took a few breaths. 'Amazing!' she relayed over the

transmitter, her voice appearing through the speaker on Cosmos. 'It works!'

'They knew how to make things that lasted in those days,' said Cosmos approvingly. 'But don't spend long on Europa – you only have a limited number of minutes before your air runs out.'

Leonia had her suit on already and stood poised. 'When I go through the doorway, you stand on the Earth side of it and hold onto my rope,' Annie reminded her spacewalk companion. 'Don't let go of it!

And Cosmos, keep the portal open the whole time we are in space. Will Rika be able to see us when we land on Europa?'

'Affirmative,' said Cosmos. 'We have to assume she will be able to see you or be alerted to your presence pretty much immediately.'

'Roger,' said Annie firmly. 'We are going to get George! I am not leaving my best friend halfway between one blue world and another. We're going to bring him safely home.'

With that, Leonia took hold of the space rope and Annie stepped through the doorway onto one of the moons of distant Jupiter – this moon being possibly the home of space dolphins, some scary robots and currently around three quarters of Annie's best friend, the rest of him still being in transit through the quantum teleportation device. Which might or might not reassemble the full George by the time his two friends, one old, one new, stepped out onto the surface of Europa in one of the most complicated and risky rescue missions that the Solar System had ever seen.

* * *

Close to the spot where Cosmos had positioned his brightly lit doorway, George's vision was clearing in the misty foggy swirl. When Rika had spotted George on the mezzanine level of Mission Control through the flying camera drone, she had immediately dispatched some of her bot helpers to capture him.

Boltzmann had been no help whatsoever. The 'nice' robot just kept clapping his hands in glee and exclaiming that 'at last!' George would meet his master. As George was led down to the ground floor of Mission Control, Boltzmann was practically skipping along behind him.

George, on the other hand, was gutted. As far as he knew, he was the only human being at large in Kosmodrome 2, which meant he had no hope of anyone coming to his assistance. Looking at Rika now, George couldn't believe he had been taken in by her when he first saw her on the screens at Mission Control. He had thought her the most amazing person he had ever seen. Now she looked distorted and strange, all her welcoming charm vanished, to be replaced by a frightening smirk.

'George,' said Rika in a threatening yet still oddly syrupy voice. 'We meet again.'

'Er, yes,' said George. 'Good news, eh?' He tried to keep his spirits up and not let her see he was frightened.

'It is perhaps more extraordinary than you know,'

replied Rika. Behind her, Boltzmann was jumping about, attempting to indicate something via a series of gestures and expressions that George couldn't read.

'You're the head of Kosmodrome 2, I'm one of the junior recruits,' pointed out George. 'It's not that surprising.'

Rika smirked again. 'I agree,' she cooed. George noticed with alarm that her face appeared to be caving in. 'You and Rika Dur coming across each other is no surprise to anyone.'

'Are you OK?' asked George with some concern. 'Your nose seems to be slipping off your face.'

'That's because it isn't really my face,' said Rika in quite a different voice, a much deeper voice and one that gave George a cold shiver as he remembered where he had heard it before. He looked over at Boltzmann, who was nodding manically and grinning in a blissed-out fashion. The nice robot looked like he was dancing to a music of his own.

'Whose face is it then?' said George slowly. 'It looks like it's falling to pieces. Have you had plastic surgery?'

'Oh, it's much cleverer than that,' said the deep-voiced person in front of him. 'I've had Rika's face 3D printed and transplanted onto my own face.'

George felt sick. Who would possibly go to such lengths? But he didn't need to wonder for long – he already knew the answer.

'And before you ask, I have a computer implant in my throat which allows me to speak with the voice of a woman.'

'Alioth Merak,' said George. 'It *is* you, isn't it? You've escaped from prison and disguised yourself as Rika in order to take over Kosmodrome 2, get rid of Eric and put yourself in charge of all the space missions launched from Planet Earth.'

'Oh, LOLZ,' said Merak, 'as your friend Annie would say. It is me. You are so right, George. Even though you defied me once before, turned down my offer to be my heir, destroyed my spaceship and my quantum computer, caused me to be arrested and imprisoned and lose control of my robot army, it's still so *very* nice to see you again.'

George blanched. He had managed to forget the pure horror of his last meeting with Merak. But once Alioth reminded him of how dramatic and how dangerous it had been – and how much Alioth Merak had lost in his previous encounter with George and Annie – George realized that Merak himself was not about to forgive and forget any time soon.

'What happened to your onesies?' he asked, trying to play for time. When he had met him before, the crazy squillionaire had worn only onesies, in the colours and patterns of the planets of the Solar System.

'Onesies are not Rika's style,' replied Merak haughtily. 'And as I have been impersonating the eminent scientist herself, I have also been making use of her wardrobe.'

'What have you done with the real Rika?' George queried, almost too terrified of the answer to ask. 'You haven't killed her, have you?'

'Of course not,' snapped Merak. 'Brutality is not my style. I'm anti-violence, if you must know.'

'You!?' said George. 'Anti-violence! After everything you've done!'

Rika/Merak tried to look down her/his nose but couldn't quite manage it as the nose had veered off so drastically to the one side. 'Rika is still alive,' he/she said. 'I have not killed anybody. The face I am wearing is a copy of Rika's face – she still has the original.'

'Then where is she?' demanded George.

'Perfectly safe,' said Merak. 'She is with some people you know – some people you know very well indeed. They're all together, in a nice contained cosy environment where they have all they could need to stay alive. For now.'

George realized he had no idea what Alioth Merak meant by this.

'Oh, blank face!' said Alioth. 'WOOF-er? Ring any bells, George? Family suddenly summoned to an organic farm in the Faroe Islands? Wonder how that happened, huh?'

'What?' said George slowly, half-astonished, half-furious.

'And Annie's mum! How sweet. She'd always wanted to play a solo while on tour with her orchestra. So I made her dream come true!' said Merak. 'That's what I do. Make dreams come true. Want to farm on a remote island? I can fix it for you! Want to play your violin in Mexico City? Oh yes, I can do that too. Want to join a training programme to be a Mars astronaut, children of the world? Come right this way . . .'

'Where are they?' asked George, his voice choking in his throat. 'What have you done?' He just couldn't bear to think of his mum and dad and his little sisters Juno and Hera, along with Annie's mum, having to encounter this man. He was more worried for his family than he had ever been for himself. Even when he had been on his most dangerous space mission with Annie, he had never felt this spinning sense of fear.

'Well now,' said Merak confidingly. 'Wouldn't you like to know?'

'Yes, I would,' shouted George. 'Tell me!'

'Um, well, what's it worth?' Alioth smirked, looking at his bright red, glossy fingernails. 'To me, that is. Because right now, George, the way I see it, I hold all the cards.'

George looked around him. He was completely surrounded by a robot army that he knew was tightly controlled by Merak – and which would react to his every command. The only ally he had was Boltzmann, and even he seemed to be entirely in thrall to Alioth.

'Let's see,' continued Merak, taking off his blonde wig.

As he did, George wondered how he could ever have thought the person before him bore any resemblance to Rika Dur, one of the world's most respected scientists. George kicked himself. How had he fallen for it? How had he been suckered in by a fake Rika Dur? He couldn't believe he had been so stupid.

'You can do something for me,' the evil Alioth purred. 'And in exchange, I will tell you where your family, Annie's mother and Rika Dur are. Is that a deal?'

'What do I have to do?' asked George, gulping. He knew that whatever Merak suggested, he would have to do it, however awful it was.

'Can't tell you that!' sang Merak. 'You have to agree first – or you never see your mother, father or sisters again. And your dear, lovely little friend Annie will never again see her mother.'

'Deal,' said George quickly, not giving himself time to balk.

'Oh, good,' said Merak. 'I've been wanting a real live human being to test out my quantum teleportation device on for some time now. It's fiendishly clever but I know you expect nothing less from me. Basically it allows you to transfer exact electronic states across space through quantum actions. I have successfully bootstrapped my robotic army and their equipment into space using this technique after the replacement Cosmos machine fell short of expectations. But so far, I have not sent living cells. You, George, will be the first! A space pioneer! And for such an exalted role, I hardly want to use coercion. It would be so much more fitting to use a volunteer. If you could just sign here!'

A robot quickly produced a lengthy contract,

which ran to pages and pages. George started to look through the small print.

'Oh, don't bother to read it all,' said Merak. 'Basically it says you are going through the quantum teleportation device of your own free will and choice.'

'But it's not true that I'm going through of my own free will!' said George.

'Fine,' said Merak. His robot snatched back the contract. 'I don't mind if you never see your family again. It doesn't bother me in the slightest.'

George hesitated. 'Why don't you go through the portal yourself?' he asked. 'If it's such a great step for mankind, then why don't you do it?'

'Oh, George!' sighed Alioth, smiling. 'I thought you would realize. It's still in the experimental phase. Now, fond of you as I am, I could lose you and not forfeit any sleep over it. But I couldn't say the same for myself. I'm much too valuable to be a test pilot.'

'Has no human ever done this before?' asked George, the hair rising on the back of his neck.

'No,' said Merak thoughtfully. 'I did try to interest some of your little companions from the training programme in volunteering – those who were asked to "leave" the camp. But they all refused – some of them quite rudely! And such a voyage must be undertaken by someone who agrees to go out of their own free will. Willingly *and* nicely, in fact. It would spoil it all if I felt I'd forced the issue.'

What is Quantum Teleportation?

Suppose Alice and Bojing work in laboratories in different cities (or planets) and Alice has a particle in an interesting quantum state. By a quantum state, we mean the state of a quantum system, such as an elementary particle, at a moment in time. If the particle were described instead by classical, not quantum, physics, its state would be described by precise values for its position and velocity. The quantum state of a quantum particle looks very different – you can imagine it as a complicated wave spread out over space, without a definite position in general. So what can Alice do, if she wants to give Bojing precise information about this state so that he can create it in his lab and study it too?

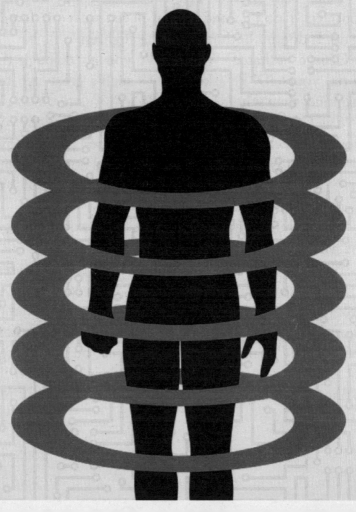

Unfortunately, she cannot simply measure the state of her particle without destroying the state (unless the state is a special kind of state called an *eigenstate*) and the measurement itself would provide incomplete information due to the uncertainty principle, which says that the more precisely you know one property of a particle – like its position – then the more uncertain you will be about another property, like its velocity. For example, an absolutely precise measurement of the particle's position would have to destroy all information about its velocity, and indeed the original complicated wave would be collapsed down to just a thin spike over one point – the position reported by the measurement.

There is a solution for Alice; a way for her to communicate the exact state to Bojing. This is quantum teleportation.

Earlier, Alice sent Bojing one of a pair of particles in an 'entangled' quantum state, while keeping the other of the pair herself. In an entangled state, each particle separately is not in a definite state – only the pair *as a whole* is in a definite state. A measurement on one member of the pair, however, obliges both particles to enter definite states – even if they are light years apart! Also the result of the measurement on one particle determines the definite state of the other particle. Alice can make use of this by making a particular measurement jointly on her original particle and her particle from the entangled pair.

The result of this measurement she then sends to Bojing by ordinary means (e.g. email or radio transmission). From this, Bojing can deduce both the definite state of the particle in his possession, and how to transform it into an exact replica of the state Alice wanted to send – but by making her measurement Alice is forced to destroy her initial state. Quantum information can be transferred, but not copied.

The end result is that Alice's particle state has been teleported to Bojing! But only information – not matter – has been teleported; unfortunately for science fiction, this is not a way for people to travel. Instead, quantum teleportation is like faxing a letter – the information is printed on new paper at the receiving end, and the sender shreds the original letter.

Personally, I'd rather go by post!

Stuart

'What?' said George. 'The others knew?'

'No, not while they were actually in the process with you,' said Merak. 'What you won't know is that I've kept all of you from the Challenges phase. We sent the duds home after the training stage as they were no use to anyone. I just kept the crème de la crème. So when a trainee or pair of trainees failed a challenge, I just popped them into a safe holding pen, in fact, to keep them until everything was ready for their great adventure.'

'Where are they now?' said George. 'And what is this great adventure?' If he thought he'd felt cold and scared before, it was nothing to how he felt now.

'Well, you'll never find out, and neither will anyone else unless you sign this document!' said Merak affably, waving the pen at George.

'I'll sign,' said George snappily, reaching for the pen. This, he figured, was it. This was the challenge he had come here for, not to fly to Mars or create a 3D printer that would work on another planet or mend a solar array. His challenge was unique and a test he mustn't fail. It was to save the other trainees who had stayed behind at Kosmodrome 2, falsely imprisoned, as he now knew, by Alioth Merak. And to get his family and Annie's mum released from wherever Merak held them captive.

'A-hem,' said the evil genius, holding the pen out of reach. 'What did I say about "willingly and nicely"? It matters enormously to me that this great step is undertaken by someone with gladness in their heart.'

'I will sign,' said George as nicely as he could, given the circumstances. 'Gladly,' he managed to force out.

'That's better,' said Merak, proffering the pen.

George took it and scratched his name on the contract, wondering as he did whether he would ever return. As much as he wanted to run screaming from Mission Control – and keep running and running until he was safely home at his funny, sweet-smelling, scruffy house in Foxbridge – he knew he couldn't. The only way he would see his family again – and perhaps the only way the other kids would ever see their mums and dads again – was if he went into space through Alioth's dodgy doorway. There was, he figured, nothing else he could do. He felt so desperate that everything seemed to white out in front of him.

But he didn't get much time to think. A couple of robots behind him stuffed him into a spacesuit, strapped some spare weights onto his legs, popped a space helmet on his head and zipped him up. Gesturing with his hands like the conductor of an orchestra, Merak then seemed to give a series of commands, which created a cone of light just next to where he had been standing.

Guided by two robots, George took up a position in the centre of the cone. He had no idea what would happen next, where he was going or whether he would

ever come back. It was so terrifying that he couldn't think about it at all. Instead, he tried to focus on the face of Boltzmann, thinking that he wanted what might be his last sight to be something friendly, even if it was also horribly misguided. But as he gazed at the battered and blackened features of the only sentient robot in the world, his vision started to blur. Boltzmann seemed to fragment into tiny little pieces which began to whir around in a swoosh of colours.

And just as George had time to think what a pretty pattern it all made, everything went dark, as though the lights had gone out, or he had fallen very suddenly into a deep and fitful sleep.

Chapter Twenty

Annie and Leonia stood either side of Cosmos's doorway, with Leonia holding in both space-gloved hands the rope attached to Annie's spacesuit. Under Annie's feet lay the thick icy crust of one of Jupiter's largest moons. When she looked down at the mottled and ridged icy sheet underneath them, she wondered if she had imagined the dark shapes moving beneath. She looked up. The very thin oxygen-light atmosphere of Europa meant that the dim rays of the

distant Sun was diffused, to create a smoky glow across the sky. Through the smog, she could see Jupiter, the most magnificent of the planets in the Solar System.

Annie looked back to Leonia and pointed at Jupiter – and the two girls gasped. Tall, skinny Leonia seemed to sway a little in her suit, and Annie felt uneasy at having got her new friend mixed up in this adventure – she wished she had left Leonia out of it. The situation they were in was scary enough already without throwing a sudden and totally unexpected trip to one of Jupiter's moons at even the super-competent Leonia. But as Annie floated gently away from the surface of Europa and only her space rope, held onto by Leonia, tethered her to something solid, she suddenly felt very glad to have her as back-up. It wasn't a moment to be operating alone.

'Stay right there,' Annie instructed Leonia, her voice going to Cosmos and bouncing back through the transmission device also fitted in Leonia's space helmet. The spacesuit technology they were using was certainly antique but it also seemed to be totally functional and very tightly stitched. It needed to be! In the freezing conditions of Europa, even a tiny leak would be the end of one or the other of them. She mustn't, she knew, take a big step or she might float away across Europa and never make it back to the portal doorway.

'Why are the robots using heaters?' asked Leonia.

Annie turned to look at the robot army and their

encampment. Now she was actually on this side of the doorway, she could make out far more detail than when she had just been looking through the portal from the Earth side. Some of the robots were holding mechanical devices, which they seemed to be wielding around the edges of the very large gaping hole in the ice.

'I expect they're trying to make the hole bigger,' said Annie. 'If they didn't apply heat, maybe it would freeze over again.'

By now, the robots had managed to get what looked like a net into the dark liquid. The girls watched as it sank beneath the ice. Around the edges of the robot-made hole, waves smacked at the hem of the circular incision in the ice. Annie floated a bit closer, paying out a little more rope. She had just seen something – or had she? – and she wanted to get another look. The glass in her space helmet wasn't very clear – it was scratched and old – so she couldn't tell if she had spotted something or whether it was a flaw in her space clothing.

'What was that?' It sounded like Leonia behind her had noticed the same thing.

'I don't know,' said Annie. 'It might be a bit of the machinery the robots are using.' But she still felt a sense of rising excitement. If she had just seen 'something' in the dark liquid which lay under the surface of Europa, then she would be the first human being ever to have seen an alien! For years, there had been theories that alien life forms could live under the icy crust of the moons of Jupiter and Saturn. Had they seen an alien? Did they look like dolphins in the oceans of the Earth? 'I've got to get nearer,' she said to Leonia. She edged away, rising gently from the surface in the low-gravity environment.

At that same moment, the shimmering white figure on the other side of the robot-made lake – like a ghost of a spaceman – became more defined. It was growing into its outline as it became more opaque.

'George,' called Annie. 'George!' She waved. Perhaps if she caught his attention, he would fully arrive on Europa – perhaps she could summon him fully to the surface of this little moon by projecting her wish for George to be whole again onto the wavy humanoid shape on the other side of the dark, frothing pond.

It seemed to be working. Bit by bit, as though he was an illustration being coloured in, George's form fleshed itself out. It seemed agonizingly slow to Annie. She wanted him to arrive in solid form on Europa, so she would know he was in one piece. When all of him had arrived, Annie could start to work on getting all of him home. What scared her the most was the thought that part of George could get lost in space for ever.

'C'mon,' she muttered to herself, willing George to make the transfer, whole and intact. 'C'mon!' she said again to herself frantically. If she lost George, would she spend the whole of the rest of her life flying around space, looking for him like a lost soul? It was too horrible to contemplate.

But little by little, George was taking shape. First his arms seemed to become three-dimensional and solid. Then his legs, followed by his torso and at last, his head and the round space helmet!

Annie gave a cry of joy. George had made it – and unlike some of the robots on Europa, who seemed to be missing limbs, it looked like all of him had arrived!

On the other side of the lake, in his spacesuit, George's newly formed body plus head fully materialized on the icy ground. He felt himself ping into his own body with a sickening lurch. Until he was sucked entirely into his own being, he had been lost in a world of strange dreams as particles of him transferred themselves across the Solar System. It was as though he had seen his own life played before his eyes like a film.

He had seen himself as a small baby, held in the arms of his proud parents with their hippy smocks and their wide young smiles. Then George had been a chubby toddler, playing with the family goat which had been

kept tethered at the back of the wattle and daub hut where he had lived with his mum and dad. The hut had been part of a camp where families had lived in the same way as early Britons in the Iron Age had done, producing all their own food, heat, light and clothing from what they could cultivate on the scrubby patches of land they had marked out for themselves.

But as a small child, George had fallen terribly ill and been rushed to a brilliantly lit hospital where his life had been saved by doctors using huge quantities of medicines and medical equipment. George saw his pale-faced mum and dad weeping by his bedside as they urged him to pull through. He saw his gran, the fierce but loyal Mabel, arriving at the hospital and shouting at his mum and dad for endangering their son's life with the way they chose to live.

Mabel had finished by insisting that they move to a house – a proper house with electricity, running water, heating and a roof! She had even bought it for them. In his dream George saw Mabel hand over the documents for the house. And he saw his parents give in and resign themselves to a life more ordinary, taking him from the hospital to the cosy little house that Mabel had given them.

But it wasn't really a normal life. Despite moving into an ordinary suburban house in the town of Foxbridge, George's mum and dad had continued to live their eco dream, using the back garden as their own little farm, attempting to generate their own electricity, making their own clothes and trying to use as few resources taken from Planet Earth as they could. And one day George saw how the pig they kept in the back garden – another of Mabel's thoughtful gifts to him – had run away, making a huge hole in the rickety fence which separated his back garden from the strange and over-grown world of next door. Following the hoof prints of Freddy the pig had led George through the jungle-like back garden of the deserted next door house right up to the back door where he met . . .

'George!' someone was shouting at him as though from the bottom of a lake. The voice was unclear and distorted, just like his vision, but still something seemed familiar to him. 'George!' it came again. He didn't know if it was part of his dream or whether he could really hear it. There was a strange ringing in his ears. When he tried to focus on anything, he just saw a swirl of darkness flecked with brilliant lights which flashed and whirred in front of his eyes.

But gradually the whirligig slowed down and the world stopped spinning. Through a haze, he could now make out a pale landscape with darker holes in it, and above, a greyish blue sky. Movement caught his attention – he could see darker dots, like ants, which seemed to be scurrying around the edges of the round holes in the greyish white surface.

And then he saw one figure more clearly than the rest. A white figure, waving at him from across a black expanse. 'George!' he heard again, only this time he knew he wasn't hearing this as sound. He was hearing it as a call from somewhere inside, as though his own self was calling him back into his body. He concentrated on the figure waving and realized it was coming towards him from the other side of the black hole. Was any of this real? He took a tiny heavy step forward, the space weights anchoring him to the surface, and then came to very suddenly.

And just in time! Once he looked around properly and saw where he had landed, George realized that one more step forward would have tipped him straight into the lake itself. Looking at the hostile liquid, which seemed somehow thicker and more viscous than water, George wondered what lay below! Was he imagining a

mass of marine bodies seething just under the surface, twisting and turning in a bubbling soup of something indescribable. He couldn't tell if he was still dreaming or whether he had seen this for real. But he could at least tell that on the other side of this lake-like expanse stood a small figure that he had seen in space before.

The figure waved at him, using both arms, floating away from the ground as it did so. Behind, in the distance, George could see another, tall figure in what looked an enormous spacesuit, clutching onto a rope, standing in a faintly glowing doorway. 'Annie!' said George to himself. Was it really her? Had his best friend come all this way to get him and take him home through the space doorway? Or was he hallucinating? Was this another strange dream? If the family goat from when he was a tiny kid turned up, he would know it was a dream. And if it didn't, would that mean all this was real? How could he know for sure what was real and what was not?

The floating figure kept on waving. Either side of the figure and by the black lake, robots continued their work, unbothered, or so it seemed, by the presence of George and whoever else had made it to this weird world. George scuffled round to Annie's side of the lake, the space weights heavy on his legs, without any of the robots seeming even to register his presence.

The robots all seemed to have different roles – some of them were using heat sources to make the lake larger. Others seemed to be holding onto an enormous net which seemed to have got stuck in the water. Some of the robots were reaching over the liquid to try and

haul the net back onto the icy banks. But as they were struggling to pull it in, the effort and the icy bank meant robot after robot was toppling into the liquid, where they promptly sank without a trace.

As a whole cohort of robots vanished into the dark liquid, Annie and George both gave a huge sigh of relief as they met by the side of the lake. Annie was floating at head height by now, so George had to pull on her space boot to bring her back down to the surface. Hugging each other very briefly – and clumsily, since both were wearing spacesuits – George held on tightly to Annie and started walking her back towards the doorway. There, Leonia, the figure in the large old-fashioned spacesuit, waited for them on the other side. But before they could reach the doorway itself, they both felt, rather than heard, another presence behind them. They turned – and saw a shimmering apparition begin to take shape. The figure got rapidly clearer and clearer, until they saw that another person in a spacesuit was joining them, also arriving via quantum teleportation from Earth.

'Not so fast, George,' this new arrival said. Annie could hear the voice perfectly clearly too. 'Have you forgotten?' it said. 'Have you forgotten our deal?'

'I've done my part,' said George, hanging onto Annie for dear life. 'I've travelled into space in the quantum teleportation device – and proved to you it can work with a living human being. So now you have to do your part of the deal and tell me where my family – and Annie's mum – are.'

This was the first Annie had heard of any of this. George knew her hair would be standing on end – if that were possible – inside her space helmet.

'No, that's not the full deal,' said the apparition regretfully. 'If you'd read the small print – as I advised you to – you would have found that you signed up to go into space, collect an alien extra-terrestrial being and bring it back to Earth for me. If you don't meet those exact conditions, I am under no obligation to do anything at all for you.'

George ground his teeth. It was so typical of Alioth Merak to change the conditions of the deal once the action had already started. 'That's not what you said,' he persisted. 'You only said I had to travel via the QT into space and then you would tell me where you are holding my family and Annie's mum. That was all.'

'What!?' said Annie. 'What do you mean, *my mum*! What's she got to do with any of this? And *who* is that?'

'I can't explain everything now,' said George, not letting go of his friend. They stood together, arms around each other, two small figures in their white spacesuits. 'But we need to get out of here.'

'Cosmos,' said Annie. 'And the portal – it's just over there.' But she was still trying to understand what George had just told her. She stared at him. 'You went through that teleport-thingy to *save* everyone!' she said. 'George, how brave is that!'

George gripped her tighter, so happy to hear that he *hadn't* let everyone down after all! But right now, they needed to get away from Alioth and his robots or it would all be in vain . . .

They started to edge away, but more and more robots were starting to materialize as they travelled from Earth via the quantum teleportation device. Annie and George realized, to their horror, that in a very few minutes they could be overwhelmed. Annie looked behind her and saw Leonia was frantically gesticulating, but Annie couldn't make out what she meant.

The next moment Annie knew what Leonia must have been saying. The portal doorway vanished entirely, taking Leonia with it – the door from Earth closed, leaving Annie and George alone on Europa with an evil robot army manifesting itself ever more distinctly by the second, and a crazed and very angry control freak, intent on revenge, just about to become fully fleshed in front of them.

Chapter Twenty-one

'**S**o, my little friends,' scooed the rapidly solidifying form of Alioth Merak, formerly disguised as Rika Dur, head of Kosmodrome 2, now wearing a space-suit and appearing via quantum teleportation on Europa. 'We meet again. How charming this is!'

'It's you!' said Annie in horror. The real voice was unmistakable. 'Alioth Merak. How did you get here?'

'It's been him all along,' said George grimly. 'It was never Rika, at least not lately. I don't know what he's done with the real Rika. But he escaped from prison and he's been impersonating her, using a 3D printed face transplant, her clothes, a wig and a computerized voice box.'

'Wow!' exclaimed Annie. She glared at Merak. 'That's why Rika turned against Dad when she came back from her holiday – it wasn't Rika at all who got him sacked. It was you! You kidnapped Rika while she was on holiday and took over her role, didn't you?'

'Then you had to get Eric out of Kosmodrome 2,' said George. 'When he confronted you about *Artemis* because he realized that it had already started, you had to get rid of him, so you made it look like he was being retired.'

'And,' chimed in Annie, 'I bet you made sure we got places on the astronaut training scheme!'

'Yes, yes, yes,' sighed Merak. 'Though I do feel that including you on the programme proved to be an error – one that I took steps to rectify with a little accident.' He sniggered.

'But hang on,' interrupted Annie, not only angry to have her suspicions about the plane 'accident' confirmed, but also suddenly remembering what George had said. 'What's this got to do with George's parents. And my mum? And where is Rika Dur?'

'He won't tell me,' said George. 'He's holding them somewhere. But my mum and dad never went to an island to farm, just like your mum never went on any concert tour. It was just his way of kidnapping them so that no one tried to look for them. He even sent us messages from them himself! But I don't know where they are now.'

'Argh!' cried Annie, realizing. 'Noooo!'

'What?' asked George.

'The boxes!' said Annie. 'There are boxes in a hospital block in Kosmodrome 2 with people in them! They're in suspended animation – they're alive but they are fast asleep! And he's sending them to space! It must be your family, George – and my mum! It is, isn't it?'

'Oh, well done,' crowed Merak. 'Quite right. Your families are safely tucked up in those lovely custom-made boxes where they will remain "asleep" until the spacecraft they are on reaches Europa.'

'I don't believe it,' said George slowly.

'Believe it,' said Merak. 'It's not just the other trainees that I'm sending out to Europa. Just in case the live astronauts don't make it, I've taken the precaution of sending some sleeping ones.'

'But our parents didn't choose to go into space!' said George furiously. 'They didn't want to leave Earth – so why did you kidnap *them* and put them to sleep? You said you wanted volunteers!'

'They did volunteer,' said Merak casually. 'Sort of. When I explained to them the other options . . .'

'You are horrible,' said George slowly. He felt numb with fear.

'What about Mars?' asked Annie bravely. Suddenly Mars didn't sound too far away. If her family and George's got sent to Mars, there was a chance they could get them back.

'Oh, we will get to Mars!' said Merak. 'We're just going the long way round.'

'I knew it!' said Annie. 'I knew there was even more to this plan than we realized.'

'So true!' said Merak. 'Life from the oceans and life – human *and* synthetic – is what interests me . . . so I want the blue planets.' He sniggered. 'I want the blue moon, I want the red planets, the grey ones, the stripy ones, the upside-down ones. Frankly, I want them all.' Around him, more and more robots were appearing, until battalions of the shadowy figures were lining up. For the moment they were still semi-transparent as the quantum teleporter did its work in sending them out to space.

But George and Annie could see that in just a few moments' time, when the robots had finished their teleportation to Europa, they would be completely outnumbered. Glancing behind them, they saw no sign of Cosmos's doorway. Was this it? Was this their final journey into space?

Just then, Annie noticed something very interesting behind Alioth Merak. Their old enemy and his horde of rapidly teleporting robots were all facing George and Annie, paying no attention to what was happening behind their backs. But Annie had seen that some of the robots which had fallen into the hole earlier must have dropped their portable heat sources before they fell. At different locations around the ice hole, heat machines

LUCY & STEPHEN HAWKING

lay on the surface and continued to melt the thick ice, perilously close to where the robot army were standing. Once the full weight of the robots arrived from Earth,

Annie reckoned the ice wouldn't hold firm under them for much longer.

'Keep him focused on you,' Annie murmured to George. 'And walk very slowly backwards, with me.'

'You promised you would let our families go if I went through the QT!' said George bravely. He and Annie took a baby step back. George hoped his statement would give Merak something to get stuck into. 'You can't take revenge on our families. They're completely innocent.'

As he spoke, both friends took another millistep backwards, slightly further away from the rapidly enlarging ice hole.

'So sweet,' murmured Merak as his robots became solid forms around him. 'Revenge, that is. Not you. I don't want you to think this was all about you – it really wasn't. You're just not that important to me.'

'It was about getting control of Kosmodrome 2,' guessed Annie. 'So that you would be in charge of all the space missions in the world.'

'Exactly,' cried Merak, oblivious to the enlarging gulf behind him and his robots. 'Only *I* could be trusted with such an important job. All the rest of the work I've done here has been clearing debris out of the way – such as your father! He had to go. He would never have allowed Mission Artemis to happen in the way I wanted. He would never have agreed to send children into space or allow me to put unsuspecting people to sleep. I had to get rid of him – and once I had done that, I had to use everything at my disposal to act fast, before anyone uncovered my plans.'

'Too bad we spoiled it all for you – again,' said Annie casually, not sounding sorry at all.

Her tone was not lost on Merak. It clearly irked him. 'Enough of this chatter!' Even through the voice transmitter, they could hear his rage. 'My robots have now arrived.' Around him, the extra-heavy robots had fully emerged, their metal boots firmly planted on the icy crust beneath them. 'Robots, seize them . . . !'

But as Merak gave the command, two things happened at once. First of all, he himself seemed to be teleporting in reverse. Much more quickly than he had arrived, he started vanishing into thin air in front of them. As he did so, the robot army tried to take a step forward in unison, but were immediately flung into confusion. Those on the back row had slithered backwards as the ice gave way beneath them. As they fell, they reached forward to try to hold onto the robot in front to stop themselves from disappearing into the subterranean sea. But their actions caused a domino effect as the rows of robots dragged each other into the rapidly widening hole beneath them.

As they fell, Annie and George moved swiftly backwards to avoid following them. They didn't think they would be able to move fast enough as the ice seemed to be crumbling away as the robots thrashed and struggled. Suspended now above the surface of Europa was the half-translucent form of Merak. It was a terrifying sight!

But as the two junior astronauts reversed as rapidly as they could, they felt a hand grab them and pull them backwards. They just had time to register that they were being hauled back through the doorway to Earth, which had opened again behind their backs.

As they stumbled through the portal, the last thing they heard was a scream of horror from the suspended semi-transparent form of Merak as his robots dived to their end in the murky oceans beneath the ice.

Then the doorway to Earth slammed shut.

The two friends collapsed backwards onto the floor of Eric's office, landing at Leonia's feet. Annie was the first to jump up. She tried to rip off her space helmet but the old-fashioned version was much harder to release. George was quicker to get out of his heavily weighted space costume. As he undid the helmet and slid it off his head, he realized he could still hear Merak's unearthly screaming.

'How come I can still hear him?' he mumbled.

'Because he's half here – and he's half there,' said Leonia, beaming from ear to ear. 'I started to quantum teleport him while you were still on Europa. I did it while Cosmos closed the doorway. So he's at least sixty-five per cent returned to Mission Control right now . . .'

'But how?' asked George. 'How did you know what to do? And why didn't you just leave him out there? Why did you have to bring him back?'

'I thought we might need him,' said Leonia quietly.

'Did you know that the robots would fall through the hole and into the pond?' George asked Annie, helping her to pull off the old space helmet.

'I thought it was our only hope!' said Annie, emerging, blinking and a little dizzy from the vintage spacesuit.

'Um, you guys,' a voice broke in.

'Leo!' said Annie, hugging her. 'Thank you! You got us out of there! It was amazing! What you just did saved our lives! And I think we beat him. All we need to do now is find out where the other trainees are, and our families – and get them

resuscitated. And then we're all good!'

'Yeah, that's all very well,' said Leonia urgently. 'But you seem to have forgotten something else.'

'What's that?' said George, looking perplexed.

'*Artemis*,' said Leonia. 'I think your intervention has caused Merak to accelerate his plans. It looks like the spacecraft launch is set to go. It's leaving. And we don't know how to make it stop!'

Chapter Twenty-Two

'Mission Control!' said George. 'Now!'
The three of them ran out of the room, only pausing to gather up Cosmos as they ran into the huge room with its banks of screens and monitors. The last time George had seen this room, it had been stuffed full of robots. This time, it was very nearly empty.

'Did all the robots go into space?' asked Annie as they surveyed the abandoned room.

'Not quite,' said George. 'They left someone behind.'

Boltzmann Brian was standing near the cone of light, which still shone as brightly as when it had transported George to Europa. 'Take me!' he seemed to be pleading. 'Please let me go with the other robots! Don't leave me here alone!'

But the only figure other than Boltzmann in the room didn't care about Boltzmann's emotional appeals. In the centre of the cone of light, the 65% of Alioth Merak that Leonia had forced to return to Earth twisted and turned, gnashing its teeth and screaming in horror.

'I'm entangled!' the hideous apparition yelled. 'I can't go forward, I can't go back! I'm half on Earth—'

'More than that, actually,' supplied George helpfully. 'Only thirty-five per cent of you remains on Europa! That's good news, isn't it?'

'No, it isn't!' howled Merak. 'Bring me back! I demand that you complete the transfer.'

Leonia, meanwhile, was typing rapidly on one of the computers. As she did so, the pictures on the screens changed. Instead of a view of Europa, with robots sliding helplessly into an ice hole filled with a dark swirling liquid, the image changed to show a launch pad with a spacecraft preparing for takeoff.

'It's the one I saw!' cried Annie. 'That's here, at Kosmodrome 2! That's *Artemis*! How long until takeoff?'

'It's running final checks now!' said Leonia.

'We must be able to stop it,' said Annie, gazing at the huge screens, which now showed nothing but the launch preparations. One of the screens was streaming from the inside of the spaceship.

'Look!' said Annie. Robots were lumbering on board, loading the long rectangular boxes Annie had seen in another part of Kosmodrome 2 onto the ship. 'Oh no!' she breathed, her heart breaking. 'Those boxes might be our families! George! George! We *must* stop the ship from leaving!'

'OMG!' said George. 'Is that my family?' His eyes filled with tears as he saw two smaller boxes being loaded. 'My little sisters . . . it can't be! It just *can't* be!'

'And look!' said Annie desperately. 'There are live astronauts on board as well.' The camera changed view and showed a row of kids in spacesuits, strapped into their seats, their heads lolling as though they were drugged. 'That must be what Merak meant – he's kept all the trainees here and now they're on *Artemis*. He's sending them to space, to found a colony on the blue moon! We've got to stop them!'

'But how?' said George. He had joined Leonia at the computer monitor. 'How do you stop a space launch?'

'There must be a way,' said Leonia determinedly. 'It has to be possible to cancel it.' She tapped away at the keyboard, but came up against a stop sign. 'There's a code,' she said. 'We need to input a code to change the launch protocol.'

'Tell us that code,' Annie shouted at the three-quarters form of Alioth Merak. 'What do we have to input to stop the launch?'

'Bring me back to Earth,' entreated Merak. 'It's the only way you will stop *Artemis* from leaving . . .'

'T minus five,' the automated countdown read, meaning there were now only five minutes until the spaceship launched.

'We can't!' said George. 'We can't bring him back – can we? It's too dangerous!'

'If we don't,' said Annie, 'we can't stop the ship!'

'Rescue me . . .' said Merak, who was getting fainter and fainter. 'If you want to stop the ship, you have to bring me back to Earth! It's the only way . . .'

But Merak's own technology had let him down. The quantum teleporter, already over-used far beyond his projections, had decided to put itself out of service – permanently. With a gargling scream of horror, Merak disappeared entirely as the quantum teleporter distributed all the molecules of him randomly around all the locations where he had ever been.

He was gone.

'What now?' said George in shock. He would never have thought he would be sorry to see the end of Alioth Merak, but the fact was that he had vanished, taking with them their last chance of stopping the spacecraft *Artemis*. Soon it would be leaving for Europa, with his and Annie's family on board, and also the other kids from the final week of the astronaut training process.

'We've lost,' said Annie dully. Her mind was whirring with thoughts – if *Artemis* launched, could they open Cosmos's portal up on the ship itself and bring everyone back through the portal? It was notoriously hard to open a space portal on a moving object – Cosmos wasn't the greatest at pinpoint accuracy for his portals when the place they were trying to reach was in rapid motion itself. She wasn't sure whether they would manage it, or whether the portal might just dump her and George outside the spacecraft, to drift around in deep space while *Artemis* powered away from them at enormous speed.

Would they have to wait until *Artemis* landed on Europa in order to try and recover their loved ones and the other kids from the training programme? Would Cosmos be able to transport so many people? The quantum teleporter obviously wouldn't work safely for human beings, so they wouldn't be able to risk mounting a rescue operation using that.

'We've lost them,' repeated Annie. Even Leonia had stopped frantically typing on the computer.

'Excuse me,' Cosmos piped up. 'But I don't think you have.'

'Really?' Annie gave a start. 'You can stop the launch?'

'Er, no,' said the supercomputer. 'Sadly not. I had my information banks wiped. I think someone suspected that my loyalties might not be to her or him entirely.'

'So . . . can we ask Tablet Cosmos then?' Leonia ventured.

Cosmos made a funny sort of noise, rather like a sniff, and said haughtily, 'That upstart fried its own operating system after Alioth Merak tried to use it for something *far* beyond its limited capabilities.'

'Oh, no!' said George, also reeling with the shock of the situation.

'I think you are forgetting something,' said Cosmos politely.

'Which is?' said Annie.

'I sent you the activation code for the launch commands already,' said Cosmos. 'Predicting that there would be some kind of hostile event, and that at some point I would be required to forfeit all the security information I possessed, I took the precaution of sending you the code before my system was cleared.'

'You did?' said Annie.

'On a "family" message,' said Cosmos. 'It's a very simple code – you just have to transpose each letter of the alphabet with its numerical value.'

Annie rootled around in her pocket and pulled out the scrunched piece of paper. 'Here it is!'

'Read it out!' said Leonia.

'You do it,' said Annie rapidly. 'You'll be faster.'

'*And the cow jumped over the Moon!*' said Leonia, with a sideways glance at Annie.

'No, you have to do it in numbers,' said Annie. 'A is one and so on.'

'OK,' said Leonia, scribbling down an alphabet rapidly. 'Try this – 1144208531523102113165415225188 208513151514.'

'OMG, that was fast!' said George. 'I'm still on "cow"!'

'Ha!' said Annie as Leonia typed in the code and the computer accepted it, activating a command screen. 'Who says girls aren't good at code!'

'What do you want me to do now?' asked Leonia urgently.

'Cancel the launch!' said Annie. 'Shut it down!'

'That option isn't here,' said Leonia, peering at the screen. 'But I can delay it.'

'Do it!' said Annie.

Leonia selected the right command and they saw a message flash up on the screen: LAUNCH DELAY THIRTY MINUTES.

George felt like he let out a breath for the first time in hours. He was so relieved that, for now at least, the spacecraft wasn't able to leave before they had a chance to get there and unload his family and the other kids.

'We have to go!' he said. He turned to Leonia. 'Can you try and get hold of Annie's dad through Cosmos?' he asked. 'I'm sure *he* could tell us how to halt the launch for longer.'

'I've already tried that!' Leonia said sadly. 'Unfortunately I think that there must be some kind of blocking device around the facility to stop anyone calling him. I can't get through at all! But I will keep on trying, of course.' Her brow knitted. 'I do not like to fail,' she muttered.

'Then we are on our own. And we don't have much time,' said Annie. 'How are we going to do this?'

'I know!' said George. 'Boltzmann!' he called over to the robot, who was slumped in a dispirited manner in the corner.

'Yes?' said Boltzmann sadly, raising his great big blackened head.

'Boltzmann,' said George, using what he knew were the magic words. 'Would you like to help me?'

'Yes!' said the very nice robot, jumping up. 'Do you have a task for me?'

'I do,' said George. 'And it's very important and only a very nice robot could manage it.'

'In that case,' said Boltzmann, 'I am your bot!'

Leaving Leonia operating the computers in Mission Control, George and Annie, with Boltzmann leading the way, shot off as fast as they could towards the launch pad. It was a huge advantage having Boltzmann with them – the distance between them and the spacecraft looked so huge that they feared they would never cover it in time, but Boltzmann simply picked them up, one under each arm. Carrying both kids, the robot ran in great long strides, covering the ground at least five times more quickly.

When they reached the spacecraft, which was simmering on its launch pad like a dog straining at the leash to go for a walk, it was Boltzmann who guided them up the complex path through the umbilical tower to the bridge, still connected to the spacecraft itself. Leonia managed to open the hatch just as they arrived, so they flew into the spacecraft itself and pulled out dazed-looking kids in spacesuits, who seemed disorientated and confused, though totally obedient to anything asked of them, as though still partly asleep. To George's amazement, the last spacesuited astronaut off the ship was the small figure of his friend Igor.

Ushering them off *Artemis* and sending them back down the tower with instructions to move away as fast as possible, Annie and George searched for their families.

'What are we looking for?' asked George as he clambered further into the spacecraft. It was an awkward climb – they had entered the spacecraft near the top and were now progressing downwards into the cargo hold. Of course, when the spacecraft was actually flying, it would be horizontal, where it was now vertical, which made it even more difficult to explore.

'Boxes!' Annie, who was on the level above George, shouted down to him. 'Can you see some large boxes, kind of people-sized and white?'

'Yes!' George's voice floated back up. 'I've found them! Do you think it's safe to move them?' He touched the boxes gently, trying to communicate with the sleeping people within – his mum and dad! And in those smaller boxes beside them – were those his little sisters? He felt a big lump in his throat and swallowed, almost choking back tears. How would he get them off in time? Could he save them . . . ?

'I don't think it's safe to leave them,' said Annie, horribly aware that the minutes were ticking away and they didn't yet know if Leonia had managed to cancel the launch or delay it any further.

Boltzmann climbed down with George. 'These have self-contained circuits and power sources,' he said confidently. 'They have been designed to be moved so they will be entirely self-sufficient provided that each box is fully charged.' He checked. 'Which they are.'

'Ugh, they're too heavy,' huffed George, trying to lift one of the bigger ones.

'They're automatically loaded,' said Boltzmann cheerily. 'And can be unloaded the same way. Like this!' The robot pressed a button set into the wall of the spacecraft and each box rose, like on a stairlift, up to the exit again, where it was laid flat and pushed back out onto the bridge. One by one, to George's astonishment, the boxes seemingly levitated out of the spacecraft and back onto the connecting bridge again.

Annie started to scramble out after them. 'C'mon!' she shouted back down to George. 'We've got to get

ourselves off the ship too! We don't know if Leonia can hold it on the launch pad for much longer!'

'Coming!' Now that George had seen all the boxes off the ship, he felt surprisingly carefree. He had never really understood until that moment how being afraid for someone else is even scarier than being afraid for yourself! Now that he thought – and hoped – that his family were out of danger, he felt a huge weight lift. He sighed with relief, and took just a tiny moment to enjoy the fact that he was in the belly of a real-life space-ship, one with the capacity and power to fly through the Solar System at great speed! Then he started to clamber upwards, following the huge plate-like metal feet of robot Boltzmann, who seemed to be humming to himself.

'We did a good job,' said Boltzmann from above. But

then his huge foot slipped and he tumbled backwards a little. It wasn't a serious fall, but it held him and George up for an extra minute while he regained his balance.

As the nice robot steadied himself, George thought he detected a change in the rumbling sound of the spacecraft's engine. It had been active all the time they were inside it, grumbling along at a low-powered hum. But now it seemed to get deeper and more resounding, as though the beast was rearing up for action . . .

Above George, Annie had already exited the spacecraft. Worried that this was all going too slowly, George climbed onto Boltzmann's shoulders and peered upwards. Through the open hatch he could see

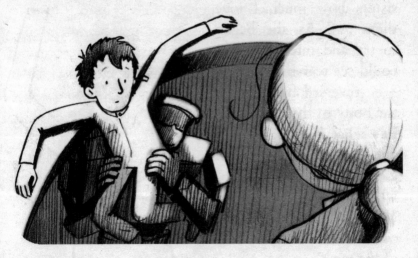

Annie's face peering down from the connecting bridge she stood on.

'Hurry up!' she urged him.

But George suddenly paused. This was what he had always wanted, wasn't it? To travel into space, to explore unknown worlds, to use all the skills and science he had been learning to find out the answers to some of the great unanswered questions about our solar system? Could he turn his back on all of that? Could he walk off the spaceship now, knowing this was probably his biggest chance ever to depart from Earth on a voyage of total adventure.

He made a sudden but very clear decision.

'Annie!' he called up. 'I'm not coming home. I'm going to stay on board! Tell my mum and dad and little sisters how much I love them ...' As she began to try and interrupt – he could see tears in her eyes – he reversed further into the body of the spacecraft. 'It's what I *want*, Annie!' he shouted, filled with glorious excitement. 'And we'll be doing it *together! You and Eric and Cosmos can be with me every step of the way!'*

The hatch started to close and George heard Annie scream, but knew there was no way that human power could stop the mighty door closing. It slammed shut, and the engines revved hungrily beneath him and the only other being left on the ship, Boltzmann Brian, the terribly nice robot.

An announcement came over the tannoy inside the spacecraft: '*Cleared for takeoff. Takeoff is active now. T minus sixty seconds.*'

And as Annie scrambled away from the tall rocket, racing for safety as the gantry fell away, George strapped himself into one of the seats and prepared himself for the journey of a lifetime.

'*Five . . . four . . . three . . . two . . . one . . . we have takeoff!*'

Mission Artemis had begun.

The Overview Effect

I think almost everyone dreams of going into space at some point in their lives. Sadly, though, most give up on that dream when they determine that the odds of going seem so small. In my case however, my father and both my next-door neighbours' fathers were astronauts. In my neighbourhood, it seemed normal to believe that all of us would go into space someday.

When I found out that I did not qualify to be a NASA astronaut, due to my poor eyesight, I decided I must build a private space agency, so that I could fly. I invested the money I earned making computer games in companies that eventually made it possible for me and others to fly to space privately. In October of 2008, I flew to the International Space Station, and became the first second-generation American astronaut, and I flew with the first second-generation Russian cosmonaut!

Preparing for, and making a trip to space, is an amazing experience! Many of the details of the experience were very different from what I expected, or the impressions you get from watching television or movies about space.

Before you fly, you must train to operate the spacecraft. Training was a great deal of fun, and I was amazed how most of it was very similar to activities students do at school, or in some after-school clubs. For example, many people like to scuba dive, as I do. When you get a scuba diving licence, you learn about air pressure and gases like oxygen and carbon dioxide, expanding on what you learn in school chemistry and physics. This is almost exactly the same as the life support on board a spacecraft. If you can get a scuba licence, you can operate life support in space! Similarly, if you can get an amateur radio operator licence on Earth, you can operate the radios on a spacecraft. Learning to be a qualified astronaut was more fun and less difficult than I had imagined . . . as long as you are a good student in school!

Then there is the space flight itself. When you watch a rocket launch into the sky, in person or on TV, it is *very* loud, and you can feel the massive vibration. However, on the inside, when I launched into space it was quite the opposite. When the engines lit up, we could barely feel or hear it. When the rocket began to lift off, it was very gentle. I have often described it as feeling like 'a confident ballet move, lifting us ever faster into the sky'. For just over eight minutes you feel about three times the force of gravity, then the engines cut off . . . and you are floating weightlessly in orbit over Earth.

The view is, of course, spectacular, but I was immediately struck by how close we remained to Earth. Airplanes can fly almost ten miles above Earth, and we were orbiting about twenty-five times higher than that. However, that is still close enough to see many of the same details you see from a plane, yet far enough to see the whole Earth below you. It is a strange feeling to be both unexpectedly near Earth, but also totally isolated from anyone down there on the surface. You clearly understand that if an emergency arises, you and your crewmates must solve it, for there is little help that can come from the surface. Learning to be both self-reliant, and to be a reliable team member, is also essential preparation for a space flight, and for life in general!

Many astronauts are deeply moved by seeing the Earth from space. There is even a term called 'the Overview Effect', which refers to how people are changed by this experience of seeing Earth from space. I too experienced this, and think it is worth sharing.

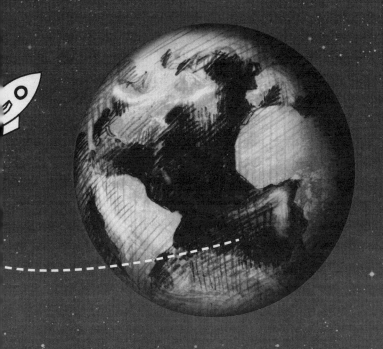

When orbiting on-board the ISS, you are travelling around Earth at about 17,210 miles per hour. At that speed you go all the way around our planet about every 90 minutes. That means you see a sunrise or a sunset every 45 minutes, and you cross entire continents in 10–20 minutes. Yet you are close enough to Earth to see clearly more detail than you might expect, even things as small as the Golden Gate Bridge in San Francisco (though you cannot see the Great Wall of China, as many have believed). Looking out the window at the Earth, seeing it in great detail while it smoothly rolls by, was like having a fire hose of information shooting into your mind about the Earth itself.

One of the first things you notice about the Earth from space is its weather. This is because a large portion of the Earth is always covered by clouds. From space you notice things like how, over the Pacific Ocean large smooth or geometric patterns of weather form, as the ocean is free from large islands or surface temperature variations. On the other hand, the Atlantic Ocean is filled with more chaotic weather patterns. This is due to the highly varied surface temperatures and shapes of nearby continents that interrupt the smoothness you see in the Pacific.

The next thing I noticed was how beautiful the deserts of the Earth are, as they are generally not covered by clouds. Sand and snow on Earth is blown into small drifts, then bigger dunes, then even bigger ridges, and from space you can see the rolling hills of sands that make similar patterns that scale all the way up to being seen from space! It was amazing to see these 'Great Fans' caused only by the winds blowing across the deserts of the Earth.

From space, it also became clear how completely humanity now occupies the whole surface of the Earth. Every desert I saw from space had roads across it, also often farms growing crops with water pumped up from deep within the Earth. Every forest, even in the Amazon basin of Brazil, had roads and cities within it. Every mountain range had roads through passes, and dams along its rivers. I saw very little 'open space' left on the Earth.

Finally, I saw an area I knew very well, the area of Texas I grew up in. I saw my home town, and nearby towns I had driven to many times, as well as the long Texas coastline where I used to visit beaches. And in the same view I could see the whole Earth, which I had now orbited many times. Suddenly it hit me . . . I now knew the true scale of the Earth by direct observation.

I had a huge physical reaction to this moment! It was like watching a movie, where they might zoom in the camera lens, while moving the camera backwards. It creates an effect where the hallway seems to collapse and shorten while the actor stays the same size. It was like that as I looked at the Earth; it remained the same size out the window, but the reality of scale around it collapsed. Suddenly to me, the Earth, which had been unimaginably large, became finite . . . and in fact, rather small.

Since my return from space, I have grown to learn that many astronauts express a similar 'epiphany' from this 'Overview Effect'. Many astronauts, including myself, come home with a renewed sense of the importance of environmentalism, to protect this fragile world we have. It seems to me that if more people had the chance to see the Earth from space, we would all take better care of our precious planet and of each other.

If space travel is a dream of yours, as it was of mine, I hope you will fulfil it someday. The opportunities to do so are getting easier every year. However, space will always be harder to reach than the next town, country or continent. You will still have to work hard to be prepared to earn a place on a team which is expanding human knowledge of and presence in locations ever farther from our home planet. You won't have to be so 'lucky', though, to be selected as many early astronauts were.

Work hard, and I believe each one of you reading this can build your own destiny in space!

Richard, ISS astronaut

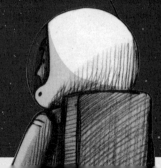

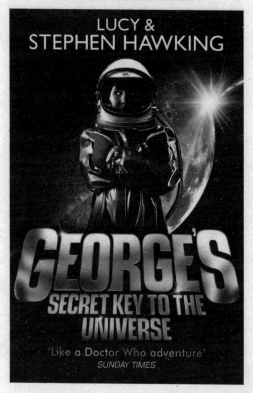

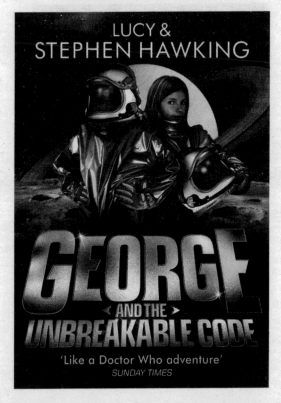